Author of the debut phenomenon *Dear You* and other bestsellers, Emily Blaine has become, with over 600,000 copies sold to date, the queen of contemporary French romance. A Breton by birth and a Parisian by adoption, her greatest pleasure is writing, and hearing from her readers.

www.emilyblaine.com

facebook.com/EmilyBlaineoff
twitter.com/blaineemily
instagram.com/emilyblaine1

THE BOOKSHOP OF FORGOTTEN DREAMS

EMILY BLAINE

Translated by
WENDELINE A. HARDENBERG

One More Chapter
a division of HarperCollins*Publishers* Ltd
1 London Bridge Street
London SE1 9GF
www.harpercollins.co.uk
HarperCollins*Publishers*
1st Floor, Watermarque Building, Ringsend Road
Dublin 4, Ireland

This paperback edition 2021
First published in Great Britain in ebook format
by HarperCollins*Publishers* 2021

A catalogue record of this book is available from the British Library

ISBN: 978-0-00-848592-4

Printed and bound in Great Britain by
CPI Group (UK) Ltd, Croydon CR0 4YY

We are often deceived in love, often hurt, often unhappy. But we love, and when we are on the edge of the grave, we turn round to look back, and say, "I have often suffered, sometimes made mistakes, but I have loved. It is I who have lived, not some artificial being created by my pride and my despair."

Alfred de Musset (trans. Peter Meyer)

Chapter One

I slouched a little further into the black velvet sofa and stretched my arms out along the back. From behind the balcony railing, I was watching the dense crowd on the floor below gyrate to the rhythm of pounding music. The overpowering bass made the dark walls and gleaming floors shake. Colorful spotlights alternately illuminated bare legs, exposed cleavage, and faces shiny with sweat. Their bodies were packed together, sometimes touching, flashing lustful smiles. In passing, I got a wink or two from girls locked in steamy embraces.

I loved this atmosphere with its intoxicating scents – sex, alcohol and the heady aroma of money in the air. I was light-years away from my first night out at a club: small-town, unhip, and stinking of cheap beer. Back then, it was the only distraction around. As wretched as my life was then.

In that other life, my professional prospects were limited to a job in the warehouse of a superstore in Charentes. From Tuesday through Saturday, eight hours a day, I would move wooden crates around. I stacked them up, emptied them out, broke them down, carried them in piles of five. I'd get ten splinters a week, hands all bloody, and a salary so meager I ate it up in ten days. Even though I wasn't doing the same work, I basically had the same life as my father, and I was angry, scared of ending up like him, stooped with fatigue, crippled with pain. I hated my life. I hated it so much that I sabotaged it: I argued with my parents, got into fights as often as possible, insulted anyone who looked down on me, and drowned it all in alcohol.

Every morning, I'd examine my reflection in the mirror of my parents' bathroom. A scar above my right eyebrow, a chipped tooth, dark eyes glassy with fatigue, a muscular body – the only positive aspect of my job – and a tattoo of a thorny vine encircling my left bicep… No wonder I gave most people the creeps.

I freely admitted it: I'd been lucky. So enormously lucky that I sometimes felt like it was all a big hoax. I might be a fraud, an impostor. Rich and famous, sure. But still a crook.

I was unloading a pallet when I'd been spotted by a casting director. After two auditions and a final screen test in Paris, I'd been catapulted into shooting my first feature-length film – and into a life where work no longer damaged my hands. That was the best part: I was paid to play angry guys, get into fights, and kiss girls who would never have glanced at me under normal circumstances. A glorious scam.

I'd said goodbye to my outdated country habits, cheap threads, stale beers, and loser friends. I'd walked away from my past and had no intention of going back. I'd almost forgotten the contempt I spotted in every look that had crossed my path. For all those people, all the ones who'd seen me carrying boxes, I was nothing.

But now I was the one on top of the world. In every way.

A glass of cognac in my hand, I relished my new life. I had money, I was admired, I was recognized. I went from bars to nightclubs, movie sets to interviews, fashion shows to society parties. To be honest, I hadn't seen the shelves of a supermarket in nearly eighteen months. A cleaning lady, an assistant, and my agent took care of that kind of tedious errand. My fridge was full, my bar well stocked, and the picture windows of my apartment overlooking the Parc Monceau were spotless.

I had everything and missed nothing from my previous life. And yet, my rage was still just under the surface, ready to ignite at the smallest spark. My meteoric success hadn't extinguished it in the slightest; all those years of brooding over my miserable life had left a mark. I missed the adrenaline sometimes, and even away from the cameras I always liked to fight. After two scandals picked up by the press, my agent had quickly found an outlet: a private boxing gym twice a week for four hours. Enough to discharge my destructive energy, all while staying in shape.

When the press wasn't feasting on my stunts, it was marveling at my determination, my obvious desire to succeed, my innate talent. Maybe. In reality, I just wanted to stay here, looking down on the world, surveying the crowd, and taking my pick of the women who offered themselves to me. Sitting on this velvet sofa, in designer jeans and with an outrageously expensive watch on my wrist, I was determined not to give up my seat to anybody.

"Which one is getting lucky tonight?"

I turned toward Simon's voice. Without waiting for my response, he leaned against the railing, staring into the crowd. A predatory smile graced his lips and he took a swig of that vile, overpriced whisky he loved so much.

"The blonde in the denim shorts?" he suggested.

"Brunette. Gold minidress."

He squinted, trying to locate my target in spite of the blinding spotlights.

"The one dancing with a guy?"

He turned toward me as I nodded. Simon, an actor who played the sidekick in my last film, barely stifled a laugh. He finished his drink in one gulp and wiped the back of his hand across his mouth to remove all trace of it.

"He doesn't look like he's her brother," he continued.

"A bit of a challenge never hurts," I said.

"You're not looking for a challenge. You just want a fight."

Simon cracked a smile, while I willed myself to stay calm. After the last fight, the press had questioned my future in the movie business – I was too unstable, too difficult, too disturbed. I'd noticed, ironically, that both in my former life and in my new one, I continued to be scrutinized and judged. Villagers or paparazzi, deep down, not much different.

I took another swig of cognac, absently watching an appealing waitress. I'd have fought for her, too. After this last grueling shoot, I needed to let off steam. It had been almost a month since I'd last been boxing and I was tense, feeling like my whole body was under pressure, on the verge of imploding. I made a fist and took a deep breath.

"Sooner or later it's going to end badly for you. Why are you doing it?"

"To blow off some steam. I like fighting. And I do it on the quiet now."

"Normal people take holidays, you know. You could … take a trip to Canada or go round the world."

"I'll think about it," I lied.

Quitting the movie business now would mean the end of my career. The artistic world abhors a vacuum. If you're not on a project, you don't exist. Taking a holiday was not on the agenda. I signaled the waitress and gave her a generous tip in exchange for two more glasses. She flashed me a cheeky smile, looking me over with interest.

With a little patience, I could have gotten this girl without even having to take her back to my place. My car, an alleyway, or the club bathrooms would have done the trick. But Simon was right – I felt like fighting.

"Do you have a shoot coming up?" I asked, in the vague hope of calming myself down.

"In two months, in Greece. I'll go with Emma."

I grimaced. I couldn't understand why Simon had become infatuated with her: a clingy airhead who expected people to curtsy instead of just saying hello. Unbearable ... and snooty: she knew perfectly well where I came from and took insane pleasure in reminding me.

"You're not going to ask her to marry you, are you?" I muttered.

Beneath my feet, the floor vibrated harder and the crowd went wild under the lights. The temperature climbed by several degrees, making the atmosphere suffocating. I caught sight of Simon's face; he took a drink from his glass before answering me.

"Not a chance," he assured me. "What about your schedule?"

"Two shoots, one in South Africa. The director is on the rise, should be a nice one. We're looking at Cannes."

Simon cocked an eyebrow. He was more skeptical

than surprised. My first movie opened numerous doors to me, and every week I received a script. I always picked the harshest roles – I loved difficult characters and twisted plots. I lost myself in the dangerous storylines.

As for Simon, he alternated between comedies and dramas. An actor since the age of five, he embodied the ideal son-in-law and inspired confidence thanks to his nice-guy looks.

"Cannes? Really?"

"Cannes. I've always wanted to show up at one of those obscene parties at the Hotel Martinez and raise hell."

"You're just into making people talk about you."

"Oh! You don't approve?"

Simon was the cautious type. The kind of guy who helps little old ladies across the street, buys organic, and doesn't make waves.

Clean, smooth, and accommodating. Everything the industry and the press liked – at least outwardly.

Our friendship was a mystery, but after a few parties together, we'd managed to forge a real bond. He shared his experience, while I took him outside his comfort zone by challenging him regularly.

Once, I'd even succeeded in dragging him along to the boxing gym to give him a memorable drubbing. For the first time in his career, Simon had put a whole film crew out of work for a week, while his nose returned to a normal size. Initially, he blamed me. Then, after downing a couple of beers, we'd laughed about it.

"You know exactly what I think," said Simon.

"That sooner or later I'll be kicking myself. You feel like you have to lecture me?"

"I've seen guys lose it all. Like on a roller coaster: you plummet so fast you can't even see where you are. You're a dangerous guy, Max, almost reckless."

"You're a boring guy, Simon. Almost deathly. You should have a little fun and stop being a nice guy."

"People like nice guys."

"And you do everything you can to keep them liking you. That's worth a visit to a shrink," I said with a smile as I got up from the sofa. "I'll leave you alone, I've got a girl to pick up."

Simon's gaze turned toward the gold minidress. I went over to the railing, to confirm that she was dancing closely with her boyfriend, eyes riveted to his. The challenge was getting more and more interesting.

"Asking her name is going to be complicated," Simon said sarcastically.

"Works for me, I don't give a damn about her name."

I raised my glass to him, declaring an end to the discussion. I wanted that girl, and it wouldn't be her boyfriend who stopped me. I grabbed my leather jacket, then charged down the stairs. The music was deafening and the packed dance floor prevented me from reaching the bar. I looked up toward the balcony. Simon lifted his glass in my direction, then pointed to my right.

I nodded and cut through the crowd to my target. The slim young brunette was still gyrating, lost in the sound of the bass. Luck was on my side: her boyfriend was no longer in the vicinity, probably off struggling with the bartender to order two glasses. I went over and did my best to end up facing her. When her glance met mine, she paused and blinked several times.

"I'm Maxime," I said, my mouth close to her ear.

A slight smile graced her lips. I didn't back away and she started to dance again, undulating lasciviously for me. She plastered her body to mine, while my hands found her hips. The whole boyfriend thing didn't seem to bother her. She didn't push me away, and instead looped her arms around my neck.

My movie career had given me work and money; it also made relationships easier. In my presence, most people were uninhibited: no suspicion, no restraint. Celebrity appeared to make them forget basic social rules. So, I'd adopted this way of being, completely indifferent to the names, virtues, and even lives of the girls I screwed.

"Did you come alone?" I asked, to make conversation.

She shook her head, pointing out her boyfriend. He was still waiting at the bar, jostled by the lively crowd.

"I know who you are," she murmured into my lips.

Her hands slid from the back of my neck to my chest.

Her eyes glazed over and I moved in a slow rhythm against her. With her long legs and mouthwatering lips, this girl was sexy. I was almost disappointed she wasn't more worried about the man she'd come with. I'd hoped for a bit of resistance, a bit of a game. But this girl was clearly ready to give in without a second's thought.

"Want to go somewhere?" I suggested, already tired of how easy it was.

She undulated again, sensuously caressing my body with hers. I let her do it, looking down from my height of six feet, as she straightened up. She lifted her gaze to mine and bit her lower lip. My urge to fight was fading, replaced by excitement and desire; I was seriously contemplating making her keep her high heels on for the rest of the night.

I turned my head toward the bar, noticing that the boyfriend had left his post. I searched for him for a few seconds, making a fist, ready for battle. With a little luck, my physique and an angry look would be enough to ward him off and save me from a new scandal.

"Let's go," gold minidress ordered.

I grabbed her wrist and aimed for one of the club's emergency exits. The crowd parted at my determination to get out. Behind me, the girl's high heels clicked on the tempered glass floor. I felt hands clutch at me and heard my name whispered like a shameful secret. I ignored the disapproving murmurs and pushed open the heavy door that led outside.

The fresh night air caught me for a brief instant and somewhat dissipated the effects of the alcohol. I took a few steps and found myself in a dark, dead-end alley.

"Here?" said the girl's voice.

"Here."

I pushed her up against the building's concrete wall and ran my hands over her body. The thrum of the bass still reached us. She made a hissing sound and complained about the temperature being too cool. I pressed my lips against her neck, noticing a layer of sweat mixed with luxury perfume. Her annoyance changed into arousal and she let out a moan laden with desire. My hands slipped down to her waist, then her ass. She rubbed up against me, lustful and willing. I found her naked thighs and slid my fingers up under her barely-there dress.

The girl arched into me, giving herself up to my appetite. I didn't really care about what she was feeling – I just wanted her body and to do whatever I felt like with it. I brushed my hand against her crotch, while my lips traced a path down to her small breasts. I seized the fabric of her strapless dress with my teeth and yanked; now it looked more like a wide gold belt. She let out a little cry of surprise while I admired her nipples, erect from a mix of chill and arousal.

My tongue did a number on her breasts, while my fingers stroked her pussy through the fabric of her panties. This was all just too easy.

"Hey!" shouted a male voice from nearby.

"Shit," said the girl in a panic.

She shoved me away and hastily readjusted her dress. Out of breath and annoyed at being interrupted, I turned toward the intruder. My arousal rocketed straight down: the boyfriend. Of course.

That added spice to the situation.

"What's going on here?"

He glanced at his girlfriend and shook his head, somewhere between disgust and disbelief. Within seconds, he pulled off his shirt and gave it to her.

"Cover up, you tramp! We're going home."

He headed toward me, eyes blazing with fury, shoulders tense, jaw clenched. His anger seemed to radiate outward in ever stronger waves. I straightened up and looked him over. Usually, just a look was enough to calm things down.

"The actor, is that right?" he asked.

"That's right. Look, this wasn't her fault," I said.

Behind him, the poor girl slipped on her boyfriend's shirt. Eyes fixed on the ground, she oozed humiliation the same way her man was dripping with rage.

"Give me one good reason not to punch you in the face," said the man in front of me. "And you!" he added to his girlfriend. "You just wait."

"Leave her alone," I hissed.

A second later, his fist crashed into the side of my head. I staggered, surprised by the force of the impact, and took several steps back. When he took his second shot, I managed to block it, and drove my fist into his stomach. He gurgled in pain before doubling over, short of breath. He straightened up and yet another punch struck my jaw, then my cheek. He trapped me against the wall, and his hand closed over my throat to suffocate me. My skull collided with the concrete and I felt the shock reverberate through my whole body.

I stumbled across the alleyway, to a safe distance from my opponent. I wiped my hand over my mouth; the familiar, metallic taste of blood fueled my anger and re-energized me. I charged at the guy, determined to unleash all my rage on him. I could detect a spark of fear in his eyes; now he regretted starting things. He backed away, ready to flee, but tripped and ended up with his butt on the filthy ground.

He lifted his arms to protect his face, but I hit him anyway. My breath was coming out as a wheeze and my head was buzzing, but he was going to pay. Pay for anybody who'd condescended to me. Pay for being dealt a better hand than me from the get-go and for his perfect life. And for a while, I was satisfied. I'd had my revenge.

The girl screamed, begging me to stop, before threatening to call the police. When I straightened up, I was out of breath and my shirt was stained with blood. My knuckles were skinned, but I was relieved. The pressure that had overwhelmed me in the club had finally subsided.

On the ground, the guy was whining, filling the alley with gasps and groans. I stared at him while his girlfriend, stooping over him, cried her eyes out. I spat and assessed the damage: my shirt was in a sad state, and I'd undoubtedly have a nasty bruise the size of Australia on my face within a few hours.

"I like to fight," I said finally. "Since you wanted a good reason…"

"Go fuck yourself," he growled.

"I'd be happy to. But your girlfriend seems less into it now."

The gleam of red and blue lights on the brick wall erased my victorious smile: the police barging in hadn't been part of the plan. It'd take them five seconds to understand what had happened here. I was already making a list of the problems I'd have to deal with: prosecution for beating this guy up, my blood alcohol content, a big scandal in the press, a delay in my next movie shoot, my agent's incandescent rage, hypocritical side-eye from the profession. It would last a few days, then everyone would forget about it.

That was the advantage of this business: you could be a horrible person, push boundaries, hit a guy in a dark corner, and they accepted your mistakes, calling them "misconduct". After a couple of apologies and a vaguely contrite demeanor, everything would go back to normal. It was easy to wipe the slate clean.

With the help of his girlfriend, the guy got up and

staggered over to the wall, which he leaned against. I weighed the odds: did I have time to run away? I was in a dead end. In every sense of the word. Considering my condition, even if I made it back into the club, I'd be quickly tracked down. The blood was already drying on my hands and lips. I headed up the alley, thinking I could evade the police and leave the pair of lovers behind me. I came out onto the avenue that ran behind the club and glanced around.

If the cops had shown up, they now appeared to be lying low. Surely, they must have been called for something more important than an actor in a street brawl.

Wishful thinking. I barely had time to take two steps before an officer called me by name, ordering me to stay put. I ignored him, pulling out a pack of cigarettes from the back pocket of my jeans.

"Stop right there!" yelled a firm voice.

I kept walking, turning my back on the cops, and lit my cigarette. I didn't get a chance to put away my lighter. I felt myself suddenly flung forward and my face crashed into the hood of a car. I grimaced at the abrupt, icy contact with my bruise.

"I told you to stop," spat the man standing over me, one firm hand between my shoulder blades.

He searched me, feeling my pockets and the small of my back.

"You have anything?" he asked, tossing my pack of cigarettes on the ground.

"No."

This wasn't my first arrest. I was well acquainted with what would happen next: I was going to be subjected to a lecture in the middle of the street, and then they'd let me go if I promised to stay out of trouble.

Abruptly, the officer grabbed my right wrist and I felt the touch of handcuffs. The other hand followed, and I was yanked roughly backward by the little chain linking my fists. The icy metal cut into my wrists, and the brutality of the arrest made me grunt disapprovingly. Nothing was going as planned.

"Take it easy," I growled.

"Dream on," he immediately retorted. "You're about to spend the night on ice, to cool off."

"Let me call somebody."

The cop's only response was to tug sharply on the little chain, and all the muscles in my body rebelled; my shoulders, in particular, did not appreciate such treatment. The officer opened the door of an unmarked car and made me duck my head so I could get inside.

"Is this really necessary?" I asked.

Looking up, I noticed a row of photographers on the pavement, standing ready to sell the photo of the century. Mathilde was going to tear strips off me for this.

"Get in!"

The car sped off, and I barely had time to see the paparazzi running after us, armed with their cameras.

"Where are we going exactly?"

"Ninth Arrondissement police station. Very friendly, you'll see!"

Chapter Two

"Good grief, how many did you order exactly?"

"They're sold by the pound. I got a really good deal!" I argued, shoving the gray velvet sofa out of the reading nook.

Baptiste shot me an exasperated look. I hung my head, vaguely embarrassed and a little bit ashamed. I felt like a kid caught with her hand in the biscuit tin. Except my biscuits were second-hand books.

Today's delivery bordered on ninety pounds.

Okay, fine: this wasn't a jar, it was a straight-up biscuit factory, and my arm was stuck in there up to the elbow. I took full responsibility, and the shame was quickly replaced by a feeling of unshakeable pride.

"Reading is a wholesome addiction," I pointed out as my neighbor added a fourth cardboard box to the stack. "I ordered enough to last several weeks."

"Sarah, you have to resell these books, you know."

Tall and strong, Baptiste ran the only acceptable restaurant in town. Also very considerate, he was my father's age and loved treating me like a daughter: he made sure that I ate at mealtimes, and regularly lectured me about the bookshop. According to him, I had no business sense and ran the risk of going bust before the end of the year.

"I know that. But first I'm going to make sure they're good."

"Sarah," he chided me, frowning.

I ignored him and opened the first box. Paperbacks were what sold the best. I'd even wound up creating a special offer: buy a book and get a free hot drink. That rewarded readers and attracted coffee fans, who, cup in hand, would end up roaming around the bookshelves.

Buying second-hand books in bulk was cheaper, and I felt like I was doing a good deed by saving them from the bin. I would sort them, repair them, display them in the shop window, and sometimes include them in theme nights for the book club.

But my favorite part was this one: the moment of discovery, when the books and I made our acquaintance and I tried to imagine whose hands they'd passed through. I'd breathe their scent, stroke the paper, and get lost looking at the covers.

I'd never had the opportunity to travel. But I read,

and it was almost the same – minus the jet-lag, plus the comfort of my sofa.

I pulled a book out of the box and flipped through the pages before continuing:

"I have to check their general condition, the covers. Did you know there are cruel people who dog-ear the pages of books?"

"Dangerous criminals, definitely," Baptiste teased.

"Like the ones who water down your Bordeaux."

"Those people deserve to die in excruciating pain. I don't think dog-earing a page …"

I raised a hand to silence him. Wordlessly and as delicately as possible, I unfolded the corner of a page that had been desecrated by a wicked soul. I was outraged that someone could have so little appreciation for a book.

"I'm going to get the rest of the boxes," my neighbor said finally.

I nodded absently, absorbed by the yellowed pages.

"Sarah?"

"Yeah."

"Stop reading. Just get them out of the boxes, you have work to do."

I was already in the midst of devouring this new story, gladly forgetting that I'd have to take everything out and catalogue it before I could enjoy reading. Baptiste made three more trips back and forth and I soon found myself sitting on the floor surrounded by a wall of boxes. I kicked off my shoes and emptied the first box, reverently placing each of the books on top of the stack.

"Do you have enough room?" asked Baptiste, leaning against the wall.

"Anita is supposed to bring back some old shelves for me. Could you come and install them afterward? I thought I'd put them under the staircase, to fill in the gap."

"If you want."

He sighed and his answer seemed to hang in the air, as if he were waiting for some comment from me. I stared at him for a few seconds, then smiled. Seeming preoccupied, he said:

"A few of us are going out for a glass of wine, do you want to come?"

I looked up at him. I was surrounded by boxes, in a full-on treasure-hunting trance, already coming up with thematic groupings for all of these marvels, and he was inviting me to go for a drink? At my silence, he moved toward me, sporting his disapproving dad face.

"We're worried about you," he said at last.

"I'm fine."

"I know the bookshop isn't exactly thriving right now."

I was getting ready to reply when he held up an authoritative index finger. Baptiste was taking this substitute father role a bit too seriously; sometimes I found it exasperating. For years my grandmother had run this bookshop. When she died, she'd passed it all on to me: the store, her love of books, her desire to share it. Everything. Ever since then, I'd been doing my best to ensure the shop's continued existence.

"It'll be okay. Summer holidays are coming, that's always better for sales."

"Sarah…"

I busied myself emptying the second box, ignoring my neighbor's inquisitive gaze. He didn't need to know that the accounts were in the red and my bank was badgering me for a meeting "to take stock of your situation…" A very convenient way to get me on my knees and finish me off by asking me to sell.

Baptiste snatched the book I was examining right out of my hands. I looked up at him, mildly annoyed.

"I can see what's going on, you know. Do you want to talk about it?"

"Everything's fine, I promise," I said with conviction.

I stood up and dusted off my light blue jeans. Pushing aside a pile of boxes with my foot, I tried to make a little space. The reading nook, which consisted of a sofa and three mustard-yellow wing chairs, was inaccessible. I'd have to clear everything out between now and tomorrow morning in order to open.

"Maybe you should meet new people."

"Why? I have you. I have Anita and the whole gang. I don't need any new people. I already have enough to do with all of you!"

"A bunch of senior citizens, half of them deaf and arthritic?"

"What about the other half?" I asked, amused.

"The other half have memory issues or prostate problems. Or both, if they're lucky. Sarah, nobody wants to hang around with people who consider their doctor a close friend. You should spend time with people your own age."

I stiffened, somewhere between amusement and bewilderment. I enjoyed being involved with the town theatre group. I liked the bookshop, and I liked living here. In my view, I had everything I needed: why seek out complications?

"I don't have the time," I said evasively.

"Have you thought about using the internet? You could socialize, find people who share your passion."

"I'm not interested, Baptiste."

"Why not go to the party before the grape harvest? There are plenty of young people…"

"… who are dead drunk, mindless, and smell bad. For someone who wants what's best for me, you have pretty questionable ideas."

"Okay, okay. But you can't stay here all by yourself! You could do with a man to fix things up … and carry boxes."

"I'm going to pretend your comment wasn't at all sexist and recommend you for the female lead in our next play."

"You know very well what I mean," he sighed. "I'm worried about you. We're all worried. A pretty girl like you..."

"A pretty girl like me doesn't need anyone else to validate her existence."

This conversation was getting tiresome. For several weeks, the theater group had been taking perverse pleasure in trying to get me out of the bookshop, but I'd held my ground. I liked being here, I liked being alone. The shop was a full-time job. Honestly, I didn't see how I could devote time to a relationship.

"I'm happy here, among the books and far away from reality. And I'm sorry about your prostate," I continued, changing the subject.

"But ... but how..."

"Simple deduction. Now, can I finish putting things away? I'll never sell them if they stay in the boxes!"

"Not even one drink?" he insisted.

"No. Thank you, Baptiste."

To end the conversation, I dropped a kiss on his lightly gray-stubbled cheek. I heard my neighbor sigh again, a sign that he was accepting yet another defeat.

"Do you still need help?" he asked, heading for the door.

"No, it'll be fine. Go home. Gloria will be waiting for you."

"She's part of the deaf half: at this hour, she must be

asleep in front of her TV show. The sound of an airplane taking off wouldn't even make her flinch!"

"I'm going to tell her you said that..."

"I'm sure you will."

In the bookshop's doorway, he smiled at me one last time and gave me a warm, friendly hug.

"Don't go to bed too late," he advised me. "And keep the doors locked."

I stayed on the doorstep while he zipped up his jacket and got into his truck. Without Baptiste, I would've had to request a delivery that would have cost a fortune. He was already helping me a lot without even knowing it, and I loved him all the more for it.

I gave him a little wave and waited for him to disappear around the corner before going back inside. I shut the door behind me, letting my gaze wander over my near neighbors through the glass: to the right Baptiste's restaurant and flower-bedecked patio bordered the square; to the left stood the bakery, side by side with the grocer. Finally, across from me was Frédéric's shop. Despite Baptiste's hints, I wasn't completely immune to the charms of the male sex. A smiling florist with a wicked sense of humor, he would have been perfect had he only returned my regard. We did have some things in common: he loved to read and took his morning espresso without sugar. From time to time he'd bring me flowers, heartbroken at the idea of putting them in the rubbish. The thought made me smile as I locked the door.

I went back to the reading nook and cautiously opened all the boxes. Among the books, I felt safe and calm. Baptiste worried about my solitude, but in truth it gave me relief. This way, I no longer had to put up with pitying looks or the mutterings of people who'd known my parents. Sometimes, I thought it would've been easier to leave, to give myself a new life, free of my family's escapades. On several occasions, I'd packed my suitcase before thinking better of it: where could I go? My whole life was here.

I spent much of the night putting away my latest purchases. After breaking down the boxes and cramming them into a corner of the shop, I climbed the stairs up to my apartment. In addition to the bookshop, my grandmother had left me a place to live on the floor above. After her death, I'd done some renovations; the yellowed wallpaper had given way to a coat of white paint and some black-and-white photos. The living room was overflowing with books that also invaded my office. Most of the time, I worked from my sofa, making plans for the book club and suggesting new activities for the regulars.

The rest of the apartment consisted of two bedrooms: I slept in the one with a bay window overlooking the park behind the building, while the second warehoused even more books.

I made myself a light supper and a to-do list for the next day. I conspicuously ignored the two bills –

telephone and electricity – waiting patiently for their turn. I'd find a solution eventually.

The next day, I took advantage of the bright sun to set up some tables outside. I also brought out the basic drinks menu and laboriously rolled out a display rack to prop up in front of the window. Yesterday's books were on it, perfectly lined up, fragrant with the smell of old paper and faded ink, ready to be bought.

As usual, Anita waltzed into the shop at eleven o'clock, full of fifty-five-year-old exuberance. Always dressed eccentrically – today she'd chosen a denim jumpsuit customized with embroidery and bits of plaid fabric – she was brimming with perpetual cheer, and had a wicked sense of humor. Since her third divorce, four years ago, she'd decided to settle in the country and help young people train for new jobs. Her ex-husbands took care of her financial comfort. After a warm embrace, Anita examined me from head to foot, then grimaced.

"I'd say … less than five hours' sleep?"

"Three and a half," I said, suppressing a yawn.

"Baptiste told me you'd bought some books."

Despite her casual manner, Anita knew perfectly well how to express her disapproval. Between her half smile and that slight brow wrinkle, I'd learned to decode the signs; this time, it was the tone of her voice, pitched a little lower than usual, that had given her away.

"Don't lecture me," I said immediately, diving back into my work. "You know I need to keep refreshing the inventory to develop customer loyalty."

"You already have miles of shelving. You could be more rational."

"I know where this conversation is going," I dodged.

"Really?"

"Really. You're going to talk to me about books, then you're going to tell me you're worried about the shop. You'll follow up with a vague suggestion regarding my non-existent love life—"

"Sarah," she interrupted me.

I held up a hand and continued:

"It will obviously be something specific enough to upset me and simultaneously fuzzy enough for me to come to my own conclusions. You'll point out the fact that I've been single for a long time and suggest a date with someone my age, like your son's best friend."

Anita stared at me, mouth agape, clinging to the counter that served as my work station. She stood up straight and a delighted smile stretched across her face. I caught my breath, satisfied with warding off her attacks.

"Coffee?" I offered.

"Decaf. And I was going to mention my nephew," she corrected.

I pivoted to the coffee machine, turning my back on my friend.

"Why do you want to marry me off to somebody so badly?" I asked her as I filled the tank with water. "I like being alone, I have work to do and no time to frolic about with the first person to come along."

"Frolic?"

I gave her a dirty look before getting out a cup and sliding it underneath the coffee spout. I tried to suppress my irritation, but in vain. I'd always hated people meddling in my business. And this obsession with my love life was getting a little hurtful: either they wanted to get rid of me, or they thought I was too awkward to seduce a man.

I'd never admit to them that the second option was the right one. I was incapable of being one of those feminine women, relaxed and at ease with their bodies. I dressed in jeans and T-shirts, I let my hair air dry, and my skin was devoid of all makeup. I envied women who knew how to show themselves off, the ones who played with their hair, with a meaningful look and a sensual smile.

My life was this bookshop. I thought about books every minute of the day … and I talked about them just as much. Even to men I might like. I was the one and only obstacle to my love life, a certified competition-caliber mood-killer, in thick socks and a woolly sweater.

"Frolic, yes," I continued. "I don't have time for all

that! Anyway, no man is going show up *here* to ask me to dinner."

"Sarah..."

"Or rather, the ones who *would* are as old as my grandfather and pervs. Believe me, Prince Charming is not—"

I broke off in the middle of my tirade, holding Anita's cup, as Frédéric, my florist neighbor, traded a conspiratorial glance with my friend, a bouquet of red peonies in his hand. I set Anita's decaf on the counter and rubbed my hands nervously on my jeans.

Not only was I a walking mood-killer, I was also gifted with a prodigious talent for gaffes.

"Hi," I whispered.

"Hi. These are for you, I thought you'd like them," replied Frédéric, handing me the bouquet.

I could count on one hand the number of times a man had given me flowers. Frédéric represented four-fifths of them by himself. It was depressing. Nevertheless, I accepted his gift with a big smile. He kept his eyes riveted to mine and our hands briefly touched when my fingers closed around the flower stems. Embarrassed and with my heart beating as though I were running a marathon, I lowered my eyes and abruptly yanked the bouquet out of his hands.

He, of course, didn't even blink and stared at me while almost certainly wondering about my mental health.

"Thanks," I muttered, my cheeks hot.

"You should buy flowers more often!"

"I'd do it if I could afford it. Thank you for these!"

"No problem. I thought you'd like them. I saw you put the tables out on the pavement."

"This afternoon is going to be beautiful, I think. What about you, got any orders coming up?"

"I've got a wedding this weekend, that should keep me busy for the rest of the week. I'll probably have a few extra flowers, I'll bring them to you."

In spite of myself, I felt a slight pang in my heart.

"Busy for the week" mostly meant he probably wouldn't be visiting me. Frédéric had a habit of popping in at the end of the day; he'd order a coffee, wander around the shop, and eventually ask me for book recommendations. Tall, dark-haired, muscular, thoughtful, funny, clever, and engaging, he was everything I liked in a man. Well, almost. If he were interested in me, he'd definitely be my ideal man incarnate. But I'd very quickly realized that he only saw me as his nice, helpful neighbor.

"Oh. Great!" I enthused to hide my disappointment.

"So, what's this about a man asking you to dinner?"

My eyes darted to Anita who, prudently, even as I cursed her and all her progeny, backed up a few steps and took refuge in the thriller section. I picked up a pencil, grabbed my planner, and pretended it had to be updated right away. My hands were shaking with panic as I crossed out two calendar squares, scribbled an unintelligible note, then turned the page to write down two novel titles.

When I looked up, Frédéric was still there, an amused smile on his lips. My heart panicked a little more when I discovered the irresistible little dimple in the hollow between his cheek and his laughing eyes.

"Am I imagining things, or are you acting like I'm not here?"

I am the girl who keeps digging, even at the bottom of the hole.

"I… It was… Nobody asked me to dinner," I said finally, twisting my pencil.

"What are you doing tomorrow?"

My pencil leaped into the air and I found myself wringing my hands. I was simultaneously terrified by that innocent little question and dismayed by my behavior. My pathological shyness was going to obliterate my slim chances with this man.

Suddenly, Frédéric's smile became a frown.

"I forgot, you have the book club."

"Ah … um … yes. But…"

"And I know you never cancel a book club meeting."

"Oh?"

"That was one of the first things you told me when I moved here. I wouldn't want to interfere with your schedule or anybody else's."

Holding back a whimper of frustration and despair, I

tried to find a way to salvage the situation. "Another evening maybe?"

I was amazed I hadn't stammered or squeaked like a teenager. Frédéric hesitated briefly, before nodding and suggesting:

"Why not lunch?"

"Yes, perfect! Tomorrow?"

I chastised myself inwardly for my unmistakable excitement and pressed my lips together to keep from coming out with yet another outrageous remark.

"I have an appointment tomorrow, but … how about the day after?"

"Yes, perfect!"

"I'll bring flowers," he promised, heading back toward his shop.

"Yes, perfect!"

I could have slapped myself. I sounded so happy that he was going to start thinking I was on uppers.

In reality, he was the only one who put me in this state.

In reality, he was the only one interested in me. I liked losing myself in his azure-blue gaze, all while foolishly daydreaming about the touch of his hand against mine.

"I'll be back tonight, for my coffee," he promised with a final wave.

"Yes, perfect!" came Anita's voice from my right.

Frédéric crossed the square at a brisk pace, while Anita shook her head in shock. She set her still-steaming cup down on the counter, then retrieved my pencil from the middle of the aisle and gave it back to me.

"That was appalling," she commented.

"I know," I moaned. "I'm hopeless with men."

"Apparently. Why didn't you drop the book club to go out to dinner with him?"

I buried my face in my hands. I wanted to disappear for good and forget the whole thing. Unfortunately, with Anita as witness, that pathetic exchange with Frédéric was forevermore etched in stone. She'd make sure to remind me at her leisure, just to torture me.

"I wasn't expecting it," I protested.

"That's the problem with men: as soon as they take the initiative, it gives us a shock. You still should have taken him up on the dinner."

"I got a lunch."

"You go to lunch with friends, Sarah. Lunch is chaste and pointless."

"You're exaggerating."

In spite of my disastrous exchange with Frédéric, I maintained some pride that I'd actually agreed to a private meal with him. It was more than I ever could have imagined. My gaze drifted toward the flower shop. Frédéric was bustling around, getting out buckets and flowers to arrange in front of his shop. I sighed wistfully, then turned to Anita, who rolled her eyes.

"So, you have two days to learn not to hyperventilate in front of him."

"You want another coffee?" I asked, changing the subject.

"No. This is fine. You should wear your yellow dress, it suits you."

"Anita! This isn't… Well, it's just that…"

"I know. But believe me, that ridiculous business about inner beauty will go perfectly with that yellow dress. Then you'll be able to focus on all your qualities, like your kindness, generosity, and organizational skills. Or your serenity," she added.

"My serenity?"

"I'm trying to decide between serenity and resilience in the face of adversity," she continued, pensive.

Serenity? I was a ball of anxiety. Everything scared me: from the bills piling up, to the weather, to my impending lunch with Frédéric. Every evening I checked twice that the doors were locked and the slightest creaking of the parquet floor frightened me to death.

I was the exact opposite of serenity, and Anita knew it perfectly well.

"Come on, Anita, what are you talking about?"

She finished her coffee in one gulp, then pointed behind me.

"Your reading nook is flooded."

Chapter Three

My night in jail had lasted longer than I'd imagined. Usually, somebody would tell me I was free to go after an hour or two. It was almost a game: for each lock-up, I'd try to guess whether they'd let me out faster than the last time. The blood on my forest-green shirt had dried after a while, leaving a bunch of blackish stains. The police had made sure to remove my shoelaces, so my feet were loose in my heavy boots.

After a couple of hours, I finally lay down on the grey concrete bench. With my leather jacket rolled into a ball underneath my head, my ankles crossed, and my damaged hands folded over my stomach, I even managed to fall asleep for a few hours, hoping that Mathilde would finally show up to get me out of there.

"Come on, get up!"

The neon lights flickered before blinding me

completely. I sat up with a grimace and wiped a hand across my grimy face. Sweat mixed with dust and dried blood formed an unpleasant film on my skin. I needed a shower and very strong coffee.

The police officer unlocked the door, thus notifying me that my night in the drunk tank had come to an end. I flashed him a victorious little smile and walked past him. As we navigated through some nondescript hallways, I took the opportunity to question him.

"Immediate trial?" I asked.

"Maybe."

We came out into the station lobby. I expected to see Mathilde, my agent and guardian angel, fairly annoyed at being woken up so early on a Sunday. If she'd had to leave her kid with the neighbor lady, too, then she was going to be downright furious. I was going to get a serious clip on my ear.

"They're waiting for you in this room," the copper pointed out.

I paused for a second, surprised. Over the past few months, I'd spent several nights in jail, and this one wasn't turning out like all the others. Most of the time, Mathilde would bellyache, open the door for me, and give me an endless lecture over espresso. Occasionally, I'd end up in front of a judge, get a slap on the wrist – an official warning – and then I'd go home. That's how it worked: one way or another, they wiped the slate clean and I took full advantage.

The fuzz opened the glass door to the room and shut it behind me. I made a face at the musty smell of industrial disinfectant. My mood darkened when I saw the three people waiting for me.

"Pulling out all the stops, I see," I said sarcastically.

"You should sit down," replied Mathilde icily.

I glanced at my lawyer and Damien – an old friend from back home. I couldn't account for his presence; I hadn't spoken to him in forever. He greeted me with a nod, his big hands, hardened by manual labor, folded on the table.

"Or what?" I said provocatively.

"I'm not in the mood to play games, Maxime."

"Sit," interjected my lawyer.

Normally dressed to the nines in a tailored suit, this morning he was in jeans and a sweatshirt. I'd apparently forced a bunch of people from their comfortable beds. With a sigh, I eventually obeyed. I pulled a chair out noisily and sat down. I stared at my lawyer, trying to decipher his mood.

"What the hell is going on?" I finally asked.

"Simon called me," explained Mathilde.

"Good old Simon," I said with a smile.

"At least he doesn't make me leave my house on a Sunday morning."

"He doesn't know what he's missing. Just tell me what you're doing here, I want to hit the sack."

"We've worked something out," replied my lawyer.

My eyes flicked back and forth among the three people in front of me. Mathilde's presence wasn't at all surprising, and my lawyer's was also predictable. But I still didn't understand what Damien was doing there.

"Did you abandon your vineyards?" I asked him.

"Just for two days, so I could come here."

"You picked a good time," I complimented him. "I'm at my best."

He just smiled enigmatically. The explanation I was waiting for didn't come.

"Maxime?" said Mathilde.

"What?" I sighed. "You going to lecture me again?"

Mathilde was only a few years older than me. Apparently, that was enough for her to act like my mother, doling out reprimands and tiresome advice. I was an adult, I didn't need a permanent chaperone.

"No."

"Great. I don't feel like listening to you harp on about how I'm jeopardizing my future. Can I leave now?"

"No," answered Damien.

The finality in his voice surprised me. Back in the day, we'd been friends. His father, the owner of a vineyard in Charentes, had twice hired me for the harvest. Damien and I had gotten along, but he was much more straight-laced and honest than I was. I'd never managed to lure him into my questionable activities.

"I'm *quite* aware," retorted Mathilde, her voice tinged

with bitterness. "I pick my battles, Max. Since I have no hold over you, I've decided to tender my resignation."

A snicker slipped out of me.

"If I had a euro for every time you threatened to resign…"

"Here's my letter," she cut me off, slapping it down on the table.

I sat up and skimmed the letter. I didn't give a damn about Mathilde, just as I didn't give a damn what she thought of me. I brushed the sheet of paper off the table and stared daggers at my now ex-agent.

"Because you think that's going to upset me?"

"I still harbored some vague hope."

"I don't care if you're with me or not. I'll find a new agent in a day."

"Maxime!"

My lawyer's hand slammed down on the table. Though Mathilde jumped in surprise, Damien didn't even blink. In his shabby clothes – a T-shirt frayed at the collar and a denim jacket – he stuck out like a sore thumb here. Everything about him screamed bumpkin. And yet, he wasn't at all intimidated. In fact, he seemed to be enjoying the show.

"What?" I grunted at him.

"Nothing. You should listen to what we're telling you."

"I couldn't care less, okay? I don't give a damn about any of you. Now, will you explain what the hell is going on? Mathilde, if you want to leave, I won't hold you back. Obviously, you have no desire to work with me."

"I have no desire to witness your downfall. You can do you what you like with your career, but don't wreck mine."

"I don't give a shit. I already told you!"

"Here's the situation, Maxime…" my lawyer began again.

He opened a folder and methodically laid three pieces of paper in front of me. I didn't even take the trouble to lean over and look at what was on them. I knew Claude would eventually tell me my sentence in barely comprehensible legal jargon. And then, to put my best face forward, I'd use my acting talents and offer my humblest apologies, promising never to hit anybody ever again.

I'd probably last a week before my next indiscretion. If that.

"Is that dramatic tone really necessary?" I laughed.

He glared at me furiously, then resumed:

"The couple you assaulted are going to press charges: assault and battery, plus sexual assault."

"What? She was fully consenting," I hissed, my teeth clenched.

"Her fiancé has a broken nose and two fractured ribs," he cut in. "We're still waiting for the full report from the hospital. In any case, even if the judge doesn't accept the sexual assault, which I doubt, you'll of course be blamed for the rest. And that's not even counting fleeing the scene."

"Fleeing the scene?"

"The officer says he had to run after you. Maxime, I assure you that this time it's very serious. You've got a lot on the line."

"Your whole career," added Mathilde.

"Since you're no longer my agent, what the fuck do you care?"

"I thought we were friends. Actually, I think we are, otherwise I wouldn't have come to try and bail you out."

"How nice of you. But I don't need anybody," I said, getting up from my chair. "I don't see what we're doing here. If it's as bad as you say, I'd already be in immediate trial, right?"

I stretched my arms up over my head, getting rid of a vague ache in my back. I was suffocating in this windowless room. I dug through my pockets, searching for a cigarette. To no avail, the fuzz had confiscated everything when I arrived at the station. I sighed, truly ticked off.

"That's right, you should already be in front of the judge," my lawyer confirmed as I paced up and down the tiny room.

"We negotiated a deal," continued Damien.

"Did you write them a check?" I sneered.

"We talked to the judge. Maxime, before explaining

what's expected, you have to know that this latest transgression could land you in prison."

My nervousness returned. I paced faster and ran a hand through my dirty hair. I'd gotten a little taste of the slammer while I was still living with my father and frankly didn't feel like repeating the experience.

"And there's already been collateral damage: your shoot in South Africa has been canceled."

"Canceled? You mean postponed until I'm out of prison?"

"I mean totally canceled. They're going to recast the lead. They don't want any bad publicity around the film."

I absorbed this news. Under normal circumstances, I'd probably have told Mathilde to go to hell. This time, I just looked down at the floor.

"I don't know if I can save your next two films. The producers are getting cold feet at the idea of entrusting their movie to a guy who might end up behind bars," my agent clarified.

"Well, I hope I can prove them right, at least. Am I going to see this famous cell?"

"We've done what we could to get you out of it."

My lawyer took another sheet of paper out of his folder. With a look, he invited me to sit back down. I complied, waiting for the rest while ignoring Damien's oppressive gaze.

"The judge has agreed to allow you a reduced

sentence. That will let you avoid prison, and especially the scandal of possible incarceration."

"I don't trust that sort of plan," I warned him.

He slid the sheet toward me so I could see the conditions of this agreement.

"Just sign on the dotted line," my lawyer clarified as I scanned the legal gobbledygook without understanding a word.

"What does this say, in plain language?"

I looked up at my lawyer. He glanced at Damien, who nodded.

"In plain language? Instead of going to prison, you'll do two months of community service," he answered.

A smirk stretched across my face. Once again, I was escaping the worst. Community service. Fine. I'd do it for a few days, then make a public apology and ask for a reduced sentence. Nothing too serious.

And nothing that would keep me from living my life as I saw fit. I'd maintain my nightly habits, keep my appointments. At worst, I'd have to regularly check in at the police station.

"Obviously, you'll wear an ankle monitor," continued my lawyer.

"Which means?"

"No going out between 10 p.m. and 8 a.m."

"I'll just get drunk at home."

"You won't be at home."

I swiveled toward Damien, staring at him

uncomprehendingly. Something was off. This whole community service thing was much too good. And it didn't explain this amateur little courthouse scene at all.

"You'll live in Charente," he added.

I pushed my chair back violently and tried to collect my thoughts. I hadn't seen the trap coming, and now it was closing on me.

"I'm not going back there," I growled.

"Damien found a solution," said Mathilde.

"I knew you wouldn't want to go back to your father's place. I have a friend who could really use a hand with repairs at her bookshop."

"A bookshop? Are you kidding me? Why not your place?"

"The judge didn't think it could be secured well enough. The vineyards aren't fenced in, while the confines of the bookshop are completely identifiable. They want to guard against any flight risk."

My breathing sped up. In the space of a second, my perfect life had just fallen apart. Into freefall, with no parachute, and a violent landing that would definitely leave a mark. I got out of my chair and picked up the piece of paper with the agreement on it.

"So, this is your … arrangement? I have to leave everything here behind for two months, and go back to some hick town? I hope the hotel is nice, at least!"

"The bookshop will provide you with a room."

"What if I don't agree?"

"You go to prison," my lawyer concluded. "Your choice."

"Really? What a fucking choice! The slammer or rot in the ass-end of Chateaurenard?"

I kicked the chair, which went flying across the room with a clang. Once again, Damien didn't even flinch.

"Obviously," my former friend said, "in an ideal world you'd agree to see a therapist there."

"And I'd try to come see you, to bring scripts for you to read."

"Fuck off! You resigned, remember?"

Mathilde's face darkened and she gathered her things. Her movements were jerky and peevish as she crammed folders into her handbag. She got up and headed for the door.

"I really don't know why we bother trying to bail you out. In the end, if you keep on destroying everything around you, it must be because you actually do want to go back to your village and schlep fruit and veg for the rest of your life, right?"

"Get out," I said icily.

"Fuck you, Maxime. You're nothing but trouble anyway."

She left the room and slammed the door. I suppressed a laugh, inwardly congratulating her on her talent as an actress. I turned back to my other two associates.

"So, what's Plan B?" I asked them.

"There is no Plan B, Maxime. Either you go back to

Chateaurenard and help my friend the bookseller, or you go directly to prison."

He got up from his chair, stretching out his heavy frame. The room seemed even smaller now. From a young age, Damien had worked in the vineyards, building up broad shoulders and impressive musculature. He was most certainly the last guy I'd pick a fight with. Despite my experience and height, I wouldn't have a chance.

He stepped in front of me, forcing me to stop pacing.

"Max…"

"Is that why you came here?" I cut him off. "To relish this humiliating little scene where I have to go back to the country with my tail between my legs?"

"I came here because you need help. You can still save your career."

"By going back there?"

"By making amends. In two months, everyone will have forgotten that you busted that guy's nose. You'll be able to get healthy in private."

"In private?" I repeated, somewhere between amusement and anger. "Are you fucking with me? How long do you think it'll be before reporters start showing up and writing pieces on my descent into hell?"

"Do you think it would be any better in prison? Do you think those jailbirds wouldn't take advantage and sell photos or interviews to the highest bidder? Come on,

Max, we're giving you a second chance! And honestly, I think it's your last."

Damien gestured toward Claude.

"Mathilde is already gone, do you want to chase away the last people who care about you?"

"I'm very popular," I assured him.

"With who? Who else is here this morning?" he retorted, furious. "Mathilde left her son with a friend, Claude canceled his weekend time with family, and I just drove all night to get here in time. We're here for you, Max. But we won't be able to help you if you spend your time pushing us away."

I glanced at Claude. As per usual, he was unreadable. His lawyerly mask prevented me from detecting the slightest emotion.

"I didn't ask anyone to come."

"That's true. But we're still here. So, what do you want to do?"

A heavy silence fell. The feeling of suffocation from earlier intensified. The trap was closing on me, and I had no way out.

"Either you come with me, we pack you a bag, and this evening you're in your new room with a view of the park … or you fly solo and we call the judge to cancel this agreement."

"What does she get out of it, the girl taking me in?"

"We're paying her," replied my lawyer. "Enough that

she won't be tempted to sell pictures to reporters and for her to keep an eye on you."

"Oh. Great. Some old bag will make me watch TV game shows and teach me to knit while drinking schnapps. And then she'll go tell her friends all about it?"

Damien smirked before shaking his head.

"She signed a confidentiality agreement. But I'll tell her that, she'll definitely be thrilled."

"I don't want to go back there!" I proclaimed in a last fit of pride.

"Maybe you should have thought of that last night…"

"… and all the times before that," my lawyer finished. "You have to sign this agreement. Believe me, you won't get another chance like this."

"Now I'm supposed to congratulate you, too," I scoffed.

"I'm not asking for much, Maxime. A simple 'thank you' would suffice."

With a sigh of defeat, I approached the table. I hated feeling cornered, hated being deprived of my freedom to choose. I wanted my independence and my current life. I was losing everything, and I wasn't sure I'd get it all back in two months.

"I assure you, Max, this is the best solution. You'll be able to get away from Paris, live a normal life, get back in touch with your roots."

"Except I did everything I could to get away from there," I muttered as I signed the legal agreement.

"Do you want a copy?"

"What for? To fall asleep faster in a town where all signs of life vanish after the evening news?"

Shaking his head, Claude slipped the agreement into a folder. He stood up and extended his hand for me to shake. I ignored it and glowered at him.

"I won't hold you back any more than I did Mathilde, you know."

He dropped his hand and I thought I detected a little disappointment in his eyes. I couldn't even feel guilty. Disappointing the people around me had become a habit of mine. My mother, my father… Mathilde and Claude were just two more names – and certainly not the last – to add to the list.

"I know. But I also know that you need reliable people around you. I'm sure within a few weeks you'll understand that we only want what's best for you."

He stuck out a hand to Damien and thanked him warmly.

"Call me if anything goes wrong."

"No problem," Damien said.

My lawyer left the room, leaving me alone with one of my oldest friends.

"Well. Now that the hired help is gone, can you explain what you're doing here?"

"I'm helping a friend solve her money problems. And I'm helping another friend solve his own problems… That's it."

"Who called you?"

"Your father."

I tensed up immediately and ran a hand over my face. I hadn't had any kind of relationship with my father for years and I didn't expect to resume contact. Since my mother died, I'd given up on family altogether.

"He asked me to help you. Since we're friends and Sarah really does need help, I came up with this solution."

He shrugged and suppressed a yawn. Given the time, he must have driven all night to reach Paris so early. As a token of gratitude, I gave him a weak smile. Damien was the loyal, reliable type, a force of nature who placed honor and sense of duty above all. I shouldn't have been surprised to see him here.

"Let's go to your place. You have to pack a bag."

"I can't even have a day to … transition?"

"I don't have time for your transitional day. We poor people have to work every day."

He jerked his chin toward the door. I slipped on my jacket and found myself out in the fresh air of a Parisian morning. The sun was barely up and I would've given my right arm for a cup of coffee. At the square, I climbed into Damien's truck, shoving yellowed delivery slips and two empty water bottles out of the passenger seat.

"Didn't have time to tidy up, hope you'll forgive me."

"I'll live," I muttered.

I was still stunned by what awaited me. Two months

in my dreary backwater province. Two months. Practically a lifetime for an actor. And without Mathilde by my side, I had nobody left to bail me out.

"Will you give me directions? Or are you going to bellyache the whole way?"

"There has to be a solution," I sighed.

"Yes. Prison."

"Going back there is worse than prison."

"Sarah is a sweet girl. I'm sure once you're there you won't want to leave! But you have to stop doing that."

His eyes had darted to my damaged hands. Going back there wouldn't calm me down. Just the opposite – more than ever I'd have to release this rage and energy.

"Don't ask too much of me. Turn left."

The rest of the ride went by in silence. Less than ten minutes later, I was back in my spotless apartment, nothing out of place. Damien even allowed himself an admiring whistle.

"The next time I'm in the market for an investor, I'm calling you. If I'm in the market for a decorator, for that matter. I didn't know you were into paintings."

"I don't know a thing about them. The apartment was like this when I got here," I explained as I got a suitcase out of the hall closet.

"You didn't change anything? Add anything?"

"Not a thing."

Damien headed to the balcony and pulled back the curtains. The early morning light streamed pleasantly into the living area. Meanwhile, I shuffled to my bedroom. Packing this suitcase was going to hurt me more than my night in a cell or our too-early conversation at the police station. I was still looking for a way out.

I tossed my clothes in a jumble into my suitcase, then headed for the bathroom. Everything there was also perfectly immaculate. I took the bare minimum, convinced I wouldn't be spending the next two months down there.

"Hey," I yelled, "do I have time to take a shower?"

"Do it quick!"

I shrugged out of my clothes and didn't wait for the water to get hot before slipping into the shower. It didn't extinguish my anger. Instead, I replayed recent events in my mind, hoping to understand when my luck had suddenly abandoned me.

"Ready?" asked Damien when I came back to the living area.

"Can I have a cup of coffee at least?"

"Of course!"

For a moment, I almost could have smiled. It was the first time in two hours that I was finally getting my way. I was heading for the kitchen when Damien stopped me. He shook his head and tapped his watch.

"On the road. It'll take five hours to get there."

Chapter Four

After surveying the damage – flooded parquet, waterlogged wall, and ruined furniture – I'd contacted my insurance agent. He was supposed to call me back. To say I was on the verge of a nervous breakdown would have been an understatement. In front of Anita, I'd tried to maintain my dignity. I didn't shed a tear. I grumbled, and cursed both my rotten luck and the bookshop's medieval plumbing.

Anita had helped me and we'd ended up on our hands and knees, using towels to sop up all the water that was threatening the books. At least I'd managed to save my rack of books-in-waiting. As soon as my friend left, I double-locked the door before collapsing onto the only dry spot on the sofa.

There in front of the wall of blistered beige paint, I set aside my pride and wept. I wept for the bookshop, my loneliness, and my life here. I looked around the shop with misty eyes. I had too many books. Too many for this medium-size town, too many for all those people who thought I was a little odd. I was aware of how irrational all those purchases were, but I couldn't help it. Being here, surrounded by novels and stories, comforted me.

The flood had brought me back to reality. I was already in a very precarious financial situation. Frankly, I was in the red, and I owed my survival purely to my status as a property owner and the fact that Baptiste fed me for free. Even if the insurance company was going to take care of the repairs, I'd surely have to put up some cash. Cash I didn't have. I buried my face in my hands and sighed.

Despair was followed by anxiety. Nobody came to wander around bookstores anymore. And even fewer people came to ask me for recommendations. I'd always thought of reading as a passion to share. As a matter of fact, that was why I'd created the book club. Sitting on the parquet already warping from the damp, I felt more alone than ever.

Eyes stinging with tears, I finally got up. Crying had given me some relief, but it hadn't changed anything about the situation. The beginnings of a migraine clamped down on my skull and I decided to pull myself together. It was a tough break, to be sure, but I could manage. I could make this place turn a profit; I could run this bookshop and attract crowds.

I took a deep breath and mounted the stairs leading to my apartment on the second floor. A glance in the bathroom mirror confirmed what I feared: my face was all puffy and my eyes were red. My nose was inflamed from too much wiping. I splashed water on my face and brushed my hair. After making some tea, I went back down to the shop. I walked past the disaster area without even looking.

That was my signature move. As soon as I encountered some bad luck or a potentially dangerous situation, I buried my head in the sand. I pretended everything was fine. I was the kind of kid who, when I played hide-and-seek, took cover behind my hand, convinced no one could see me. I knew it was childish, but it kept me from thinking too hard and getting depressed.

I reopened the shop, leaving the door wide open. The summertime warmth chased away the last of my worries. I ventured a smile as I arranged the tables and chairs on the pavement.

"Hi!"

I froze when I heard my neighbor's voice. What were the odds that my face had deflated enough that I no longer resembled a scarlet balloon?

"Hi," I mumbled, uselessly shifting a chair.

Head in the sand, like always. I already had trouble facing my neighbor under normal circumstances. This time, between the evidence of my crying fit and the reading-nook flood, I was this close to hiding under a table.

"Is everything okay?" he asked.

"I … yes."

"Anita told me you had a burst pipe…"

I finally turned toward him, almost relieved I didn't have to put on an act. My smile widened and my mood lightened when I saw the bouquet of wildflowers he was holding.

"It won't help with the mopping up, but I thought it couldn't hurt."

"Thanks," I murmured appreciatively.

I brought the flowers to my nose, soothed by their scent after all. Within seconds I was already feeling better.

"You shouldn't have," I said, entering the bookshop.

"Anita told me it was serious and you were going to have to close?"

"A major flood. Not too nasty, but it'll require some work. I'm waiting for the insurance agent to come assess it."

I put the flowers in a vase while Frédéric paced back and forth in the entrance. I made a face, then dismissed the subject with a wave of my hand. If I was going to stick my head in the sand, it wasn't so I could pour salt in the wound with the florist.

"Really, nothing dramatic."

I moved toward Frédéric, who was weaving in and

out of the low shelves. The entrance to the shop was the area I had worked on the most. I liked it to be welcoming and make you smile right away. I'd tried lots of different things before settling on what worked the best.

"Blind Date?" asked Frédéric, pointing to a shelf in front of him.

"For anybody who comes here and says, 'I don't know what I want.' Which is what people do most of the time…"

After a long pause, Frédéric picked up one of the gift-wrapped books. Every week, I would choose five titles – new and old alike – wrap them up and add a card with just a few words about the contents. The customers' curiosity and surprise would do the rest.

"And then, when they give them as gifts, they have the perfect excuse for a blunder. They can just blame chance and me."

"Let's avoid giving a medical thriller to a nurse…"

"Or erotica to a nun," I hooted. "That's happened before," I continued, seeing my neighbor's utterly dumbfounded look.

"Really?"

"She came back to exchange it afterward. She got a travel guide. Much … better suited to her."

He laughed along with me and opened the little card attached to the book, which contained the keywords. He raised an eyebrow, then went on:

"Okay. So, perhaps 'an unexpected meeting', 'a taste

of Italy', and 'families suck', is … a locked-room mystery set around a family barbecue gone wrong? Or maybe an intergenerational cookbook?"

"It's *Romeo and Juliet*," I replied, laughing.

"Too bad. The cookbook would have been more useful, especially for our lunch."

An embarrassing silence settled over us. I just smiled, pretending my blood pressure wasn't going through the roof … not because of the lunch, but because of me. I just didn't know how to interact with men. The slightest friendliness made me panic. I was afraid of misinterpreting signals, tripping over my tongue, and sinking into the depths of humiliation.

Frédéric must have interpreted my silence as a wave of doubts, because he started in again:

"Are you okay with having lunch together?"

"Um… Yes, of course…"

"I thought since you eat alone almost every day, you'd like a little company."

"Oh, yes. Of course! Well, let's keep it simple, eh? A sandwich will be great!"

Anita would have hit me for ruining the moment like that. A man was finally inviting me to share a meal, and I suggested sandwiches. I should have gagged myself, then hightailed it to the "self-help" section to find a practical guide on male–female relationships.

"I was aiming a little higher, actually."

"Okay. But, really, don't go out of your way, I—"

"Sarah, I'd like very much to take you out to the restaurant," he cut me off gently. "I'd like to spend some time with you."

"Aren't we already doing that?"

The second I answered, I kicked myself. Frédéric was going to start believing I didn't want to go to lunch at all. Except it was the exact opposite. I wanted it so much that it scared the pants off me and made me nervous and defensive. And, inevitably, I blurted out a whole bunch of nonsense.

"I meant, more … privately."

A hot flush gripped me, and my throat tightened. This man was just *talking* to me and I was already on the verge of fainting; a lunch would sign my death warrant. Another silence slipped between us. I stared at the "Blind Date" books without really seeing them. The only thing that reassured me was glancing at my neighbor. He seemed just as uncomfortable as I was, arms hanging at his sides.

"What about the play?" he asked.

"The play? Oh … you know about that?"

"Anita is a real blabbermouth. She'd give up the nuclear launch codes to anybody who asked. She told me that every year, at the end of the summer, you put on a play. Have you already started rehearsals?"

"Not really. The book club hasn't decided what to perform yet."

"Do you have a preference? Is there a role you'd like

to take on?"

"Not on your life! I'm happy with managing the volunteers and yelling at them now and again like a good, temperamental director."

"You'd rather be in the background, then?"

"It's not really my thing to be … in the spotlight. I like to stay in the wings."

Frédéric looked at me curiously. His eyes darkened slightly, and I held my breath as I felt his thumb brush my cheek to push back a rebellious lock of hair.

"To be honest, I think that's kind of a shame."

His voice was soft as silk. It lasted half a second, but to me it seemed like time stopped. Just like my heart. I'd had plenty of conversations with Frédéric before: we'd talk about our respective businesses, the weather, our customers, life in the neighborhood … but we'd never had such intimate contact.

My heart raced with panic and I took a step back, ready to hide behind my counter.

"You want it?" I asked, gesturing toward the book in his hands.

He paused, still shocked by the change of mood. I pasted on a professional smile and whipped a paper bag out from under the counter.

"My treat!" I offered, a little too enthusiastically.

I couldn't handle the situation. It was a real Catch-22: I liked Frédéric – and it seemed as though he liked me, too – but the prospect of getting close to him terrified me.

For me, men were a little bit like heights. I knew they existed, and they fascinated me, but as soon as I got anywhere near them, vertigo would throw me so off balance that I found any excuse at all to run away.

"I want to pay for it, Sarah."

"No, it's fine. It's my pleasure!"

"Is there any chance this play will get chosen?"

The abrupt change of subject unsettled me. It took me a second to understand: the book, the play, Frédéric, the flood. Today was exhausting. I almost regretted reopening.

"Because if you play Juliet, I could make sure to learn the part of Romeo in the next two days," he joked.

I was convinced my heart was going to give out because of this emotional roller coaster. I'd managed to tamp down my panic, and now it came back with a vengeance, ready to trample what was left of my pride. I cleared my throat and tried not to let my voice quaver.

"I told you, I prefer not to be on stage. And besides, this play wasn't on the shortlist."

I reached out, silently urging him to give me the book. Slipping it into the bag and handing it back to him had to be enough to make him leave.

"Well, I can't wait to see it!" he said, finally giving me the book.

He stepped up to the counter and I laid the bag with his book on top of it. I thrust my hands into my pockets and managed to breathe normally. Was it normal to be so out of sorts? To alternate between acute tachycardia and unpleasant heat waves? My experience was so limited that I couldn't even understand my own body.

"See you at lunch?"

"With pleasure," I trilled.

With one last smile, he slipped out. The very next instant, I collapsed behind the counter, exhausted from my performance.

I was a walking disaster.

I groaned with frustration, cursing my ability to ruin a relationship … even one that hadn't started yet. After a few minutes of self-flagellation, I got back to work, writing up two recommendations and making lists of possible future themes for the display window.

At the end of the day, my insurance agent – a tall, thin man – showed up at the bookshop. His snooty attitude told me immediately that he wouldn't do anything to make my life easier. Besides, I remembered his last visit perfectly well: a nonexistent sense of diplomacy, no empathy, and zero flexibility. I didn't stand a chance.

"Well, then, what's going on here?" he asked, cleaning his glasses with his tie.

I led the way to the reading nook. Silently, he pulled a file out of his satchel and took a few notes. His khaki-green suit was so big he was swimming in it. An odor of mothballs mixed with tobacco made me wrinkle my nose. I already couldn't wait for him to leave.

"Tell me what happened," he prompted.

"There are three rows of pipes that run behind this wall."

"And they date back to the construction of the building, I imagine?"

He swept a condescending look over the space around him. I'd never been ashamed of the bookshop or my apartment – until now. I crossed my arms over my chest to regain some confidence. He could do his job, but belittling everything I'd built here was out of the question.

"Yeah. I assume one of the pipes broke."

"And then flooded part of your store. And where is the leak?"

"I cut the water to that section."

"Good."

He jotted a few more notes down in his file, then prodded some of the furniture I'd cleared away into a corner. A long, heavy silence fell, during which he looked everywhere, like a Grand Inquisitor.

"And this has happened before?"

"Two years ago."

He frowned. I added quickly, "Road construction caused the leak; too much vibration. My kitchen upstairs was flooded. The damage was very limited."

"And since then you haven't had any work done to …

reinforce your facilities? They're obviously in bad shape. There should be a complete renovation."

"Of course. But the cost of that renovation is too … high. It's impossible for me to finance such major work."

"But you understand that our company cannot cover the damages as a matter of course?"

I stared at him, the reality hitting me. After two floods, the insurance company could actually slam the door in my face and cancel my policy. As if reading my thoughts, the insurance agent said:

"To renew your policy, we'll of course have to review the property beforehand. If the work hasn't been done…"

He didn't finish his sentence, and his threat remained unspoken. I hid my anxiety and went back to surveying the damage.

"So, there's the wall, the floor. A few books were affected. The furniture, too, obviously."

He took down my remarks religiously, while I nibbled nervously on my thumbnail. This man, with his questionable smell and hideous suit, had my fate in his hands.

"Good. Mademoiselle Lacoste, here's what I suggest: I'm going to advise my company to cover the expenses for the damages incurred by the leak. For the leak itself, you'll have to have the repair work done."

"What about paying for it?"

"I encourage you to inquire with the appropriate

agencies. Your town hall, the housing authority ... A whole host of agencies can help you finance the work. On my end, I'm going to consult with the company's social assistance department. We'll certainly find a solution."

"Except I don't have six months to do this," I cried. "I don't have the money for plumbing!"

"Then maybe you should think about whether you want to maintain this shop?"

His tone froze me in place. He closed his writing pad, slipped his pen into the pocket of his suit, and nodded at me in farewell. I squeezed my hands into fists and managed, with difficulty, to hold back the stream of insults on the tip of my tongue. Now it wasn't just my future that was uncertain – I wasn't sure I'd make it through the end of the day.

"We'll send you a check for the repairs. For the rest, you know what you have to do."

"You can see yourself out," I snapped, furious.

He left my shop in an instant and I closed the door behind him. In two sentences and ten minutes of assessment, this man had just shattered everything I'd built here: the bookshop, the book club, my apartment, my childhood memories.

I went back over to the reading nook. Of course, I could always keep the bookshop open during the renovations ... but that was just postponing the inevitable. Without insurance, I couldn't stay here. The bank would eventually hold me to account, and I'd no longer have access to credit.

I was trapped and didn't have the faintest idea what to do.

I dissolved into tears on the sofa; it was ruined, in any case, with its sodden fabric already smelling rancid. Worn out from sobbing, I finally sat up. I'd hatched a bunch of plans as absurd as they were improbable, from fraud, pure and simple, to prostitution.

My inability to lie made me abandon the first one.

The prospect of having my insurance agent as a client made me forget about the second.

I could also have a big clearance sale, in hopes of bringing in enough money to make the repairs and get back on the right foot. The situation was desperate, but I could still come out with my head held high. If I was going to lose everything, I might as well choose the moment.

Sell everything. Including the bookshop. It broke my heart into thousands of tiny pieces, but I had no other solution. The books, the furniture, the shelves, the coffee cups. Everything. And then, find a job and forget this disaster. It was my best hope. The plan that left me with nothing, but saved my pride.

Relieved that I'd made a decision, I went up to my apartment. I checked the state of my face. It was obvious I'd cried too much today. I opted for a nice bath, trying to forget that this place would soon no longer be mine.

An hour later, I was on my way to Baptiste's for dinner. My hair still damp, I suppressed a shiver as I felt the cool evening air caress my cheeks. Upon entering the restaurant, the smell of roasted meat seasoned with *herbes de Provence* made me smile. I needed comfort, and a hearty meal would surely do the trick.

"I'm sitting in the back," I informed Baptiste as I wended my way between the tables.

"I'll bring you a glass of wine!"

"Bring the whole bottle."

The hearty meal would do me good, the alcohol would make me forget this day, and I'd end up in my bed poor and drunk. Baptiste met me at the table, promised bottle in hand. While proceeding with the corkscrew ritual, he explained:

"A 2012 red, fantastic Bordeaux. Tonight, lamb shank confit with rosemary and mashed potatoes. I can make you a salad, if you prefer."

"Lamb, potatoes. Perfect. Double the potatoes!"

He stopped short and frowned. I was more of a fan of green vegetables and salads; Baptiste could likely count on one hand the times when I'd allowed myself the famous truffle tagliatelli, his wife's specialty.

I held out my glass, encouraging him to continue. I didn't want anyone to ask questions, let alone try to make me change my mind. Just silence, lamb, potatoes ...

and this delicious wine I was tasting half-heartedly. Baptiste watched me.

"If you have a problem, we can talk about it, if you want."

"We could, yes ... but it won't be enough!"

A fresh frown crossed his face. He opened his mouth, about to ask me a question, but he was interrupted by a customer calling for him. He grumbled into his beard and poured me a glass.

"We'll talk later," he warned me.

"Bring some cognac, then!"

This time, he was downright furious. Baptiste had this adorable tendency to protect his own – his wife, his family, his loved ones – and he could prove particularly tough and aggressive when people he liked were attacked. I knew that I must be worrying him, and he was surely conjuring up a whole pile of scenarios to explain it.

When he returned to my table, he set my plate down in silence. He'd probably end up asking me questions again with dessert.

"Hey."

I stopped playing with my meat and lifted my gaze toward Damien, another neighbor and the owner of a local vineyard. Seeing my face, he frowned, and without asking permission grabbed an empty chair from the next table. He sat down across from me, a worried expression on his face.

"The last time I saw you like this, your favorite TV show had just been cancelled and one of your suppliers had dared to unceremoniously chuck a box of books on the pavement."

I shivered at the memory. The box had broken open immediately and books had ended up in the gutter. Two thirds of my order had been destroyed and I'd griped for two days while wishing the ten plagues of Egypt on the delivery man.

Without saying a word, I poured myself another glass of wine. A smile flickered across Damien's lips, and with a wave of his hand he signaled Baptiste to bring him some of what I was having. He turned the bottle toward himself, nodding with appreciation when he saw the provenance of this fabulous red wine and its powers of amnesia.

"You know it?" I asked.

"Made by a friend of mine."

"It's excellent," I complimented him and raised my glass.

"It's made with love," he exclaimed with a laugh. "Winegrowing is nothing but that!"

"That's something we have in common! At least, for the moment!"

I brought the glass to my lips and tried to drain it in one go. Damien stopped me in an instant, seizing my glass and shaking his head. I grumbled but didn't rebel. I didn't have the strength anymore.

"And it's made to be savored," he said.

"That's what I'm doing!" I protested thickly. "I'm savoring it!"

"You're knocking it back! If you're really feeling awful, stick to cocktails and save this wine for a special occasion!"

He moved the glass away from my grasping fingers, then rested his elbows on the table. Baptiste brought him a whole place setting and he ordered a salad. From that point, I concentrated on carefully shredding my lamb. My stomach was too knotted up to eat. The wine at least had the virtue of making me forget this disastrous day.

"How about telling me what's going on," Damien offered. "You seem like you're at the end of your rope!"

"I don't know where to start."

"I'd say 'at the beginning' but I'm afraid of being too clichéd!"

To encourage me, he put his hand over mine and patted it gently. Through the bookshop, I managed to establish a host of relationships. I had friends, loved ones I could count on. Most of them were my parents' age. Damien was one of the few exceptions. Barely three years older than me, he managed the vineyard he'd inherited with a professionalism and perseverance I admired. He'd suffered terrible weather and major setbacks with customers, but he'd held his ground, without letting it get him down.

Across from him tonight, with the several glasses of

wine I'd gulped down and my dejected appearance, I felt a little bit pathetic. In his eyes, I probably looked like a self-pitying diva.

"I'm going to sell the bookshop."

That was both the beginning and the end of my story. Except telling someone made the situation real and irrevocable, as if it confirmed my decision. Damien looked at me, confused.

"I really did want the beginning, actually," he said calmly.

"The insurance company is threatening to cancel my policy. The bookshop is too dilapidated."

"Make some repairs!"

"Oh! Thank you, I hadn't thought of that," I said sarcastically with a grimace.

I took another swig of my glass of wine and my anger receded instantly.

"I have nothing, Damien. Not a cent. Nothing. Nada. Zero. The bank can turn a blind eye to my overdraft, but they'll never agree to finance a loan. The plumbing leaks and needs to be completely refurbished, the roof could use a good cleaning. I don't even have enough to change the two bulbs that burned out last week."

"No one here will accept you selling."

"No one here is helping me," I said, a little bitterly.

"You're drunk and irrational. You can't sell the bookshop. You're the heart of this town. Everyone knows it!"

"I'm not doing this lightly, Damien. I've turned the situation over every which way: I don't see any other solution. Do you see one?"

"Do the repairs yourself!"

"With who? I'm all alone, Damien. I don't know how to do that sort of thing… I … I can't do it," I repeated, stifling a sob.

His silence confirmed what I feared. There was no other solution. It broke my heart to admit it. I swallowed my tears and took refuge in my glass of wine. Out of the corner of my eye, I saw Damien calling to Baptiste.

"Bring us another bottle," he ordered.

Drunk, I was incredibly cheerful and ready to fall asleep anywhere. Once I was in my bed, I buried my head in the soft pillow with a happy moan. Here, at least, nothing could happen to me.

The bookshop doorbell pulled me from sleep a few hours later. I grimaced, covering my ears with my pillow. My head was buzzing and weighed two tons. This racket was doing nothing to soothe my impending migraine. I cursed the neighborhood kids and pulled the comforter up.

But the bell rang again. A long, strident, intolerable buzz. Clearly one of the kids had found a way to stick a piece of tape on it. Wrapped in my comforter, hair tousled, stunned by a hellish hangover, and dazed by lack of sleep, I hurtled down the stairs to the door.

I unbolted it and nearly tore it off the hinges. To my great surprise, I found Damien, breathless and with dark circles under his eyes.

"What?" I barked.

"I found a solution," he panted.

"For?"

"For you to keep the bookshop. I have the money."

He doubled over, out of breath, hands on his knees. I pulled the comforter more tightly around me, glancing quickly around. This might be a joke.

"Damien, it's not even morning yet!" I groaned as I shut the door on him.

With a firm hand, he pushed it open and gave me a dark look as he straightened up. I took a step back, to avoid an unfortunate encounter between the door and my face.

"No time to wait. We have to talk about it now."

He entered the bookshop purposefully and headed for the coffee machine. After closing the door behind him, I followed and climbed up on my stool, eyes still half shut. Damien handed me a steaming cup of coffee, then sat down across from me.

"I have a solution," he said again. "And you'll be able to keep your bookshop."

"You met the devil and I'm going to have to sell him my soul?"

A smile quirked across his lips and he shook his head. I took a sip of my coffee. Though it didn't wake me up completely, the bitterness at least made my mouth taste less like cardboard. I shivered and rubbed my eyes. I wasn't a night owl, preferring the early morning light for contemplation.

"Almost," he said with a laugh. "Does the name Maxime Maréchal mean anything to you?"

"The actor?"

"The actor, yes."

The shock sent my mouthful of coffee down the wrong pipe. A coughing fit shook me and tears of pain stung my eyes. Damien waited calmly for me to recover before going on. I still didn't see the connection between the bookshop and Maxime Maréchal.

"He's having some problems with the law."

"That's not new, is it? Isn't he the one who punched a photographer?"

"Yes," he sighed. "He's … currently, he's in the drunk tank. We're trying to find a way to keep him out of prison."

"We?"

"His agent, his lawyer, and me. Maxime and I were childhood friends. He was always … impulsive. But this time, he's got a lot on the line. His career could be over if he goes to prison."

"What does that have to do with me?"

I still didn't understand. My hands closed around my

scalding cup as Damien caught my eye. Exhaustion warred with worry across his face. He took a deep breath, as if he were about to jump into a pool, then said:

"We could offer him community service. He'll serve his sentence, but outside of prison. I thought… I thought he could do it here."

"Here? In Chateaurenard?"

"Here, with you."

In one second, my hangover vanished. The fog keeping my brain from functioning correctly dissipated. Maxime Maréchal. With me. I thought furtively of my allusion to the devil. Maxime *was* very nearly the devil. The mad dog of the movies, a womanizer, unstable, impulsive, violent. I had no desire to welcome that guy into my bookshop. Desperate, maybe, but not raving mad.

"In the bookshop, then? Doing what?"

"Well, helping you. You were saying last night that you didn't have anyone, that you needed a hand! Maxime could help you here and do some repair work."

I stared at him incredulously. After everything I'd been through the day before, this proposition was surreal. A movie star was going to come do my repair work – a scenario straight out of my list of absurd plans.

"Damien, this is crazy! That guy is berserk! How could I control him? And what would I do with him? What if he got violent with me?"

"Control him? With money. He'll pay to be here and

that will finance your renovations. The slightest mistake will send him to prison. Believe me, he really doesn't want to go there. His career is all that matters. You're in a position of power."

"Are you joking? Is he at least knowledgeable about plumbing?"

"Frankly, I don't know. But we'll work it out. What matters is that his mere presence will boost traffic in your shop."

"And reporters? Photographers? I don't want to be spied on forever. And where will he stay?"

Damien rubbed the back of his neck, visibly embarrassed. When he looked back up at me, I realized that the trap was much more vicious than I'd imagined.

"No," I replied, as soon as I understood.

"We don't really have a choice. The ankle monitor will limit his movements. And since you have a spare room…"

Damien took my hand in his and his voice softened.

"Listen, Sarah, he's a friend. An old friend. He has a whole lot of problems, and if we leave him down there, it'll end badly for him. As for you, you need money. You really think we'll let you sell the bookshop without a word? You think that won't mean anything to this town? It's an arrangement that suits both of you. And anyway, it's temporary!"

"Damien, I don't…"

"Let's try it, okay? In any case, if there's any problem, he goes back to Paris to serve his sentence."

I now regretted drinking too much during dinner. My mind wasn't clear enough to make a decision. The idea of having a stranger here to live with me was horrifying. On the other hand, saving the bookshop was the only thing that mattered.

"How long?" I asked, still dazed.

"Two months. It'll go by fast! And I'll be there to keep an eye on him."

Damien glanced at his watch, betraying his anxiety. I took a moment to think about the implications of such an agreement. Unlike other women, I liked my solitude, I liked the silence, and I liked being able to walk around in a bathrobe without worrying about prying eyes. But, in any case, if I didn't find the means to finance the repairs, even my bathrobe would end up being sold.

"What about the money?"

"Half of it by tomorrow, the rest at the end."

He leaned toward me and added in a low voice:

"I'm talking about an amount large enough to cover your renovations and take you on a luxury trip around the world. Sarah, please, you have to say yes."

"Why do you want to save this awful dude so much?"

He took my cup of coffee out of my hands and finally answered:

"He's not awful, just lost."

Chapter Five

"You're stopping?"

"Last rest area before Chateaurenard," Damien explained. "You get ten minutes of reprieve."

He parked the truck and took a pack of cigarettes out of his pocket.

"What do I care," I muttered. "Anyway, I thought we were late?"

"Five hours on the road and when you finally talk to me, it's to complain?"

"Go fuck yourself, Damien."

"Excellent idea. But before that, I'm going to get a coffee, because I just got saddled with almost twelve hours of driving and a sleepless night to save your ass."

"I didn't ask you for shit! I'm used to running my own life."

I was still angry with him. These five hours on the

road, in his grimy truck, with dirty tarps and a cab that smelled like hay, had reminded me of everything I'd run away from. Coming back here meant admitting that I'd screwed up.

"And look where that got you!"

"Are you gonna get that coffee or what?" I shouted, kicking the dashboard.

"You can be as mad as you want with me, but you're the only one to blame!"

I stared daggers at him before wrenching the door open to get out. Damien followed and came around the car to face me. It was the first time since I'd left my parents' house that somebody dared to look me in the eye with the firm intention of standing up to me.

"Admit it!" he shouted. "Admit you're the only one to blame!"

"That little bastard shouldn't have gone to the police! It's his fault!"

To release my anger, I slammed my fist down on the hood of the truck. The metallic sound seemed to echo around the whole car park and a few curious looks turned toward us.

"You almost killed him!"

Annoyed, I pushed Damien away by driving my fist into his shoulder. His nearness was maddening, making me feel like I couldn't breathe anymore. He took the blow, then came back at me, his chest right up against mine. Even though I was taller, I knew Damien could put me on the ground in a heartbeat. Just the look in his eyes was enough to keep my fists at my sides.

"If you want to hit somebody, take on somebody your own size," he whispered, jaw tight.

"Don't tempt me."

"You screwed up, Maxime," my friend barked as he drove his index finger into my chest. "It's as simple as that! The quicker you realize it, the better."

I took a deep breath and pushed away another wave of rage. In my gut, I knew Damien was right. But this return to the past felt like a much harder blow than any punch.

"Now we'll go get that coffee," he said.

"You've spent the last two hours complaining about traffic and how tired you are. Don't you want to just keep going?"

"Put on your sunglasses and stop griping! I'm going to buy you a cup of coffee."

"Wonderful, you're so good to me," I quipped.

"Don't make me regret saving your ass!"

We headed for the food court. At this time of year, there were already holiday-makers returning to their cottages for the summer. I'd done everything I could to leave this region – I couldn't understand anyone coming here voluntarily. There was nothing here, except maybe some vineyards and a few churches to visit. It was sad and dreary, utterly uninteresting.

Damien bought me a vile cup of coffee for forty cents.

We sat down away from everyone else, at a grubby high table. I caught a few curious glances. Despite my dark glasses, because of the newspaper headlines, I was easily recognizable.

My hell had begun the second I'd climbed into Damien's truck. Photographers were already cooling their heels in front of my place. When they saw me leave with a suitcase, a flurry of rumors must have flapped off to the newspapers. Within a few days, the whole country would be informed.

"When we get there, we'll have to stop by the police station for your ankle monitor. You'll be able to go out twice a day, for one hour. Afterward, we'll head for the bookshop where Sarah is expecting us."

"What's this girl like, exactly?"

"What do you mean?"

"The last time I saw a bookseller, she was as old as my mother and wore bifocals," I replied.

"Sarah is your age and really nice."

"Really?" I asked, delighted to finally find something interesting in this business.

"Really. And I forbid you to touch her. She's not one of those girls you can screw at a night club."

"So, I'm under house arrest and banned from sex?"

"With her, yes. Sarah is … shy. You might intimidate her, or even frighten her. So, please, don't involve her in any of your lecherous plans."

"Sounds like you've got a thing for her!"

"Don't be an ass, she's like my sister. So, if you touch her, I swear I'll kill you. Sleep with anyone you want, but not her. She's too good for you."

"Fine. Whatever."

"And for your community service, we'll go over that with her when we get there. She's had some water damage and you can expect some big renovations. I really want you to help her. She needs it."

"I thought she said yes for the money!"

"She said yes to save her bookshop and do me a favor. How long has it been since you helped somebody?"

I just shook my head. In any case, I was hamstrung and at the mercy of this bookseller. I'd just go back and forth between the bookshop and my room. Two months. Two long months of shame. I could do it.

"What about Mathilde? What do you think I should do?" I asked.

"Well, well," sneered Damien, "does Maxime Maréchal feel remorse?"

"Shove it! She annoyed me … but I don't want to sack her."

"Damn, you really are sorry? If I'd known, I would have put my foot up your ass sooner! That girl moved heaven and earth to save you. You're going to have to realize there are people around you who want to help."

"They're people I pay. Her, my lawyer. Even this

bookseller. It's the dough that keeps them close to me, nothing else!"

Damien sighed, then took a swig of his coffee. I had no illusions about my relationships with others. Upon entering this world, I'd known that money ruled everything. My only real friend was Simon: the only man in my entourage with more money than me. In this world, more than anywhere else, without money we were nothing.

"Flowers, apologies. She'll calm down eventually, but I have to say I thought you were really nasty to her. You deserve to be dropped. Apparently, you have to hit rock bottom to get that!"

I was brooding over my mistakes enough. I didn't need Damien to repeat them all. I'd behaved like a thickhead with my agent; I was going to have to repair the damage. I didn't want to leave the profession. Even though my current career owed a lot to chance, I wanted to do everything I could to stay an actor.

"For the time being, just obey your sentence to the letter. That will show your good will!"

"As if I had a choice," I grumbled.

"But you did have one. We always have a choice," Damien lectured me, then emptied his cup of coffee in one gulp. "Shall we?"

The last few miles of the journey seemed to last an eternity. I recognized the familiar landscape of Charente: vineyards, trees, greenery, and that delightful little village of Chateaurenard. Damien's winery was one of the area's few attractions. The number of residents went up in the summer, but the winter was so quiet that you could go out completely naked in the middle of November without encountering a single person.

"Here we are."

Damien parked near a flower shop and pointed across the way: a bookshop located in an old two-story building. A few tables and chairs had been set out, not far from a shelf overflowing with books. Above the door, ivy meandered along one of the windows. The sun streamed pleasantly onto the pavement, but there was no one there.

"It's deserted," I muttered.

"It's only the start of the summer season."

I looked back over at the bookshop. A dark-haired young woman, dressed in oversized jeans and a black tank top, was scribbling on a slate in the shop window. I heaved a weary sigh. Two months. Two long months.

"That's Sarah. Get your stuff, we're going to the police station!"

Nearly an hour later, I was sporting an ankle monitor. The cops hadn't been lenient with me, but under the watchful eye of Damien, I'd held it together. The instructions were clear: I couldn't leave the bookshop except from eight o'clock to nine o'clock in the morning and from seven o'clock to eight o'clock in the evening. I had to go to the police station every Monday and, obviously, behave myself on pain of returning to Paris to end up in the slammer.

I knew the local fuzz were hoping I'd crack, so they'd have the pleasure of taking me back to the capital and slathering on a new layer of humiliation.

"If you want, we can go running tomorrow morning," suggested Damien.

"I'd rather have a punching bag!"

"I'll try to find one. But I'm up for a morning jog. It'll be good for me, too!"

"Whatever."

I had very little time off the leash. Spending it with Damien would certainly keep me from getting into more trouble.

"Ready?" asked Damien as we prepared to cross the street to the bookshop.

"Do I have a choice?"

"I already told you, we always have a choice. Do you have the check?"

"In my back pocket."

Those last few yards were the hardest. As long as I was out on the street, there was still a sense of freedom. I could see the sky, feel the wind – I was like anybody else. I might even have been there of my own free will, poking around the bookshelf set up on the pavement.

"What is this thing?" I asked Damien.

"Books-in-waiting."

"They're free. For people who can't afford them," a woman's voice explained. "Someone will buy a few books and leave some of them here for the less fortunate. You can take one, sir."

I grimaced and shook my head; these dog-eared paperbacks didn't appeal. I turned toward the bookseller I'd glimpsed from the truck. Her jeans were definitely too big and her tank top had a hole in the front. Curly hair, a bit wild, framed her pale face. Her green eyes pierced me, as if trying to uncover my darkest secrets. With a little makeup and a decent dress, she could have been attractive. But here, surrounded by books, hands gray with dust and cheeks flushed with exertion, there was nothing appealing about her.

"Sarah, this is Maxime."

"Pleased to meet you," she said, thrusting her hands into her back pockets.

"Maxime, this is Sarah. She owns the place, both the bookshop and the apartment upstairs. Sarah is a village institution."

"No kidding," I muttered.

"We had a long drive," Damien said, to explain my bad mood.

"Yes, indeed. And I have no desire to be here," I reminded him. "Where's my room?"

An awkward silence descended, until Sarah opted to go

inside and show us around. The smell of old paper and ink assaulted me – this was going to give me a migraine. I spotted the staircase that must lead to her apartment, but Damien put a hand on my arm before I could make a move.

"What?" I barked.

"Sarah wants to show you around the place."

I cocked an eyebrow, not at all interested in making nice. I hated this place, and the idea of being cooped up here for two months made me want to puke. Would I have to be a model prisoner, too?

"I was actually thinking about going to sleep," I replied curtly.

"We can do the tour tomorrow," suggested Sarah. "It'll all be the same."

She punctuated her remark with a nervous little laugh, all while rubbing her hands on her jeans. Behind her, I saw a heap of boxes revealing a few books. Sarah followed my gaze.

"I received them last month. They still have to be sorted, labeled, and put on the shelf."

I shot her a surprised look.

The place was overflowing with books, every last square foot crammed to capacity. I didn't see how she could add any more.

"Maxime will help you," offered Damien.

I sighed and got a sharp elbow in the ribs.

"That's what you're here for," he reminded me.

"You'll also help her move the reading nook so she can reopen it by next week."

"Oh! But it's not really all that urgent and…"

I suppressed a victorious smile. This girl was way too nice. Within a couple of days, I'd have her eating out of my hand. This was going to be too easy.

"Sarah, you need help," Damien cut in. "Maxime will move the necessary shelves. I want to see this reading nook back up and running as soon as possible. He'll also help you with the repairs. He knows how to paint, I think."

"I'll try."

I didn't especially feel like making an effort. My sentence consisted of living here for two months, not being her slave. Besides, I'd always hated painting. It reminded me too much of my father's job.

Damien shot me a warning look and tried to mend my image:

"He'll help you," he assured her. "He's too scared I'll give him a good hiding!"

Another nervous laugh from the girl, as her eyes rolled around, looking for refuge. They ran over everything, except for me. Sarah had obviously taken pains over the décor: quotes, reproductions of paintings, book covers pieced together into mosaics. Everything revolved around literature. I wondered vaguely if she cared about anything else. I doubted it.

"Obviously, you're free to help yourself as much as you like."

"I'll be sure to," I lied.

She smiled at me hesitantly. Damien was right, this girl was a mouse. As soon as I looked at her a little too long, she dropped her gaze. I felt like a wild animal busting into a museum.

"I'll show you the apartment."

The staircase was steep and I had to duck my head to avoid the ceiling. Sarah led the way, while I followed Damien. In between two steps, he turned to me with his teeth clenched.

"Pretend to be nice! You're freaking her out."

"I'm not doing anything!" I answered in the same tone.

"At least try to thank her. She's doing you a favor," he reminded me.

The staircase opened directly into a large living area. The place was warm and contained no surprises: Sarah lived in a world of books. Piles of novels filled the walls. A wooden bookcase even seemed to be sagging under the weight of them. A sofa upholstered in black fabric and a television set marked the sitting room. Further on, a white lacquered kitchen covered an entire wall. There were no tables, just a counter with two stools.

"To the left is my room, and to the right is yours. I left the sheets on your bed. You have a closet. The bathroom is behind this door."

"What about yours?"

"This is mine. We'll share," she murmured.

Her uneasiness increased and she started doing the evasive gaze thing again. She slipped her hands into her pockets and shuffled her feet.

"Sorry, it's not very big, and it's certainly not what you're used to, but..."

"Maxime slept in my barn for a whole summer. Believe me, he's had worse!"

Sarah's face brightened, as if relieved. I stared daggers at Damien. Did he have to remind me of that? Sleeping in his barn had taught me just one thing: I preferred a comfortable bed.

"As for cooking, I confess I'm very bad at it. So, if you tell me what you want, I'll take care of the shopping."

"Sarah eats at Baptiste's pretty often. He runs a wine bar on the square," Damien explained.

"I'll go have a look around ... between seven and eight o'clock," I said between gritted teeth.

Sarah moved off toward the kitchen and checked the refrigerator. While she was occupied, Damien gave me another jab with his elbow, coupled with a furious look.

"Now," he demanded in a low voice. "And you have to give her the check."

Damien was making me do something I didn't enjoy. I hated thanking someone profusely, especially in public. That was also what I liked about the movies: they would give me directions, I'd learn my lines, and I'd say them.

No qualms, mechanical emotions, no problem. Easier than being myself.

I tossed my bag into a corner and cleared my throat. "Sarah?"

"Yes? Oh, sorry, what would you like? I can still go do some shopping and…"

Her shyness was comical. It could also be useful.

"I wanted to thank you."

"Oh! Well…"

"And give you this," I added, getting the check out of my pocket.

Her cheeks regained that tomato color. She pressed her lips together before taking the check. Oddly, Damien's warning came back to me. I wasn't supposed to touch her.

"Th-thank you, that's most kind. Would you like a receipt, or…"

I laughed at the idea of her giving her jailbird inmate a receipt. "You don't have to be quite so formal," I observed. "We're going to spend two months here together – let's not make it any harder for ourselves."

"Okay, whatever you want," she said. "Thanks again for the … uh … check."

"Perfect," said Damien. "You've got the insurance money?"

"Bank transfer tomorrow," replied Sarah. "Then I'll go buy the supplies I need for the repairs."

"Call me, I'll come help you, okay? I have to go. Maxime, I'm counting on you for our morning jog!"

"I don't intend to lose an hour of freedom," I answered.

"I'm off! See you later!"

Damien made his escape from the apartment, leaving me alone with Sarah. Her embarrassment was palpable and I decided to take refuge in my room. I certainly wasn't going to be leaving it much during the coming weeks.

"I'm going to put my stuff away."

"Okay. Do … do you want to eat dinner together? We don't have to, but I thought I could get something to go and…"

"We're not going to be friends, Sarah. Not even close."

My response stunned her. She stared at me for several long seconds, trembling all over. This wasn't just shyness, I really scared the shit out of her. Interesting.

"I'm not here of my own volition," I reminded her. "I'm serving my sentence and going home, got it?"

"But…"

"I did everything I could to get out of here and, honestly, I have no desire to stay. So, I'm going to do these two months. I suggest you stay out of the way and ask no questions. Okay?"

I picked up my bag and threw it over my shoulder. I slammed my bedroom door behind me. The little room looked out onto the street. I opened the window, tempted to jump over the railing. Except this time, I knew I wouldn't get another chance.

I opened the bag on my bed and emptied it. The room was so small I had to edge between the bed and the armoire. I could barely open the doors all the way. The parquet creaked under my feet. I busied myself for a few minutes, avoiding thinking about my anger. After unpacking my bag, I stretched out on the tiny bed – a single, of course! – and stared at the ceiling. The only distractions in the room were a vintage clock radio and a pile of books on a wobbly shelf.

I opted for music. I picked up my phone and checked my messages. What a surprise: neither Mathilde nor my lawyer had tried to get in touch with me. Aside from Simon, I had no one. I tried to call him and got sent directly to voicemail.

"Shit," I grumbled.

I ran a hand over my face and took a deep breath.

"Two months. Just two months."

Chapter Six

What a night! Between the emotional roller coaster of the weekend – the flood, the insurance agent, Damien – and the arrival of Maxime, I couldn't sleep for hours. His words and icy tone had shaken me. I'd tried to be welcoming and kind but my nerves had gotten the upper hand.

While making myself a cup of coffee, I replayed his arrival in my mind, trying to determine the exact moment when he'd deemed me so abhorrent. Sure, he hadn't chosen to come here and I could admit that Chateaurenard wasn't the most exciting town in the world … but wasn't it better than prison? He could have at least shown a little gratitude! What a douchebag!

Today's newspaper had the virtue of filling in the blanks of the story. Maxime had beaten up some poor man. If he didn't want to end up here, he should have restrained himself and not hit the guy. Let him be angry, fine. But certainly not at me. I was just like him in this situation: under duress and not very happy with my lot. The doubts I'd expressed to Damien were coming true: Maxime was unmanageable and I wasn't the one to make him stay out of trouble.

I climbed up on the stool and sipped my coffee while flipping through the local paper. I sometimes found classified ads getting rid of old furniture or books. That let me fill the shop with books … and free furniture. Money was a constant concern. Which was why, even if Maxime was loathsome, I couldn't kick him out.

I was going to have to play the pleasant hostess … even if it meant biting my tongue for two months.

The sound of a door pulled me from my thoughts. Maxime emerged from his room, dressed in shorts and a T-shirt. Instinctively, my eyes dropped to his ankle monitor.

"Hello," I said with a smile.

"I'm going for a run," he grumbled.

I checked the time. He had forty minutes until his morning curfew.

"Should I save you some food?" I asked.

"Not hungry."

"Not even coffee?"

Behaving pleasantly with this obnoxious guy was a challenge. I wondered if he was provoking me or if he acted like this with everyone. Last night, I'd seen his clenched fists and tense shoulders; he was controlling himself, holding in a resentment that threatened to explode at any moment.

"I said no."

Then, without another word, he hurtled down the stairs. In irritation, I threw my last bite of brioche into my cup.

Sixty days. Well, fifty-nine, if you didn't count the previous day. I hoped it did count.

After taking a shower and cleaning the kitchen, I went down to the bookshop to resume my normal routine. Today was shaping up to be gorgeous and I hoped the beginning of the holiday season would bring me customers. While I waited, I decided to stay busy with putting out a new selection of books according to their color … just to answer that regularly occurring question: "The cover is red/blue/green … but I can't remember the title." We were in the middle of summer, so I opted for yellow and picked out a few titles.

Thirty-five minutes after leaving, Maxime reappeared looking exhausted, his T-shirt drenched in sweat. I wondered vaguely if he'd slept that night or if he'd been too busy constructing an escape plan that consisted of tying his sheets together to abseil down the front of the building. Without glancing at me, he climbed the stairs and I heard the antediluvian boiler fire up.

Damien entered next, looking woefully unfit, the poor guy.

"Had a good time?" I joked as he collapsed onto a stool.

"Brutal," he panted.

I could only smile in sympathy; I wasn't very athletic myself. I preferred the preventive measure of eating my vegetables, rather than the cure aiming to eliminate calories. I let him catch his breath and offered him a glass of water.

"I thought running with me would help him release some energy."

"I'm not sure it's working. He looks just as angry as when he woke up this morning."

"Maxime isn't much of a morning person."

"He's not much of an evening person, either. He refused to have dinner right before explaining that we were definitely not going to be friends."

"You have to give him some time. It's complicated."

"Complicated? It's complicated for him to be nice?"

"You'll teach him," said Damien, smiling. "You can kill him with kindness."

"What if I don't feel like being kind?"

Damien failed to stifle a laugh. He finished his glass of water in one gulp, still sweating profusely onto my countertop.

"OK, then; let's see how mean you can be. Hit me with your worst insult."

"You're … red as a tomato," I said, proud of myself.

"Try again!"

"You… You look… You look like a beached whale."

"Honestly, Sarah, my eight-year-old daughter is better at this than you! Stay kind, it's more your thing."

I gave him a dark look – at least I hoped it was dark – and turned on my heel to go through the list of titles requested on the internet. That was the advantage of second-hand books: I was becoming a gold mine for collectors and could sell certain titles for higher prices. It was those few juicy sales that allowed me to keep the shop afloat.

"He'll eventually calm down," said Damien, still out of breath.

"Before or after you keel over?"

"There, you see, much better! You've got the furious look nailed, too," he added when I turned around to glare at him. "Just be yourself, Sarah. Eventually, he'll calm down."

"We'll see. Meanwhile, I don't really know how to act around him. He must be used to people doing everything for him, you know?"

"Yes, and look where that's got him. He needs a little dose of … reality. Give him work to do, it's the best way to handle him. You'll get there, Sarah, don't worry."

I stayed chatting with Damien until Maxime's footsteps on the stairs marked the end of our conversation. I didn't want to feed his anger by letting him discover that we were talking about him behind his back.

"Do you want to eat lunch together today?"

I didn't know if Damien was talking to Maxime or to me. My new housemate was in the back, probably making his way through the shelving.

"I have to stay here," replied Maxime hoarsely.

"And uh ... I have something planned," I said.

"Something or someone?" joked Damien.

"Something with someone," I answered, narrowing my gaze.

"A sort of date?"

"A date, yes," I retorted, a little offended.

"Lunch isn't a date. At best it's ... an initial interview. Max, I'll bring you a bite to eat. Meanwhile, don't forget what I said: fix up the reading nook!"

Maxime muttered something unintelligible in response. Damien ducked out with a wave. I found myself alone with Maxime, and without any instruction manual for him. I turned toward him, momentarily preoccupied by his physical appearance. Under normal circumstances, I would have admired his dark eyes, chiseled jaw, and broad shoulders. I might also have taken note of his black jeans and the tattoo on his forearm that disappeared under the sleeve of his T-shirt.

Maxime was an attractive man. Handsome, by current standards. Mesmerizing, even. The kind of man who makes your mouth go dry and your heart skip a beat.

Even so, his attitude was enough to kill any and all

attraction. I would have liked to see him smile and joke around. But I already knew there was no chance of that.

"Shall I do the reading nook, then?" he asked unenthusiastically.

"Yes, please. Mostly the flooded area needs to be cleared and the sofa moved to a new spot."

"By the window."

This was neither a question nor a suggestion. Maxime had decided that the reading nook would migrate to where my new bookshelf currently stood. After thinking it over for a minute, I realized it was actually a good idea. The bookshop's other corners were too dark, and we had some space there. Shifting small bookcases or tables would be less troublesome than moving an entire set of shelves.

"That'll work," I agreed. "Are you sure you don't want anything to eat?"

"No point."

"Lovely! Are you always in a bad mood, or is it just with me?"

"I told you, we don't have to be friends. My life isn't here."

Privately, I thought back on Damien's words. Deep down, I understood what he'd meant: Maxime was lost. He wasn't from here ... or anywhere. That was certainly one of the few things we had in common: when I arrived here, around the age of ten, I felt like an outsider too. It had taken me a long time to settle in.

Over the course of the morning, Maxime did all he could to reconstruct the reading nook. After pushing back several bookcases and two tables, he managed to wedge the sofa – the one that had survived – underneath the window. Then he suggested taking the coffee table outside to dry and left the two ruined chairs on the street until they could be taken to the dump. Finally, he helped me put back the decorations, including some string lights.

"Thanks," I murmured, as he moved a console table toward the entrance.

I stared at his tattoo, wondering if that thorny vine was a message or some kind of warning. Those thorns were certainly intended to repel the curious, like barbed wire strung along a fence.

"I'm going to close up during lunch. I'm going out," I added.

Maxime turned and walked toward me. Suddenly, standing in front of him, I felt puny and defenseless. His feline manner radiated danger.

Or maybe it was arrogance. A way of provoking me, of seeing whether he could behave with me as he did with others, ordering me around.

"Not me," he replied.

The iciness in his voice froze me in place. I thrust my hands into my pockets and tried to look confident, despite my rising blush. Revealing even one of my weaknesses would be my undoing.

"Will we have a civil conversation at any point today?"

A fleeting smile lit his face. My tremulous voice must have amused him.

"No," he said.

He positioned himself in front of me, so close that I shuddered. It wasn't out of fear, but because of his face, soulless and emotionless. As if a Siberian chill had suddenly swept through the shop, freezing out all signs of life.

"No to the conversation, or not today?"

"Both. Why would I want to talk to you, exactly?"

"To break the ice."

My answer made me smile. Break the ice, which had just taken over the bookshop, emanating from him; it was totally appropriate. Maxime stared at me, from his extra head of height and athletic build.

"We could … I don't know … talk about movies. Or books."

"Books? Very creative," he said sarcastically.

"Well, then tell me what you like, we can talk about it. Over dinner, for example."

I stopped, exhausted. I'd had enough of hitting a brick wall with each new suggestion – I was tired of his endless grumbling. He frowned, then delicately reached out to touch my hair, plucking something between his thumb and index finger.

"Cobweb," he mumbled.

I was immobilized on the spot, legs trembling. I tried to make a sound, but nothing came out. I was paralyzed, stunned to see this sullen man was capable of a tender gesture. For that brief instant, the blast of cold air had disappeared, and my heart was racing as fast as it had on the ghost train at the carnival. That had been out of fear, but now?

He stepped back and indicated the end of our conversation with a nod.

"Your date is here."

I turned immediately and through the window saw Frédéric approaching. I looked down at my outfit: stained old jeans and a sweater that was so loose, I could have made a short dress out of it. With Maxime's arrival, I'd forgotten all about this lunch. I was in a pathetic state, my hair was a mess – I hadn't even combed it! – I was barely dressed, and filthy.

"Make him wait, I'm going to change!" I shouted, running back up the stairs as fast as I could.

In ten minutes, I managed to make myself look human. I'd gathered my hair into a big gold clip, applied a light layer of makeup, and I was dressed decently, in a light flowered dress. I came back downstairs fighting with my high-heeled sandals, almost breaking my ankles on every step. Frédéric was waiting for me at the entrance, a rose in his hand.

I thanked him, nervous at the idea of our lunch. My most recent date was last year. To say that it ended badly would be putting it mildly. Behind us, Maxime was noisily stacking books.

"So you two have met?" I asked, all smiles.

"I introduced myself," replied Frédéric.

"Ah … this is Maxime."

The two men exchanged a look, and from the way Frédéric's face lit up, I knew he'd recognized him.

"This isn't—"

"Yes, it's him," I cut him off.

"And what—"

"An arrangement. He's going to spend some time here."

"A long time?"

"The summer."

"And where does he sleep?"

"I've got a spare room. He arrived yesterday."

I felt like I was undergoing a cross-examination without knowing what I'd been accused of. However, in my neighbor's eyes, I could clearly read incomprehension and doubt. I glanced at Maxime, who was engrossed in a blurb.

"He's a friend of Damien's. He's … going to help me. With the repairs to the bookshop."

"You could have asked me … or he could have stayed with Damien."

"This is more central. Shall we go?"

I had to cut this short. More questions might betray the reason for Maxime's presence here. Officially, nothing was preventing me from saying that he was serving a prison sentence. But I wanted to protect him; I knew how oppressive the curiosity of a small town could be. Shame, humiliation, whispers, gossip… In the end, it could break you.

"I'll be back in two hours, can you lock the door behind me?"

Maxime just nodded, his dark gaze darting to me. He didn't even have the courtesy to wave back at me, just slammed the door after I left. On the way to the restaurant, I ran into Damien and told him Maxime was at the shop.

At the restaurant, Baptiste seated us on the terrace and gave us menus. I ignored his conspiratorial smile and exaggerated wink. I hid behind my menu and pretended my blood pressure wasn't hitting the roof. I reread each item ten times, looking for a way to start the conversation. Obviously, I wasn't going to tell him about the last book I'd read – it was a little too corny.

The news? Too depressing.

The weather? Too obvious on this sunny terrace.

Holiday? I knew he wouldn't be taking one before winter.

My renovations? A little too self-absorbed.

My most recent experiment in the kitchen? Disastrous.

My limited experience with gardening? He'd

eventually find out that all the plants I bought wound up committing suicide. Even cacti.

"So, how's your wedding?" I finally asked.

"My wedding?"

My face heated up instantly and I cursed myself, again, for being so awkward.

"*The* wedding," I corrected myself. "The one you had to take care of."

"Oh, yes, well, it was a success."

He told me how he'd decorated the church with an arrangement of white and pale pink flowers. He was so enthusiastic, only pausing to give Baptiste his order. In fact, for the rest of our lunch, all I had to do was prompt him with questions and the occasional nervous laugh. I envied the ease with which Frédéric was talking. He was putting his passion and all his energy into it.

Books had always been my passion. I read ardently, almost in a sort of uncontrollable binge. I would have done anything to escape my life, and books had quickly allowed me to do it. And yet, when I had to defend a book I'd loved, I couldn't find the words. I could write up a recommendation, I could suggest books ... but confronted with someone who didn't share my point of view, I was tongue-tied.

Several times, I caught Frédéric focusing on my lips for barely half a second – time enough to make me panic.

"I had a great time," Frédéric said as he walked me back to the shop.

Our hands brushed against each other as we ambled slowly. Without saying anything, Frédéric hooked his fingers in mine. We weren't quite holding hands, but that slight contact sped up my breathing. I cleared my throat, already dreading the moment when Frédéric would lean in to kiss me. I was worried I might faint dead away.

"What would you say to dinner next week?"

"Oh… Well…"

A smile stretched across my neighbor's lips. His fingers closed more firmly on mine and he moved so close to me that his aftershave tickled my nostrils. I held my breath and – eyes half closed – readied myself for the touch of his mouth on mine.

But, apparently, Frédéric liked to talk.

"I'm looking forward to it, too," he whispered in my ear.

I opened my eyes to discover that Frédéric had moved back, the prospect of a kiss going with him.

"I'd like to see you sooner," he said, "but my mother is coming to visit for a few days. I don't want to leave her all alone."

"Oh! I understand, of course!"

I could have convinced him if I hadn't giggled right afterward. "Family first," I added.

"I could introduce you!"

Another giggle escaped my throat. The mortification made me want to bury myself alive. I freed my hand from his and tried to lead the conversation to a less stressful topic.

"I have to go open up … the … well, I have to go open the shop!"

"Oh. Okay. So, that's a yes on the dinner?"

"Yes, yes, perfect! Next week, right?"

I was already backing away, hands behind my back. I just wanted to hide in the bookshop and howl my frustration and embarrassment into one of the pillows in the reading nook.

"How does Wednesday sound? I'll come pick you up."

"Yes, perfect!"

"A picnic? On the beach?"

"Yes, perfect!"

I waved to him and knocked furiously at the door to the bookshop. Out of the corner of my eye, I noticed that Frédéric was still watching me. His mother must have taught him to wait until a lady was safely inside before leaving. Though it was hard to know what could happen to me in downtown Chateaurenard at two o'clock in the afternoon.

Damien finally opened the door, a half-smile on his lips.

"Move it, I have to find a shovel to dig my grave," I told him.

I pushed him aside and rushed into the shop. Maxime came down the stairs and raised an inquisitive brow.

"I didn't take my keys," I explained to the two men.

"It was open," replied Damien.

With a frustrated groan, I collapsed onto one of the armchairs, grabbing one of the cushions to hide my face in it.

"You were cute together," Maxime said sarcastically.

"Were you watching?" I asked, pulling the cushion away.

"There's not much else to do around here," he explained with a shrug.

"I have to go. Maxime, think about what I said, okay? Sarah, very pretty dress," Damien said.

He left the bookshop a second later, leaving me alone with Maxime and my despair.

"How pathetic was I?" I mumbled.

"Enough to make us laugh," replied Maxime, removing a row of books from a worn-out bookcase.

"Mocking laughter?"

"Kind of, yeah."

As he had that morning, he got lost reading a dust jacket. I watched him for a little while, intrigued by his concentration. For the first time since he arrived, he wasn't angry or in a bad mood. He looked up at me and straightaway put down the book, lifted the shelf, and turned it over.

"You can read," I encouraged him.

"Damien asked me to flip all the shelves in this bookcase and clean it, is that all right?"

"You're asking my opinion?"

"I suppose."

"Without grumbling?"

"Damien asked me to make an effort with you. So, I'm doing it. Anyway, this bookcase?"

I remained dumbfounded. It was one of the first times we'd exchanged more than two sentences without attacking each other. It almost made me forget my shameful scene with Frédéric. In a corner of my brain, I made a note to call Damien and thank him.

"Uh … yeah. There are rags under the cash register, if you want."

I got up from the chair and decided to accept this change by making an overture.

"You want some coffee?"

He looked me over for a long minute. If I'd suggested taking off for Pluto he couldn't have been more mistrustful. I smiled reassuringly, like a lion tamer trapped in a cage with an angry specimen.

"I'm going to make pastries for book club tonight, do you have a preference?"

He shrugged and then, after picking up two rags, went back to take care of the bookcase he was charged with. I sighed, before putting things in perspective: at least he wasn't biting me.

The next few days followed the same rhythm. Maxime, solidly uncommunicative, worked steadily in the bookshop. By the end of the week, he'd repaired my wobbly bookcases and turned over all the worm-eaten shelves. He did his morning run with Damien and, in the evening we ate dinner together, mostly in silence. I managed to catch up on my own activities, particularly transforming the meetings of the book club into rehearsals for the play.

"So, Anita, you'll be Dame Pluche, Camille's governess. And Baptiste, you'll be Father Blazius, then."

The play was *Don't Trifle with Love,* by Alfred de Musset. Casting the roles was the simplest part. The club divided up the characters among them fairly naturally. Élise, a student from Paris, joined the club during the summer. Her parents lived in the village and, on occasion, she also helped me out at the bookshop.

"Élise, you'll be Camille. And then Damien will be Perdican."

"I love playing bashful lovers," said the latter with a smile, before devouring a sugar bun.

"Perdican is a moron," Élise announced.

"And Camille is a sanctimonious church lady who hides behind religion to avoid facing life and love," Damien shot back.

"Great, you're already in character. Baptiste, could you rehearse the first scene with Anita?"

"Can't we swap?" Anita whined. "Father Blazius

seems much closer to my own temperament. He seems more … alive. And I'd love to play a man!"

"There's no way I'm playing an uptight, embittered goodwife. I'm keeping Blazius and she's doing Pluche!" ranted Baptiste.

The whole troupe came to life, debating the characters' virtues and failings. I liked watching them argue with each other. Moments like these made me smile and reassured me about the entertainment I offered. Seeing them put in so much heart and energy, I knew that I was right to lead my life here. Thanks to them, their laughter, their irreverence, I was happy to be here.

"Good evening," said a voice behind me.

I spun in my chair to find Maxime. The club members fell abruptly silent. Dressed in dark jeans and a Ghostbusters sweatshirt, Maxime stared at each of them in turn.

"I … I think everyone knows you. Except Élise. Élise, Maxime."

She stood up from her chair and held out her hand to greet him. Maxime just nodded, closed off as always to the slightest connection with other humans. I had finally come to terms with it. In the morning, we politely said hello, but from a distance. At night, we took care to avoid each other in the kitchen and went to our separate rooms as soon as dinner was over.

We had very little contact; I told him what he had to

do and he complied. To my great relief, he didn't grumble anymore and no longer wore his bad mood on his face. Damien, by making him run every morning, was obviously helping him channel his rage.

Élise shot me an oblique look, to tell me: "That's Maxime Maréchal, for fuck's sake!" I knew that look perfectly well – I dealt with it in all the customers who came to the bookshop. They didn't dare ask questions, but their stunned faces spoke for them. Despite my silence and that of my friends, I'd noticed that visits to the bookshop had risen. I could have chalked it up to the influx of summer tourists, but, judging by the way people nosed about between the shelves, I knew it was to bump into the local attraction Maxime had become.

"Do you want to join us?" I offered.

"You could help us, with the play," suggested Damien. "With your talent and experience, we could put on a brilliant performance."

"You could be on the poster," continued Anita. "As the director, for example… In any case, it would be great publicity…"

"No," I cut in. "We don't need that. Every year, the audience is full."

"That's true," admitted Anita. "Too bad!"

"I came to get my phone charger," Maxime explained.

"Okay. We're done anyway. We'll meet again the day after tomorrow to rehearse the first scenes."

The group stood up the moment Maxime slipped

away toward the counter. I opened the shop door and said goodnight to each cast member one by one. Bringing up the rear, Élise, all smiles, took advantage of the moment.

"I want to know everything," she murmured.

"There's nothing to tell. He helps me out around here and I'm putting him up. That's all."

"You're putting him up? So ... he sleeps here?"

"In the spare bedroom," I clarified, a little irritated.

She exited the bookshop, but didn't stop talking to me. Élise was a nosy one, with a definite tendency to gossip. I didn't much like becoming the object of her chatter.

"You do realize that you're living with one of the sexiest men in the country?"

"When he's not complaining, he barely strings two sentences together. He's not looking for friends. And I..."

"For God's sake, Sarah! Get your head out of the books and look at this guy! He's gorgeous!"

I rolled my eyes, exasperated. Obviously, I'd realized that Maxime was far from unpleasant to look at. But his appearance didn't matter much to me. I would have liked to be able to talk to him and have a real conversation. I couldn't believe he was so uncommunicative for no reason. His anger had to have an explanation ... and I would have done anything to defuse it. I often wondered what Maxime could look like silly or relaxed.

I decided to avoid the issue and find a way to head off the story that was already forming in Élise's mind.

"Anyway, I'm dating someone," I announced.

"Oh yes! Frédéric? Anita told me. That's wonderful news, I'm so happy for you. Good night, Sarah. See you tomorrow?"

"With pleasure!"

Apparently, my imaginary liaison with Maxime was already just a vague memory. I was relieved. I didn't feel like becoming the topic of conversation. Even worse, I definitely didn't want Maxime to hear that sort of thing and think that I had a hand in it. Our relationship was rocky enough already – I didn't want to damage the little bit of civility we did have.

I locked the door behind Élise and tidied up the reading nook. I turned out the lights and went back up to my apartment, hoping to encounter Maxime and make a start on a real conversation. I couldn't live like this anymore, cohabiting with a man I didn't know. We still had several weeks of communal life to go – we had to get on, somehow.

Unfortunately, when I reached the living room, everything was already plunged into darkness. I switched on the light in the kitchen and wrote a note for Maxime. The next day, I had to leave early to collect boxes of books that a friend of Anita's was getting rid of.

My note was brief:

Gone tomorrow. See you later.

Chapter Seven

It was only after hearing Sarah close the door to her room that I got up from my bed. Dressed in boxers, I cautiously opened my door and headed for the kitchen. After inspecting every cupboard in the apartment, I'd eventually concluded that Sarah didn't have a single bottle of alcohol. Even the medicine cabinet in the bathroom was devoid of disinfectant.

I'd foreseen everything about my stay here: the humiliation, first of all, the boredom, the frustrating waste of time, and being forgotten. I'd come here for that purpose … and my mission had been more than accomplished: I'd heard not a word from Mathilde, and even less from my lawyer. But it was definitely Simon's silence that weighed on me the heaviest. Realizing that our friendship had been fake, just like the world of showbiz, was painful.

I opened the refrigerator and, in the absence of alcohol or cigarettes, set my sights on fruit juice. I pushed aside the papers strewn across the countertop and piled the books in a corner. I squeezed two oranges and settled onto one of the kitchen stools. Since I'd arrived here, I'd only slept a few hours a night. I was too tormented by questions about my future to find rest. The solitude, which was supposed to make me think, was starting to weigh on me.

Worse, I was becoming almost allergic to other humans. Showing up in the middle of Sarah's book club had *not* been a good idea. I'd found myself face to face with all her friends. In particular there'd been that young woman who'd eyed me hungrily. Young. Smiling. Naive. In Paris, I'd definitely have made a move.

Here, among the books, she'd barely held my attention. Anyway, I couldn't live here the way I lived in Paris. Damien and Sarah had my fate in their hands. Committing a faux pas would mark the end of my reprieve.

"I thought you were sleeping," said Sarah, rubbing her eyes.

She turned on the light in the living room, illuminating both spaces. My eyes scanned her bare legs, only slightly concealed by a long T-shirt with the image of a pile of books on it. Her hair cascaded over her shoulders and thick black socks completed her sleepwear.

One thing I had to acknowledge about this girl: her incredible innocence. Sarah must have been a nun in a past life. Tonight, as she stood there, suppressing a yawn, I found her sleepy face rather touching. She pushed her hair back, revealing one bare shoulder.

Touching and a little bit sexy, actually. That she wasn't doing it on purpose and had no idea made her even more … attractive.

"I don't sleep much," I explained.

Her eyes roved over my bare chest and she almost tripped over the other stool. She sat down on it carefully and her eyes finally met mine. "I understand," she said.

"You're very polite," I commented.

"Normally I'd take that as a compliment. But coming from you … I don't know."

"You don't know?"

"You don't react like us other humans. Why am I polite?"

"Because you don't ask questions. Even though I can hear your brain running at full speed from here."

A small smile wandered across her lips without ever quite settling there. *Very polite,* I mused. She didn't even try to deny it. And yet, from the way she twisted her hands and shifted nervously in her seat, I guessed that it cost her not to interrogate me further.

"It's a compliment," I reassured her finally.

She blushed furiously and I shook my head. I'd come across the shyest girl in the country. Most of the time, when face to face with me, women were pretty forward. On rare occasions, they played coy. Sarah, though, was truly shy, as though she was genuinely scared of dealing with the world.

"What's your excuse?" I asked.

"For?"

"I don't need much sleep. What's your excuse for being here instead of back in bed?"

"I live here, you know. I don't really need an excuse to hang out in the kitchen in the middle of the night."

"Okay. Sure. So, you heard me and thought I was out here doing drugs? Or maybe you thought I was running away?"

"No. And … no," she replied after a moment. "If you'd wanted to leave, you would have done it a long time ago."

"So, what then? You missed my grumping?"

She frowned, a bit annoyed by my comment. She took a deep breath and lost herself in the contemplation of my arm tattoo for a while. The thorny vine wound its way from my shoulder to my wrist, without any particular direction or end. Quite a lot of women had seen it. But none of them had looked at it like Sarah did. She was neither intrigued nor curious. She followed the curve of the design attentively. Once again, I felt like she was trying to uncover a secret, like I was a safe whose combination she was searching for.

For the first time in my life, a woman's gaze was making me feel uncomfortable.

"Orange juice?" I offered.

"With pleasure. It suits you," she added after a short silence.

I stifled a laugh. This was the first time somebody had said my tattoo "suited me". Most of the time, I was complimented on the design or the aesthetic.

"And I don't think you're grumpy. I can understand your ... attitude. Honestly, I wouldn't like being catapulted into a different world than my own."

"You mean a world without books?"

She placed a hand over her heart and put on a shocked expression. I juiced the first orange while laughing. Sarah was so naive, it was adorable. My bad mood was fading in the face of her good nature.

"What you just suggested is intolerable," she murmured.

"I assure you it's possible."

"Not for me. I was raised in this place, surrounded by books. My grandmother left it all to me. I don't think I have much else."

"Your grandmother?"

I handed over her glass, curious to know more. My past had given me a lot of motivation – to escape. I didn't want to live the way my parents did. I wanted more, I wanted to get out of this mess and forget them as quickly as I could. I had trouble understanding why Sarah was so attached to this place.

"She raised me," she explained. "My parents weren't really up to it. My father left when I was four. My mother went back and forth to prison a few times. The last time I saw her, she promised to get me some sweets. It's been … a little over twenty years."

I stared at her in silence. I was even more lost than before.

"You don't react like us other humans," I said, copying her.

She grinned at me before taking refuge in her glass. She was an enigma for me. Despite her history, she didn't give off any anger or desire to leave this place.

"You should be angry," I said finally.

"I was, for a while. But it made me waste a lot of time," she said with a smile. "I preferred…"

"… to read?"

"Books saved me from the worst. Calmed me down. And my grandmother was a lovely woman. I have a lot of friends, I have this shop, I'm in good health. I learned to appreciate what I have. Except the plumbing," she joked.

Except for that exposed shoulder, that embarrassed smile, and those bare legs, I could have numbered Sarah among the saints. But I wouldn't have liked a real saint as much. Sarah had seen nothing of life, she'd never traveled, she'd never experienced what people her age usually have.

It gnawed at me. I could have given her a dream life, a luxurious apartment, outrageously expensive clothes. Everything. Including her damn plumbing. Everything. Including an ocean of books.

But I couldn't tell if she even wanted it.

"No wishes? No crazy dreams, like 'If I won the lottery…'?" I eventually asked.

"Yes, of course."

She gazed upward, playing with the book in her hands. I wondered vaguely what a girl like Sarah could dream of. The obvious answer finally hit me in the face.

"Let me guess… More books?"

Her smile widened and her eyes gleamed guiltily. I burst out laughing and managed to make her blush even more. She finished her glass and put the book back down on its perpetual pile.

"It's almost too easy," I said finally.

"Maybe. Sorry for not being a more mysterious woman."

"You are mysterious. But in certain ways, you're a bit too predictable!"

Another smile stretched over her lips. She looked at me, in that same disarming way she'd examined my tattoo. She got down from her stool and passed close to me to put her glass in the sink.

"I don't mind being predictable, I achieved my goal. I wanted to hear you laugh."

She ventured a satisfied smile, while I took in her remark. She moved away in the direction of her bedroom. My eyes went immediately to her thighs. Before entering her room, she took care to remove her thick socks and roll them into a ball.

"Did you see my note?"

I nodded, then picked it up and shook it as proof.

"I'll be back by late morning, can you open up?"

"Absolutely!"

"Good night, Maxime."

"Good night, Sarah."

She closed the door behind her, leaving me alone in the kitchen. I rinsed the glasses and returned to my room.

I tossed and turned for two solid hours before falling into a restless sleep.

When I woke up, Sarah was already gone. She'd left another note on the counter. I glanced distractedly at it, while making myself a strong coffee. I checked the time and looked out the window to see if Damien was there yet. Our morning runs helped me clear my head. In the absence of news from my lawyer, Mathilde, or Simon,

Damien remained one of the few people to make sure I was holding up.

As I brought the cup to my lips, I gazed at the books Sarah was accumulating in the kitchen. I still didn't understand what fascinated her so much about them. For over a week, I'd spent my days pulling them off the shelves only to put them right back. The task was unnecessary, but it had the virtue of keeping me from thinking.

I thought back on our conversation from the previous night. She'd been right on one account. I hadn't laughed like that, so spontaneously, in months. I was used to giving orders, laughing on command, shaking hands with people whose names I forgot half a second later. My relationships were artificial and constrained. I had to be polite, smooth, emotionless. None of which I could manage in Paris. Here, at least, my few connections were healthy. No roles to play, no image to preserve, no names to remember. I could be angry, nobody cared.

However, I was aware that it was precisely my out-of-control behavior that had led me here. I knew I had to apologize, not least to Mathilde. I'd taken it out on her when it wasn't her fault. On the contrary, she'd spent most of her time smoothing things over and making sure the industry didn't turn its back on me. I had to make it right.

I finished my coffee in one gulp and made sure my morning hour of freedom had begun. I headed down to the bookshop and unlocked the door. Damien was waiting for me, water bottle in hand.

"Ready?" he asked.

"Let's go!"

After forty-five minutes of running, we got back to Sarah's shop. Since the outdoor tables and shelves weren't set up, I guessed that she hadn't come back from her morning jaunt. However, a thick packet, addressed to me, was waiting on the doorstep.

"Delivered by courier," Damien read, picking it up. "This thing's got some weight to it!" he added.

I opened the door to the shop and got myself a glass of cold water.

"Who sent it?" I asked.

"It's from Claude, your lawyer. You want me to open it?"

"Why not! It has to be stupid endorsement contracts!"

Just the idea made me grimace. I liked acting … but I hated the side effects of this profession. I had to sign contracts to wear such-and-such a brand regularly and, on occasion, show up at company parties. Champagne, girls, canapés. At first, I enjoyed it. But, over time, boredom got the better of my contractual obligations.

Obligations that Mathilde and Claude tried to save in spite of everything.

Damien dropped the imposing envelope on the counter and shot me a knowing smile.

"It's a script. I assume Mathilde took your threat

literally and sent everything concerning you through Claude."

I slid the script out of the envelope and flipped through it. I tried to recall my last conversations with Mathilde. Had she talked about a specific project? Nothing was coming back to me.

"You'll have time to read it," said Damien.

"I was actually considering waiting a bit. Anyway, I can't do anything from here. And I don't think anybody's expecting me in Paris."

"You think? What world are you living in, Maxime? You think nobody's interested in you?"

"I fired my agent. My lawyer is definitely washing his hands of me. And my only friend – well, the guy I thought was my friend – hasn't reached out since I got here. I'm telling you: nobody's waiting for me there."

Damien chuckled, then collapsed into the armchair in the reading nook. He shook his head, then continued:

"What's it been ... ten days since you arrived?"

"Yeah, why?"

"Ten days you've been here, tons of people have potentially seen you and recognized you."

"Yeah," I said, getting upset. "It's not like I like it. I would have preferred a less ... exposed job. Like in a vineyard. I wouldn't need to talk to anybody, or worry my ugly mug will end up on the front page of the newspaper."

"Exactly, nothing's leaked out. Not a word, not a photo. Do you know why?"

"Who would come to this shithole?"

"People who want a scoop and money. You think nobody came? You're wrong! They all came! They took pictures of the bookshop and Sarah. They also probably took a few snaps of you dusting the shelves. But nothing's come out! Nothing!"

I frowned, uncomprehending. I hadn't even wondered about it. After all, I was here against my will, I didn't care if they found out. I was used to people saying anything they wanted about me, used to being something to gawk at. The press surely had the information, but why would they be interested in an out-of-control actor with criminal tendencies working at a bookshop?

"Nothing's been published because Mathilde and Claude worked like crazy since the night you were arrested. Everything's being monitored and handled. If a paper puts out something about you, they run the risk of a major lawsuit. And if Mathilde and Claude are doing that, it's to save your career."

I felt like an idiot now. An idiot and pretty ungrateful. Damien straightened up, while I quickly thought about what I should do.

"You should read that," he said, tapping his index finger on the script. "Everyone is counting on you to start filming again in September. Open your eyes, Maxime. You have no reason to be mad at us."

"Mathilde and Claude?"

"Them too. This whole situation… For God's sake, Maxime, it's all nothing! You're here for two months, and then you'll be back in your old life and getting your bearings."

I smiled at him, then pulled my jersey up to wipe my face. Listening to Damien, I immediately thought of his father. They had the same values, the same will, the same way of talking to people with minimum diplomacy. I appreciated his frankness.

"How did your father put it? Glass half full, right?"

"Right, yes. Call Mathilde. I promise, she'll come back to work for you."

I rapidly weighed the pros and cons. I had no idea what I was going to say. In theory, I knew how to make an apology and appear contrite. In practice, it was different. Mathilde and I had a professional relationship … enhanced by a very strong friendship. I knew her son, she had a key to my apartment. She knew me through and through.

"Not one reporter, then?" I asked again.

"Not one. No reporters, no photographers. You might not escape social media, but that'll be a lesser evil. Ask your buddy Simon to create a new scandal that'll get rid of yours!"

"Very funny! Simon isn't really the type to create a scandal."

"Call Mathilde and read that script, it'll get you back into the swing of things. How's it going with Sarah?"

"I've been good as gold," I said sarcastically.

Damien burst out laughing and slowly headed for the door.

"So, what's it like?" he asked finally.

The image of Sarah, last night, simultaneously innocent and alluring, came back to mind. I was still frustrated at being here, but Sarah was making the exercise less tiresome. I was hoping I could have another late-night conversation with her. Despite her inquisitive stares and inexplicable passion for books, I enjoyed her company. She lived as if she'd escaped from the turn of the last century: sweet, kind, smiling. She acted like nastiness didn't exist. It made her a pretty appealing room-mate.

"It's … different," I said eventually. "Sarah is a strange girl. I can't make her out."

"Not so easy to bark at someone who's all smiles!"

"No, but it can get a bit monotonous," I said quickly, to cover myself. "She doesn't watch TV, not even movies! Outside of books, I don't think she has a life. Oh, yes, that bloke. Frédéric, right?"

"That's right!"

"I'm not feeling it," I said, wrinkling my nose.

"You know him?" he asked, surprised.

"No. Just a feeling. He's too polite."

Damien stared at me uncomprehendingly. I turned on the coffee machine and opened the canister of coffee beans. I didn't have any real reason to distrust Frédéric. Still, when I'd seen him with Sarah, something in his too-smooth attitude had bothered me.

"He asks Sarah out to lunch, he almost holds her hand, and he doesn't even try to kiss her? It's so shady!"

"Maxime, not everybody jumps on a girl at the first opportunity. He's gentlemanly and civilized. You could learn something. Speaking of civilization…"

My friend dug around in the pocket of his tracksuit and took out a piece of paper folded into fourths. He dropped it on the counter, inviting me with a jerk of the chin to open it.

"What is it?"

"Read it, you'll see!"

"I've got my hands full," I said, pouring the coffee into the machine. "Tell me what it is, dammit!"

"A furlough."

The coffee canister crashed to the floor, spilling its beans onto the parquet. I grumbled at my clumsiness, then swore when I almost went sprawling. I turned toward Damien, who held up his hands in self-defense.

"You break it, you bought it," he said, laughing.

"I can go back to Paris?"

I was in shock. Ten days. Ten days of lonely hell, and my punishment had been lifted? Automatically, I counted it up. If I left right now, I could be in Paris for dinner, then a night club. I'd take up my life where I left off. My smile widened, but very quickly fell back to earth.

"For one evening," Damien specified.

"One evening? What the fuck do you expect me to do with a free evening, *here*?"

"The village festival is this weekend, I thought you'd like to participate."

"You thought what? What the fuck do you want me to do at this festival? Shimmy around dancing the lambada? Drink cheap punch? Meet local farmers, to rediscover my roots? Fuck, Damien, I don't want to be here! I just want … literally anything else!"

Damien's face darkened. He stared at the paper, still folded on the counter.

"A local farmer saved your butt. You might be ashamed of it, but yes, your roots are here. I thought you'd like a little excitement. Do whatever you want!"

"Damien…"

He stepped outside, but turned back one last time, face expressionless and eyes blazing.

"You're a shit, Maxime! Paris? Who's called since you've been here? Huh? Who goes running with you? Who protects you?"

His rage was palpable. As I so often did, I'd spoken without thinking, and now I'd antagonized the one person who was on my side. I took a step toward him, hoping to calm the situation. I'd gone too far. Yet again.

"Damien, it's not..."

"Fuck off, Maxime."

He crossed the street at a brisk pace. My ankle monitor kept me from leaving the bookshop and following him. Out of frustration, I threw a punch at a stack of books. They fanned out across the floor and I resisted the urge to send them out into the street with a few furious kicks.

I went back behind the counter and cleaned up the mess. I abandoned the idea of making coffee, then tidied the books and closed the bookshop door. I had ten minutes before the shop opened to take a shower.

As Sarah had requested, I opened the shop for her. I brought the tables and chairs out to the pavement, then set up two book displays. Sarah had created a table of yellow books. Some of them had little recommendation labels. In the second display, I found second-hand books. The covers were a bit crinkly and the pages bulgy from being thumbed through. I suspected Sarah couldn't bear to throw them away.

Inside, I tackled peeling off the wallpaper ruined by the flood. It took me a solid hour to remove every square inch. I threw it all in the skip outside. From the doorway, the florist gave me a little wave. I didn't even bother to respond. I didn't like the guy. The very idea that Sarah could like him, or that he could be intimate with her, gave me the creeps.

Sarah was innocent and sweet. He was much too smooth to be genuine. I was afraid he'd use her and hurt her. Sarah couldn't handle the disappointment – she was much too enthusiastic and naive.

Back inside the shop, I pulled back the baseboard from the disaster-stricken wall to check on it.

"It's worse than I'd imagined," said Sarah's voice from behind me.

"It all needs to be re-plastered. Then sanding and wallpaper or paint."

"Translation?"

"Enough work for two weeks or so," I explained, as she stepped forward to join me.

I burst out laughing when I saw her face. Her hair was covered in dust, and a family of spiders seemed to have spun miles of cobwebs. A few black lines streaked her cheeks. She shot me a glance and then a smile.

"Basement or attic?" I asked.

"Both, of course. I don't think anyone had set foot in those rooms since last century."

"A good haul?"

"Excellent. I have about ten boxes. I'll pick it all up tomorrow. Damien is going to bring them over."

"Okay. More books, then."

"Never too many! Look, you do know how to do all these things, right?" she suddenly fretted, gesturing at the dilapidated wall in front of us. "The sanding and the plastering and…"

"Yes, I know how."

She sighed with relief and brushed a lock of hair out of her face, simultaneously adding a new black streak to her cheek. I stifled a laugh, and without asking her permission tried to erase the streak with my thumb. She pulled back slightly but didn't push me away. I met her surprised gaze and gave her a conspiratorial smile. Despite all my anger, I had nothing against Sarah. She'd found herself trapped with me to save her bookshop. She didn't deserve me derailing her plan.

"I thought we didn't have to be friends," she murmured.

"Are we going to become friends just because I'm doing this?"

I tried to concentrate on the line I was attempting to erase. Unfortunately, I was doing even more damage, spreading the dust all the way to her neck.

"It's a risk, yes."

I stopped for a brief second, then resumed my task.

"I like to live dangerously," I said with a smile.

She laughed gently and her cheeks warmed under my fingers. Her shyness was coming back at top speed. As soon as we got into an intimate subject, she closed in on herself.

"Three minutes without blushing, a new record," I said sarcastically, as her blush further intensified.

"Living dangerously led you here," she pointed out.

"If I profane with my unworthiest hand / This holy shrine, the gentle fine is this …"

A brilliant smile crossed her face. It was the first time I had seen her light up like that. She pursed her lips and shook her head.

"A man who quotes *Romeo and Juliet* can't be that dangerous."

I lowered my hand and Sarah stared at me. She had that deep, enigmatic look again. Her eyes dropped to my arm and followed the line of my tattoo. A shiver went through me and rooted me to the spot.

"I'm going to get changed," she said.

The pins-and-needles sensation in my body dissipated. Sarah went off in the direction of the stairs, leaving me in the shop.

I'd never felt like such a wretched fraud before.

Chapter Eight

"Anita, do the scene again, but please, you have to be closer to Élise."

I was used to Anita's exuberance: she never took anything seriously. Tonight, we were rehearsing the Musset play and, for the end of the first scene from Act II, my friend was proving particularly absent-minded. So, I got on the stage and showed Anita what I expected of her. I did her lines with Élise and replayed the scene. Anita nodded and went back into the wings, ready for her entrance.

"You're her confidante, so you can get a little bit closer, you know? So, let's start again. When Damien exits, you come on stage. Élise, you call out to her, and at the same time please walk toward the opposite exit. Otherwise it won't work."

I went back down the few steps and watched as they

replayed the short scene. Nearby, Damien was rehearsing the next one with a friend of his brother's, who would play Rosette. After over an hour of rehearsal, I was beginning to flag.

Élise and Anita executed it perfectly and, from their sighs, I knew they were relieved. As Damien was launching into the second scene in the act, I heard the door to the theater bang and Maxime appeared. He nodded at the cast, greeting them silently, before settling in the back of the hall. I checked the time: Maxime was taking advantage of his free hour outside the shop.

I went back to the rehearsal, guiding Damien through his seduction of Rosette. Despite all my concentration, I could feel Maxime's gaze scorching the back of my neck. The memory of our late-morning exchange haunted me. While we were talking, I felt like his anger was fading, like he was almost sweet. But his tattoo reminded me that he kept his distance ... and my instincts were telling me that I should do the same. The warning was clear: nobody got close to Maxime without getting hurt.

Still, hearing him quote Shakespeare had moved me. He rarely showed his softer side. It was probably better that way. I shouldn't get too attached to him. In a few weeks, he'd resume his Parisian life and forget this provincial interlude.

After forty-five minutes stumbling over the same monologue, Damien threw in the towel, which signaled the end of the rehearsal. I gave instructions for the next one, in two days, and let the troupe disperse.

When I turned around to Maxime, he'd already disappeared, observing his curfew to the minute.

"I hope he's calmed down," grumbled Damien beside me, piling up chairs to put away.

"Maxime? Why, was there a problem?"

"I managed to get him a furlough for the weekend here but His Highness reckoned it was beneath him to spend it with us yokels."

I grimaced. I knew how cutting Maxime could be in just one or two sentences. Damien was the resentful type; weeks could go by before he'd agree to move on. He pushed the pile of chairs into a corner and put on his coat. From the look on his face, I knew he was still irritated.

"You said it yourself: he's lost."

"I told him to fuck off!"

"I'm sure he deserved it. But maybe you should have been more understanding. He's not that stubborn!"

Damien stared at me, then walked over.

"I thought you were going out with Frédéric?"

"I am. Well, more or less. That has nothing to do with this, anyway!"

"I hope so. Because Maxime is the last guy you need. He's unstable, he's violent, and frankly, he jumps anything that moves."

Damien was being hasty. Yes, Maxime was full of

resentment, but he was trying to control it, and he had never shown his rage around me. In his calmer moments, he was even … sweet.

"Sarah, don't get a crush on him," Damien warned.

"No, no. It's just that… I don't know. Was he always like this?"

"As far as I can remember, yes. Listen, Sarah, I know how you are. Don't try to … to deal with his issues, okay? He'll be out of here soon and you won't see him again. Just host him."

His recommendations sounded like orders. If I'd vaguely hoped Damien would enlighten me on the Maxime mystery, I was a bit disappointed. There had to be an explanation. No one arrived on this planet wanting to kill their fellow humans. Even the way he pushed people away, made them feel like they weren't up to the task, implied he was hiding something.

"Fine. I … I was just trying to understand."

"I know. He had a bad childhood, a father who beat him, an absent mother. Not exactly a recipe for stability. It is what it is, Sarah."

"That explains a lot."

"I think as far as defective parents go, you've had your share, too. Still, you're not ready to attack everything at the tiniest comment."

"Okay, okay!"

I gave up. Damien was too angry to listen to me, let

alone help me. I hoped another conversation with Maxime would help me see more clearly.

"I have to go, I'm already late and the babysitter is going to end up ruining me."

"You'll be back the day after next? I really need us to rehearse the scene between Perdican and Rosette."

"I'll come with Adèle," he said before planting a kiss on my cheek. "She'll do some coloring while she waits for me."

"No problem!"

He ran to the exit, pulling out his car keys before he even got out the door. For almost an hour, I tidied the theater, sliding our work table against a wall before throwing out the plastic cups. I packed up the bottles of water and the thermos of coffee. I turned out the lights and locked the door to the community theater behind me. As I walked toward the shop, I glanced at my watch.

Maxime was of course at the apartment, but I didn't have time for a conversation. I had to get ready for another dinner with Frédéric. I hoped it would be an improvement on our last date.

After dropping off the thermos on the counter, I climbed the stairs to the apartment. Maxime was in the living room, watching television, in semi-darkness.

"Hi!"

He turned his head toward me and gave me a little nod. Thanks to the halogen lamp, I could make out his wry smile. That one detail was enough to reassure me about his frame of mind: he was cooperative. A glass of water was resting on the coffee table, and without really knowing why I stared at his bare feet. This was new. From here, Maxime could have seemed almost normal, far from his acting career and unrestrained Parisian life.

The table was set for both of us and a wave of guilt assailed me. I hadn't told him I was going out and I had to be ready in less than fifteen minutes. I almost would have canceled to talk with him.

"I'm going out to dinner," I explained.

"It doesn't matter," he replied promptly. "It'll be there for tomorrow morning."

"Sorry I didn't tell you. And I … well, I have to get ready. Frédéric is going to be waiting for me and…"

"You're having dinner with the florist?"

He got up from the couch, his smile now forgotten. I pulled off my sandals and headed for the refrigerator to get a drink.

"Yes, second time. A good sign, don't you think?"

"Must be. I'm not a big fan of convention."

"You've never asked a girl out to dinner?" I asked, amazed.

"We generally have more exciting things to do."

"Like talking?"

"Not really. There's not much chance what they have to say is worth my attention."

"So, I imagine I should be flattered by our fabulous conversations?" I scoffed.

I didn't like the turn this was taking. Damien's words came back to me. I shouldn't give Maxime too much thought. I could be friendly, but I didn't have time to make a good guy out of him; I wasn't even sure I wanted to.

"It's different with you. Everything is different with you."

"Why is that?"

"I like talking to you. Because you listen to me," he answered with a shrug.

Despite his palpable embarrassment, his low-key smile reappeared. In an instant, the stifling air in the kitchen became lighter. I felt myself blush to the roots of my hair, while my heart beat madly. Maxime stared at me cautiously, as if he feared a blow.

I decided we needed a change of subject.

"Did you enjoy the rehearsal?"

"Very much. Damien could be more … regretful, right?"

"Regretful? You know the play?"

Maxime no longer surprised me. Some Shakespeare and now Musset… Sooner or later, he'd wind up reciting Rostand to me outside my window. The idea made me smile. Some women fantasized about romantic dinners, priceless jewels, or chivalry. I would be much happier with a book.

"A little. Perdican should be more tortured by the idea of using Rosette to get revenge on Cam—"

He broke off when he saw me smiling. I took refuge in my glass, but it was too late. Maxime was looking embarrassed – almost annoyed again. Talking with him was like walking a tightrope without a net.

"I didn't know you knew the play. I think you're right, Perdican is hurting himself by doing that. He should be a bit more hopeless at the end of the scene."

Maxime seemed relieved and nodded without adding anything.

"You should go get ready, you're going to be late," he pointed out, while I was still thinking about Cyrano and Roxane.

"Uh, yes. You're sure it doesn't bother you?"

"It's your house, you can do whatever you want."

I raised my eyebrows, amazed. I was starting to understand how Maxime worked. For him to be so agreeable, almost benevolent, was unusual.

"That's not like you," I said finally. "No comments? No … digs?"

"I told you…"

"No. Is it the fact that I'm going out with him that upsets you?"

I crossed my arms over my chest, ready to do battle. I wanted an explanation and I was going to get it. Unless he was making fun of me? He was making fun of my notorious failure with men. He'd already made fun of my blushing today; he must find it hilarious when I stammered and ran away as soon as a man wanted to kiss me.

"I didn't think my opinion mattered to you."

"Apparently it does!"

"Listen, do whatever you want, Sarah. Go out to dinner and have fun. I'll be safe, locked in here. Go get dressed."

He glanced at his watch and frowned. I did the same, realizing that my fifteen minutes had just gone by at lightspeed. I still didn't have my answer, but I was out of time.

"We'll talk about it later," I declared with conviction.

"Of course!"

I dashed to my bedroom and got rid of my jeans and old sweater. I slipped on a wide blue cotton skirt and a sleeveless white blouse. After checking my outfit, I snuck into the bathroom. I energetically brushed my hair and put on makeup.

Tonight was supposed to mark the true beginning of my relationship with Frédéric. We'd already shared some meals, we'd held hands – well, fingers, to be precise – so I was hoping for a kiss tonight. The first of many, if possible. I added a touch of perfume and threw a satisfied smile at my mirror.

I went back to the living room, adjusting my post earrings. Maxime was still in the armchair, eyes riveted to the screen. To be on the safe side, I planted myself in front of him to get his opinion.

"How do I look?" I asked, arms at my sides.

"Like something straight out of the 1950s?"

I took a look at my outfit, devastated. I wanted to look attractive, I wanted people to gaze at me with a glimmer of desire in their eyes, for them to wonder vaguely about my perfume, and for a man to eventually bury his nose in my neck.

"Really? But I've worn this skirt all the time and I've always had compliments!"

"I don't doubt it. Likely from seventy-year-old men!"

"Women, too," I harrumphed.

"Who won't have to worry about the competition."

"Fine. Do you think my long blue dress would be better?"

"The one that looks like a faded curtain? No, keep this one! It's slightly better."

"Lovely," I growled. "Thanks for the ego boost!"

I left the living room in a snit and slipped my sandals on. Feeling undermined, I wound up undoing the top button on my blouse. While hoping for the flame of desire, I'd only gotten a small spark of interest. I still had no idea how to deal with Maxime. By asking his opinion, I'd vaguely imagined he would give me a clue as to how to act with him.

All in vain. Maxime remained indecipherable.

I took my cardigan down from its hook and, on edge, fought with the sleeves for several long seconds.

Suddenly, the sweater slipped out of my hands, and

as I turned to catch hold of it again, I found myself face to face with Maxime. From this short distance, I could distinguish the outline of his taut pecs under the black fabric of his T-shirt. He was holding my cardigan in his hand and once again he had that smile, the one that quirked up the right side of his mouth. His dark eyes searched me.

"What's this?" I asked, tracing my finger along the scar that crossed his eyebrow.

"The remains of a bad memory."

My fingers grazed the line of his jaw before my hand fell back to my side. His unpleasant remarks were already forgotten. I was trapped between the door and his body and I didn't really feel like moving. Maxime didn't frighten me. He fascinated me. Every new clue about his life just fueled new questions.

"What time are you coming back?"

Breathing heavily, I cleared my throat to regain a foothold in reality. Just the way he looked at me made me flustered. Frankly, this wasn't new with a man. But usually it terrified me and I ended up turning tail. With Maxime, I was trusting, reassured by his gentle smile and the shape of his broad shoulders.

"In two hours, I think," I answered hoarsely.

"Okay. I'll stay here."

"Maxime Maréchal is joking. I think I'll have to call a news channel or two," I quipped.

"Turn around, I'll help you."

Meekly, I obeyed. Maxime helped me slip my arms into the sleeves and adjusted the cardigan on my shoulders. My breathing resumed a normal rhythm and I ignored Maxime's subtle scent. I pretended that I wasn't on the verge of being intoxicated by it beyond all coherent thought.

"You look very pretty," he finally complimented me.

"You're just trying to redeem yourself!" I countered, turning toward him.

With trembling fingers, I buttoned my cardigan, eyes riveted to Maxime's. His dark gaze hypnotized me. He rarely brightened, but every time I saw a burst of joy or a glimmer of sincerity, it was a real gift.

"A bit. But even wearing a bin bag, you'd be very pretty."

Our bodies were still close to one another, so close our breath was mingled. I waited for Maxime to move aside, but he stayed near, eyes examining my face. Without asking, I touched my hand to his wrist and ran my index finger along his tattoo. I went up over his forearm, traced an arabesque around his elbow, then on to his biceps.

"You should stop," Maxime warned me huskily.

His muscle twitched at my touch and I didn't hide my triumphant smile. I breathed out:

"A sign of life…"

My gaze turned away from his tattoo and toward his face. His eyes were closed, as if he were trying to maintain control. I reversed my trajectory, delicately following the line of the bramble to his wrist. I was almost disappointed at not being able to go farther. Now that I'd discovered the sensation of his skin against mine, I wanted more.

"Please, Sarah, you should stop."

That sounded like a warning. As per usual: all of Maxime's words were aimed at keeping me away from him. Tonight, I wanted to prove to him that it didn't work with me. I wasn't afraid of him.

"There's no danger," I said finally.

"Sarah, you should go to your dinner, before I detain you."

"I like to live dangerously."

His happy smile echoed my own and he undid the first two buttons on my cardigan.

"Less severe," he explained. "Have a good evening!"

Abruptly, he moved away and went back to the living room. The heat that had come over me dissipated like the fog in my brain. With him gone, I could return to normal operating mode.

"Uh ... thanks. You too!"

After a second of hesitation, wavering between wanting to stay and having to leave, I rushed downstairs. Frédéric was outside my door, a bouquet of peonies in his hand. I thanked him warmly.

"Leftovers from a birthday party," he explained.

He'd often given me flowers. Every time, or nearly, they had been leftovers. Normally, it wouldn't have bothered me, but tonight, I would have liked these flowers to be just for me. He led us to Baptiste's restaurant.

"You seem distracted," he commented as I dug into my meal.

"I'm a little tired."

Since the start of our dinner, I'd had trouble taking an interest in the conversation. Frédéric was fueling the discussion, carrying on with anecdotes, while my mind wandered, thinking about Maxime and his tattoo.

I thought again about touching his skin, the warmth of his body, even the way it had reacted, as if his feelings had betrayed him. At last I'd found a chink in Maxime's armor: he wasn't so dangerous.

"Because of Maxime?"

The name of my "flatmate" pulled me from my thoughts. I felt myself reddening and immediately took refuge in my glass of white wine.

"I mean, he's a little weird, isn't he?"

"No," I cut in. "Just … serving his time – we can't ask him to be happy to be here."

"Sarah, I'm worried about you. I don't know if you can trust him. He's damaged."

"He's helping me out, so it's not so bad. Tell me about your mother's visit instead. Did it go well?"

Straightaway, Frédéric launched into the epic tale of his mother's visit. Apparently, the old lady was hard to please and always rambled on. I absent-mindedly finished my plate, nodding at regular intervals. Maxime and his husky voice were still haunting me. Maybe I should have stayed home.

After dinner, as always, Frédéric walked me back to the bookshop door. This time, he didn't hesitate and took my hand in his. His palm was hot and a little sweaty. Flowers in my other hand, we crossed the square that led to the bookshop. Automatically, I looked up toward the apartment. The light in the living room was still shining, and I surprised myself with a smile of relief. Now I'd likely have a chance at resuming my conversation with Maxime.

"I had a really nice time," murmured Frédéric.

"Me too."

Even with my mind elsewhere and checking my watch three times.

We took our places in front of the door to the bookshop, lit by a spotlight and string lights wrapped around the ivy that surrounded the windows.

"I enjoy your company a lot, you know."

"Me too."

His eyes dropped to my mouth and my heart started up its mad panic again. Unlike our first evening out, I was dreading this kiss. I was no longer expecting it, and wanted it even less. I hadn't thought about it all night, and I would have preferred not to have to deal with it. Not with Maxime right above us.

Then Frédéric laid his mouth against mine and kissed

me. It was clumsy and hesitant. I was in shock and he seemed to be wondering if it was a good idea, like when you taste an exotic dish for the first time, not sure if your body is going to accept it.

That was it, exactly that sensation. Frédéric's lips against mine were a frigid experience, of the kind that made you grimace. It was light-years away from what any girl could hope for from a first kiss, neither unforgettable nor legendary.

A real disappointment.

"See you tomorrow," he said. "Do you want to have lunch together?"

"Uh … no. I … I have a lot of work to do tomorrow. And I'm tied up with the renovations. Let's say this weekend. At the village festival?"

"Sounds good. I'm doing the flowers there anyway."

"Great!"

I tried to speak with enthusiasm, but I doubted my acting skills. I disentangled my fingers from his, but Frédéric stole another kiss from me, just as much of a dud as the first. I gave him a smile and entered the bookshop with relief.

Good grief, what was wrong with me?

I'd spent weeks fantasizing about the florist. And now that I was getting dates and he was kissing me, I wanted to run. I couldn't even blame my inexperience or shyness; I'd actually felt a sort of urgency. I had to get away.

"So how was dinner?"

I relieved myself of the flowers by depositing them on the kitchen counter. The two place settings had been cleared, and Maxime was sitting on one of the stools, phone in his hand.

"Dinner was pleasant, afterwards was … very, very strange!"

I sat down close to him, squinting at his phone screen.

"I was trying to reach Simon. He's not answering. So, tell me, why strange?"

His sincere interest intrigued me. I stared at him, before finally realizing what had happened. It was him. This disaster was his fault. After letting me know he didn't like Frédéric, he'd put on that whole show with the cardigan to sow doubt. And I, like an idiot, had taken the bait. I felt like such a moron.

"It's your fault," I said at last.

"My fault? Why?"

"You made me have second thoughts. Everything was going well with Frédéric before you decided to emerge from your tortured silence. I was doing really well. The thing with the cardigan, do you do that often? Or is it something you stole from a movie?"

"Sarah, I'm not following you. What happened and how is it my fault?"

"I was … out of sorts. Because of our conversation and the whole thing that happened over there," I said, gesturing at the section of wall where I'd been cornered.

"I messed up the dinner. I didn't say one pleasant word or speak a meaningful sentence."

"I'm sure you're exaggerating!"

"And then, when he kissed me … nothing," I confessed, mortified. "Not even a flicker."

Maxime laughed softly and shook his head. He set his phone down on the counter and stared at me intensely. From his smiling face, I guessed that he was more than satisfied with having sabotaged my evening. I didn't really blame him. I mostly blamed myself for being so easily influenced. But I was used to living alone, making decisions alone, managing the bookshop as best I could. Maxime had succeeded in turning all of that upside down.

"Nothing?"

"Nothing."

"So, you're blaming me for a bad kiss?"

"It wasn't a bad kiss. It was the first with him. That's a big deal! It's supposed to be the one that makes you blush and stammer, makes you float, makes you forget your whole life. The one that's supposed to make you happy," I finished, out of breath, wringing my hands with frustration.

"The one you read about in books?"

I lifted my gaze toward his. I could see the glimmer of mischief in his eyes, that little spark that made him even more handsome. Next to him, I must seem very dull.

He got down off his stool and planted himself in front

of me. As close as he'd been during our pre-dinner conversation. My body warmed up and the air grew thin. In the gleam of my little living-room lamp, Maxime was superb, the line of his jaw as if chiseled from stone.

"The one you read about in books, eh?" he repeated.

I nodded, regretting my perch on a stool that felt increasingly unsteady. My whole body was vibrating as Maxime drew near.

"Very well. Since you think I stole that kiss from you, I'm going to return it."

"What?"

Chapter Nine

Sarah's eyes were as round as saucers. Breathing heavily, lips parted, and clinging to her stool, she seemed even more vulnerable. I'd waited two long hours, hoping she'd come back earlier. I'd taken a discreet peek out the window when I heard them talking and I'd felt a wave of relief wash over me when I saw that the kiss was much too short and lackluster to mean anything.

"I don't … I don't understand," she stammered.

Her cheeks reddened violently and I knew that she'd understood my proposition perfectly well. I fixed my gaze on her mouth and heard her breathing accelerate.

"I'm going to return it," I repeated.

"What?"

"The kiss. The one you didn't get. The one you dream about. Look at it as … life experience."

"You're going to teach me to kiss? Forget it!"

She scrambled down from her stool and escaped to the living room. Swiftly, she pulled off her cardigan and struggled with it before throwing it on the sofa. She paced up and down the room for a few seconds, hands hidden in her hair.

"Sarah…"

"No. Listen. Here's what I suggest: you're going to go back to your room, I'm going to go to mine, and we're going to pretend this disaster of an evening never happened."

She didn't dare meet my eyes, keeping hers fixed on the floor. Only now did I realize that I'd been too rough. Sarah had spent most of her life reading books, surrounding herself with considerate men, great romantics, passionate yet tame stories.

She'd spent her life in a world where everything ended well and no ex-cons got involved.

Obviously, I wasn't even close to an ideal man. I wasn't smooth like Frédéric, nor easy to understand. I was trouble.

Except with her. With Sarah, I was much calmer. Maybe because she didn't expect anything of me, no fake smiles or polite nods. Sarah looked at me like no one else did, digging into the depths of my soul in search of my dark secrets. Sooner or later, I'd end up confessing one or two of them to her.

When she finally looked up at me, she still seemed

just as fragile, hesitating between the disappointment of her dinner and my too-harsh proposition.

I held my hands up in front of me, as a sign of surrender. Nonetheless, I continued to reduce the space between us.

I wanted to kiss her. Just once. To see what it was like to kiss a woman with no other intentions, to check if her lips were as soft as they appeared, to quiet the voice of my conscience screaming that Sarah was too good for me, to destroy the anger mixed with jealousy I was feeling.

And above all, because I wanted to. Badly, and to hell with the consequences. Sarah deserved that kiss. She deserved it with me.

Her chest was rising and falling very rapidly, as if she'd just run a marathon. She backed away and tripped over the lamp, which wobbled on its base.

"Shit," she swore, steadying it.

We found ourselves face to face, my frustration colliding with her shyness. During our previous confrontations, Sarah had been calm. This time, I could hear her panicked breathing and make out a glimmer of uncertainty in her eyes.

"I'm sorry about your date," I murmured.

"Try saying it without smiling and maybe I'll believe you."

My smile broadened and she seemed to relax slowly.

That's what Sarah needed: time. She wasn't impulsive. I would have to try harder.

"I'd like it if you told me about this," she said, pointing to my tattoo. "It intrigues me."

"Briars keep intruders away," I explained.

"So, it's a warning to others?"

As she'd done before her dinner, she rested her hand where the design began on my wrist. At the touch of her cool skin, a shiver went through me. Her fingers studiously followed the ink embedded in my skin. I closed my eyes. That simple contact set me on fire, gave me unheard-of sensations. For the first time in years, a woman was caressing me without any other goal than to know me.

"You should stay away from me," I finally whispered.

She ignored my warning, too focused on tracking the design. The shy and blushing Sarah gave way to a more audacious and desirable woman.

"Where does it end up?"

"Chest."

Her eyes rested on my T-shirt, as if she hoped to see through it. After two seconds' reflection, I decided to pull it off. I threw the shirt on the floor and let Sarah discover the rest of my tattoo. The briar ended wrapped around another, which was itself entangled with a third. The brambles then expanded, blossoming across my chest only to trail away on the opposite side.

In silence, Sarah followed the line of each briar. Then she asked:

"Why briars?"

"Because they grow everywhere. And they survive better than humans," I added with a smile.

"You're a survivor. As long as nobody touches you."

I felt her warm breath caress my chest. An intense, burning desire seized me. Sarah was unlike anyone I'd ever met, and I had never felt anything like this before. I couldn't take it. Just the touch of her finger on my skin had been enough to push me to my limit. The thought of her whole body against mine was like a drug.

Sarah had succeeded where most people had failed … or given up. She'd taken the time, talked to me, given me time. She'd hung on, despite my warnings, and that was what attracted me to her: her selflessness.

I kept my arms at my sides, resisting the urge to touch her. I wanted to touch her. More than anything. Even more than my freedom. But Damien's words still haunted me.

"Walk away, Sarah," I said, gritting my teeth.

She took a step back but kept her eyes riveted on me. That short distance was ineffectual. On the contrary, frustration burned in my stomach. I'd met loads of women, fucked some of them into oblivion, had fun fondling others, but Sarah had nothing in common with those other girls. She was goodness incarnate.

"Does it work?" she asked eventually.

"Does what work?"

"Do people reach you in spite of this?"

"I keep them at a distance for their own good. Most of the time, I wreck my relationships. I destroy everything, Sarah. It's what I do best."

"I'm sure you're exaggerating."

"I don't have any contact with my father, I fired my agent, the guy I thought was a friend doesn't even call me anymore. I even managed to fight with Damien. I destroy things, Sarah. I destroy them."

"Fine," she said with a smile.

"Fine? That's all you have to say?"

"Maybe *I* like to live dangerously."

And as if to prove it, she took a step forward. My heart felt on the verge of imploding, unable to control my erratic thoughts. I had to protect her … but I was drawn to her. Apart from Sarah, no one had ever had this power over me.

She laid her palm over my heart and my breathing stopped.

I looked down at her. Sweet, attractive, fragile, shy. Her hold over me had developed so quickly, it almost scared me. When our eyes met, I knew I was lost. Tonight was going to change everything between us.

I leaned slowly toward her face, leaving her the painful option of fleeing.

Sarah didn't blink. She wasn't even breathing

anymore, and her hand pressed against me did nothing to push me away.

I lazily brushed against her mouth. She tasted like sugar, probably from her dessert. Her hand glided over my skin and her fingers hooked my belt. She went up on tiptoe and pressed her parted lips against mine. Slowly, my body ignited, and against my will, I finally gave in.

My palm found her cheek and I pulled her against me. A low moan escaped her. That intensified my excitement and I almost hissed as I felt Sarah's hand graze my crotch. I abandoned her lips to follow the line of her jaw. I kissed the square of skin behind her ear, then returned ferociously to her mouth. I pushed Sarah against the wall and imprisoned her against my body. Her chest rose and fell rapidly against me. My free hand found the small of her back and her body fit mine perfectly.

Her tongue slipped between my lips and our kiss became passionate and uncontrollable. Sarah's hands were all over me. My chest, the back of my neck, my face, she was enthusiastically exploring this new territory. At regular intervals, her fingers slid across my chest. When she felt the drumming of my heart, I sensed her smiling against my mouth.

To my despair, Sarah was very overdressed. I wanted to feel her curves under my hands, to savor the heat of her skin against mine, but it was much too fast for a girl like her. So, my mouth roved over what she offered me:

her neck and the tops of her shoulders. In my hands, Sarah let herself go. Head thrown back, she moaned softly. I could have done whatever I wanted.

She'd ignored my warnings.

She'd taken the risk. And that overwhelmed me.

Out of breath, I finally moved away from her. She was panting, mouth open, lips swollen. I missed the taste of her skin already. Her eyes shone with a new light, a mix of flaming desire and fear.

I didn't know what had come over me; I didn't even understand how we'd gotten here. However, I was sure that it was a bad idea. Sarah and I came from different worlds, we were total opposites, and I refused to let her become more collateral damage for my unmanageable anger.

"You're right," I said finally, still out of breath. "We're going to pretend this evening never happened."

Her eyes widened and her face fell. The light in her eyes abruptly went out and her whole body tensed like a bow. In spite of myself, I was already seeing what I feared: I was hurting her.

"But…"

"I owed you a kiss. You wanted to know what it was like, right? Now, you can reproduce it."

"So that was it?"

A sad laugh escaped her. She put her thumb to her lips, as if to erase what we'd just done. I'd have sold my soul for that simple gesture, to be able to stroke her mouth and tell myself she was mine.

I backed up again, distancing myself. It didn't change much – the sexual tension in the room was unbearable. Normally, I would have walked out the door and roamed the night, trying to forget her hurt expression. I'd have downed a few glasses and ended up finding some poor guy to fight. It would have let off steam. For at least several hours, I would have forgotten my life entirely.

But I was trapped here, with her, between her walls. Escaping would only make the situation worse.

"You just wanted … to show me?"

"It's just a kiss, Sarah. Don't…"

"I feel humiliated."

"You wanted a kiss. Something perfect, from a stupid book. There, it's done!" I said, upset.

"From a stupid book?"

"That's what you dream about, isn't it? A romantic date, a perfect man, flowers, books, dinner, a chart song to listen to on a loop?"

"Actually, I prefer Sixties hits."

She gave a bitter laugh. I recovered my T-shirt and put it back on, ignoring her contemptuous look. I knew how to detect anger from miles away – it was radiating in her tiny living room and would eventually flatten me if I didn't leave now. And Sarah hadn't said her last word yet.

"Since we're doing big revelations, rest assured, Maxime, that kiss wasn't all that perfect!"

I didn't have time to catch her eye before she was already closing the door to her bedroom behind her. I stayed standing in the living room for several long minutes. Finally, I went to my room, and in a rage sent my bedside table flying with a kick. My porcelain lamp exploded into dozens of pieces.

The only thought that came to me as I painstakingly gathered up every fragment was that once again I'd excelled in my specialty: destruction.

My night was disastrous. I spent more time staring at the little crack that ran across the wall than sleeping. I was reliving my kiss with Sarah. I'd lied through my teeth. To pretend that that kiss was a demonstration was the most ridiculous lie I'd ever told.

When I awoke, I hadn't managed to rid myself of the insane desire to get into a fight. I had to release the rage running through my veins like viscous lava. It was worming its way in everywhere, into every corner of my soul. At least serving my sentence here had the virtue of providing clarity on my situation.

It was time to resolve my own problems. I checked the time on my watch and grabbed my phone. I tried to reach Simon and was truly surprised when he finally picked up.

"Fuck, I thought you were dead!" I said.

"Busy, mostly. So, how's your sentence going?"

In the background, I could make out the sounds of Parisian life, from angry motorists to schoolyard shouts. I heard him take a drag on his cigarette, then blow out the smoke. I already envied him his freedom and anonymity while I was here in this goldfish bowl.

"Fine. Sarah is … nice."

Nice. Such a useless, inadequate word. Sarah was desirable, kind, caring. Nice, too. But she was so much more than nice. Better than anything I'd ever experienced, better than picking a fight.

Better than me, that was for certain.

"Nice? I didn't even know you knew that word. Anyway, I won't be able to talk for long, I have an audition for a movie."

"Oh! Great…"

Out of the corner of my eye, I peeked at the fat script Claude had sent me. I hadn't read it yet. I was now so far from that world, I was having trouble believing I was still part of it.

"Claude told me he sent it to you. You know, the Philippon one."

"Oh. Which part?"

"Same as you. The lead."

I ignored his conceited tone. Normally, I'd have taken

him down a peg. I didn't like people eyeing my roles, let alone stealing them out from under me. Simon knew that perfectly well. He was provoking me, as I sometimes did to him; a subtle way of reminding me that I was far from Paris, and thus far from the business. He was amazed by my silence.

"No reaction?"

"Go fuck yourself," I laughed.

"Ah, I was worried. For a minute, I thought you were going to wish me good luck."

"Take full advantage of my absence. When I get back, I'm pulverizing you."

He laughed in turn, but very quickly silence fell. Our conversations normally centered around showbiz and the girls we met. It was harder to talk when none of that was relevant.

"I just wanted to see how you were doing," I explained finally.

"Mathilde told me about the arrangement they negotiated. Not too bad, eh?"

"In any case, nothing splashed across the papers. I'll be able to save my ass, yet again."

"Yeah."

Another silence fell, barely broken by a few horns honking. This conversation wouldn't go any further. I knew that now.

"You're lucky to always have somebody there to get you out of trouble," Simon finally said.

I sat up, suddenly alarmed by the tone of his remark. Simon was much too proper to make trouble for himself. He was as smooth as the feathers on a duck; a nice boy, polite, his contact with the police limited to a parking ticket. This anxiety wasn't like him.

"Are you in trouble?" I asked.

"No, it was just a thought. You planning to audition for the part?"

"No idea. I want to read the script first! We'll see."

"How much longer?"

"Five weeks."

"Okay. Listen, I'm outside the building, I've gotta go."

I didn't have time to respond before he'd already hung up. I spent some long minutes replaying our short conversation in my mind. Something about it made me uneasy. The way Simon was hurrying, his little comments, I could sense he was having problems. But as far back as I could remember, Simon and I had been polar opposites. While I managed to make the worst trouble for myself, he was a consistent good boy.

I decided to get up and go straight to the shower. My bad feeling about Simon still didn't fade. I tried to chase the feeling away to concentrate on Sarah and this new day. The day after. The one following our kiss. I had to stick to my course of action: keep my distance, make her understand that she wouldn't gain anything from being with a man like me ...

except a heap of problems and an overly troublesome past.

From the smell of coffee wafting through the living room, I realized Sarah had been up for a while. I poured her a cup anyway; it would be a sort of peace offering that would indicate whether or not I'd succeeded in making her swallow my lie and whether or not she'd understood.

I walked cautiously down the stairs, two cups in my hands. Sarah's laugh was reverberating around the bookshop. Good. If somebody was with her, she would probably be less inclined to tell me to go to hell. That suited me.

"Good morning," I said, setting her cup down in front of her.

She shot me a surprised look, then gestured toward Anita with her pen. Obviously, she had no desire to talk with me.

"Anita was telling me about the preparations for tonight."

"Tonight?"

"The village festival. Band, big tent, unlimited cider. Hope to see you there," Anita said.

"Damien got me a furlough but… That kind of festival isn't really my thing."

I tried to catch Sarah's eye, but she was lost in a pile of books. On a sheet of paper, she was religiously recording the titles. In other words, she was ignoring me.

"Oh no, we have lots of fun. It would do you good to see people, to go out. You don't have to inflict extra punishment on yourself by holing up in the apartment," continued Anita.

"I'll think about it," I said evasively.

Anita stared at me and an embarrassing silence settled between the three of us. Maybe she'd guessed that something had happened between me and Sarah. I just gave her a forced smile, hoping she'd finally leave. I didn't like the vibe I was getting from Sarah; her whole body was tense, from her crossed legs to her too-severe ponytail. She seemed deeply upset.

"See you at rehearsal?" Anita tossed out.

"Yes. And learn your lines," Sarah sighed. "We should get this show on the road tonight. We have only one more month to get ready!"

Anita rolled her eyes and directed an irritated grimace at Sarah, who didn't even look at her. I suppressed a smile; Anita was truly enthusiastic and optimistic by nature, and I wasn't surprised that she and Sarah were friends. Aside from differing in age, they were a lot alike.

"I know what you're doing," grumbled Sarah.

I traded another conspiratorial smile with Anita.

"Camille dear, everything is ready for our departure; the Baron has finished the accounts, and my mule is equipped," Anita recited bombastically.

Sarah and I corrected her in unison:

"My mule is saddled!"

Sarah shot me a delighted smile, while Anita's eyes darted back and forth between us. She ended up shaking her head appreciatively, before bidding us goodbye one last time.

"See you tonight! Maxime, I'm counting on you!"

She slipped out, leaving me alone with Sarah, who pushed back her pile of books and took some little blue boxes out of a drawer. She hadn't touched her cup of coffee, which didn't reassure me about continuing our conversation.

"Do you know the play?" she asked finally.

"Excuse me?"

At last she looked up at me. The gleam of amusement prompted by Anita had already disappeared. She stared coldly at me, reminding me of my schoolteachers. No understanding there: they would lecture me, tell me I was worthless, and send me home. My father would then take care of kicking my ass, to improve my attitude.

"*Don't Trifle with Love,* by Musset. The saddled mule," she reminded me. "Studied it in school maybe?"

"Oh. No. Just a good memory. Rehearsal the other night, remember? You spent your time making them redo that scene. I know the lines."

She nodded, a little smile on her lips.

"I even know what you do when you're annoyed," I continued. "You curl your lip. And you roll a piece of paper between your hands, to keep from strangling Anita or Baptiste."

Another smile, wider this time. For that one smile, I could have killed a florist with my bare hands.

"Admit it, that surprises you!"

"Maxime, where you're concerned, nothing much surprises me anymore," she said, taking a sip of her coffee.

I rubbed my hand over the back of my neck, not really knowing how to bring up the subject. I'd broken the ice, and now we had to talk about last night.

"Sarah, about last night, I'd like to..."

"Don't worry, everything's fine."

I slipped behind her, picking up traces of her usual sweet perfume. Sarah was wearing an off-the-shoulder sweater that presented the nape of her neck to anyone who looked. I had a crazy urge to lay my lips there and taste her sweet skin. I wanted to feel her frantic pulse against my mouth. At the stealthy contact of my chest with her back, Sarah straightened up. Her whole body tensed and she held her breath.

"I think I owe you an apology," I murmured finally.

"Apology accepted," she replied hurriedly.

"I said I was thinking it, not that I was doing it."

She swiveled toward me, staring into my eyes. I suppressed the desire to brush away a strand of hair floating by her cheek. I pressed my lips against her forehead and kissed her tenderly. When I moved away, her eyes were closed and her lips parted, as if she were trying to catch her breath.

"I'm sorry for being … what I am," I said at last. "For destroying things, for being unpleasant, for being a poor farmer's son. I'm sorry I'm not the man you think I am. Really."

"Maxime, it's…"

"But I'm not really sorry for that kiss. I never regret … a moment's happiness," I explained.

"Okay."

"Especially with you."

Her cheeks reddened intensely. I found myself smiling. That blush, it was a sign that our normal life – forced cohabitation – was resuming. I moved away, suppressing the pleasant – very pleasant – idea of kissing her again. She turned around and went back to her task.

"What are you doing?"

"Mystery picks. Actually, you could help me. You have to create the labels, attach them to the raffia, and once the books are covered in brown paper, wrap the raffia around them. Like a present, you see?"

She showed me one of the books, while I took another swig of my coffee. Her desk was a veritable construction site, strewn with books, ribbon, scissors, and innumerable Post-it notes.

"Or you can just wrap them and I'll do the rest," she proposed as a compromise.

"I'm not sure I can do it as elegantly as you."

"Who cares! What matters is the book."

"If that's what matters, why are you wrapping them?"

She shot me an incredulous look, as if I'd just asked whether fire burned. Apparently, in Sarah's world, as soon as books got involved, there was an obvious explanation.

"Sorry for asking," I said, a little anxious.

Sarah burst out laughing and that unsettled me even more. I stared at her, uncomprehending.

"I'm not used to you apologizing. And I'm not sure I want to get used to it. Please, don't change, Maxime."

"The books," I cut in, to reorient her toward a less thorny subject than my personality.

"Most people come in here, pick up a book at random, turn it over, read the blurb, and put it down. By wrapping them and adding a clue, I give them a chance."

"Your customers?"

"The books. The customers come and make their decision based on a cover and a few lines. It's not very fair. I'm making a level playing field. And actually, people prefer mystery. Some of them get addicted. They throw themselves into it and … what?"

She stopped short at my broad smile.

"I like it when you come alive like that," I explained.

"I just don't like people to judge a book by its cover. As simple as that."

"Okay."

"Sometimes, a book seems forbidding. You just have to give it a chance."

Her gaze strayed to my tattoo before finding my eyes. My smile faded and a hot thrill ran through me. In Sarah's eyes, I was normal, and that excited me more than anything. She saw me like no one else did, with my wounds, without knowing all my secrets, but with the conviction that I wasn't a bad guy.

Slowly, her gaze slipped to my mouth and the memories of our kiss yesterday resurfaced. Then the same air crackling with desire, the same tension in our bodies, the same yearning to feel her legs clamped around my waist. If I kissed her again, my meager resistance was going to shatter. I'd take her right there, on this counter, in front of everyone, and lose myself in her.

"It's also true for people," she said.

Then, in a barely audible whisper as she resumed her mission of wrapping books, she added:

"Especially with you."

Despite the fact that I'd been terrible to her for weeks, despite the fact that I'd pushed her away last night, Sarah still trusted me. I didn't know if that was loyalty or foolishness. I'd never been faced with this kind of behavior before. As a rule, I disappointed the people close to me. It was easier to disappoint them than to maintain a relationship.

Obviously, with Sarah, it was different. In four weeks

and with a single kiss, she'd turned my universe completely upside down.

But I didn't have time to respond.

In the doorway to the bookshop stood Frédéric, with, instead of a shield, an impressive bouquet of flowers. I swallowed a smile: this guy still hadn't understood a thing.

"I… You left so quickly last night, I just wanted to make sure you were all right," he said as he stepped into the shop.

"I'm fine," replied Sarah.

"Ah, great. I … I was wondering… Well, I wanted to know if you'd like me to take you to the festival tonight."

Sarah's eyes darted from the florist to me, before returning to the florist. She rested her hands on her desk and hesitated a few seconds before answering.

I felt suddenly powerless. I had no claim over Sarah. And yet, the idea of this guy putting his hands on her made me crazy. I squeezed my fist hard enough to hurt myself, but it was still better than unloading it in this guy's face.

For the moment, anyway.

"Um, I don't know," she replied at last, after a brief glance toward me.

"I could take you there."

A wave of anger flooded me. I took a step back, trying to concentrate on something else. Normally, I would have made trouble, doing everything I could to embarrass the poor guy. But with Sarah as a witness, I was more cautious. Attacking him would only upset her and make me the villain.

"And I'll walk you home," he promised.

I moved back again, disappearing into the shadowy shelving. Sarah's answer pierced me to the core.

"That would be lovely," she said.

Chapter Ten

When I was younger, my grandmother had made me promise never to lie. Solemnly, with my hand over my heart, I'd sworn not to lie. Neither because it was easier nor by omission. Never. I'd quickly realized that my grandmother had been traumatized by my mother's continuous lies. And I'd kept my promise. No lying, no deception, no compromising the truth.

Until last night, with Maxime.

The moment the lie had crossed my lips, I'd regretted it. Lying only made the situation worse. At any rate, that's what my grandmother would regularly tell me. But seeing Maxime distance himself so easily and suggest that he'd kissed me just *for demonstration purposes* had hurt my pride. So, yes, I'd lied. I'd said that the kiss wasn't perfect.

But it was, in every respect. Between his lips caressing

mine and his possessive hand sliding down my back … that kiss was everything I'd always imagined. It hadn't just made me happy. It had transported me up and away, out of myself. Feeling his heart beat, pressing myself against his body as if my life depended on it, feeling the scratch of his three-day stubble, smelling the trace of cologne on his neck, delighting in his moans. I'd loved it all. Thinking about that kiss still made me blush.

When I woke up this morning, after a difficult night, I'd run my thumb over my lips. I'd felt it on my mouth, like a healing wound. I'd replayed the scene over and over again in my mind, overdosing on it, not understanding how I could feel such emotions with a man who didn't care about me.

I brushed my hair mechanically in front of the mirror, musing on Maxime's attitude. Everything about him screamed at me to distance myself. I'd been warned, even kept at arm's length. Anita had advised me to protect myself; Damien had recommended I not get attached. But there was nothing rational in my relationship to him. After our rough start, his icy repartee, and his anger permanently screwed into his fists, we'd managed to talk. But talking only made the situation more complicated. An innocuous sentence would lead to dozens of questions, and the slightest hint of an answer would inspire new ones.

Curiosity had given way to fascination. I wanted to know more. Always. Maxime revealed little, but when he did, I discovered the man hidden away behind the thorns of his tattoo.

I tried to chase Maxime from my mind and prowled around my bedroom. Agreeing to spend the evening with Frédéric had been an impulse, and not a noble one. When you're hurt, you do everything you can to hurt the other person back. Seeing Maxime's victorious smile fall when I'd accepted Frédéric's invitation had soothed my fractured ego. He couldn't be allowed to believe he was the only one calling the shots. He wanted distance – I'd give him distance.

I could blow hot and cold just like him.

Just like him, I could keep a poker face and act like that kiss never happened. Accepting his apology didn't mean I'd forgotten. Every second of that kiss had been etched into my very skin, into my cheeks from the contact with his hands, into my neck from the caress of his lips. But Maxime had been clear: he didn't want anything more.

So, just like him, I was getting on with life.

And getting on with life meant giving Frédéric another chance. I suspected I bore some responsibility for our disappointing kiss. I was hoping this evening would mark the real beginning of our relationship. I was convinced that in a few years' time we'd be laughing about our misadventure. Even so, I still had Maxime's comments in my head, and I decided to fight against my shyness by choosing a more fashionable outfit for this evening. I opted for a black vintage dress, which showed my back. The neckline was modest, but the flared skirt came to my thighs. I wondered if it was too much, if I was going from one extreme to the other.

After ten minutes of indecision, I finally came out of my room, putting on my cardigan. Maxime was in the kitchen, dressed in his usual night clothes: an old Stones T-shirt and stretched-out tracksuit bottoms. When he saw me, he let out a whistle of approval that made me blush to the roots of my hair.

"I didn't end up using your bin-bag idea."

"It would have been less revealing, though."

I casually pulled off my cardigan as I reached for my bag, giving him ample time to admire what he'd lost last night. My ego was still bruised.

"I assume you're not coming?"

"No."

"Because we're hicks?"

He paused, then grabbed an apple and bit into it. He studied me for a moment, probably hoping I'd ask another question.

"Is Damien still mad at me?" he asked finally.

"A little. You know, I really think he had a hard time getting that furlough. You could at least thank him for the gesture."

"I didn't ask him for anything," he grumbled.

"That's the problem with friends. Sometimes, they do

unexpected things just to make you happy. Terrible, isn't it?"

I gave him a mocking smile. Once again, Maxime didn't realize he was very popular. He created his own loneliness and used it like heavy-duty armor. Inviting him would have been futile. He would have refused on principle.

"You're not a hick," he added in a lower tone. "And you look really good."

"Thanks. Do you think … well, since Frédéric asked me out, do you think he'll like it?"

My shyness was back a hundredfold. I'd chosen this outfit for my neighbor, to please him. After two failures, I wanted this evening to go well. Maxime looked me up and down slowly. A long shiver went through me. I ignored the hot flush threatening to devour me and nervously buttoned my cardigan.

"So? You think he'll like it?"

"I think it's proper to warn you that I'm going to wind up hitting this guy," he said coldly.

"If he doesn't like it?"

"He's going to like it. He'd have to be blind or completely dimwitted not to be attracted to you."

With the tips of his fingers, Maxime brushed my cheek, and my heart immediately started racing, ready to run a marathon on the spot. How did he have so much power over my body? We were farther apart than yesterday, and yet what I was feeling seemed ten times stronger.

"I'm in the second category," he added eventually, dropping his hand.

"You could come."

My voice was so weak that it sounded like I was begging. Maybe that's what I was doing. I wanted to spend time with him, talk with him, and find out how he got the scar on his eyebrow. I was aware this wasn't very fair to Frédéric: I'd agreed to go out with him, but I was inviting Maxime along. And I was inviting him for the wrong reasons.

That must have been a new habit, because I'd accepted Frédéric's invitation for an even worse reason.

"Give me one good reason," he proposed.

His voice was gentle and warm, almost comforting. I would have liked to believe I was reason enough, but I still had the bitter memory of yesterday in mind. A kiss, then an icy wind that had left me cold and exposed. I couldn't forget my resolution, to prove to him that I'd risen above the whole thing.

"We're going to have fun," I said. "Drink, have a bite to eat, talk to people. Laugh, too!"

"Nothing new, then?"

"Why do you do that?"

"What?"

"Act like I could convince you. You'd already decided you wouldn't come anyway."

He pulled a face, then nodded. He got some leftover chicken out of the refrigerator and started making himself a sandwich. I watched him, hoping he'd resume the conversation. I suppressed the bitterness coming over me. Maxime could blow hot and cold from one moment to the next. I was angry at myself for thinking for even one second that, in his eyes, *I* could be reason enough to… Forget it!

That sandwich was definitely more interesting to him than anything I could offer.

"I'm going. The dance floor awaits!"

He looked up at me and took a bite of his sandwich, signaling his total indifference. I went down to the bookshop. Frédéric was waiting for me, all smiles. I smiled back with all the conviction I could muster. I hoped I was hiding my disappointment, but I doubted it.

"Is everything okay?" fretted my escort.

"Sure, yes. Shall we?"

He offered me his arm, and I wrapped mine around it. I couldn't help glancing toward the apartment windows. For some reason that escaped me, spending the evening with Maxime eating chicken sandwiches seemed a much more tempting prospect.

The town council had gone all out. An immense tent, like a circus big top, had been erected near the town hall.

Strings of lights had been set up, beautifully lighting up the square. Musical ambiance was being provided by a local band, while at the other side of the tent the bar was serving wine and baskets of fries. With the summer holidays, the village population had doubled, hence the crowd milling around the dance floor.

"Do you want to dance?"

I said yes, and Frédéric led me through the crowd, and we danced through several lively rock numbers. The music was loud enough to make me forget my worries. After an hour of letting Frédéric's hands grab me to spin me around, I felt him pull me against him. The music slowed down and his cool palms slid underneath my cardigan to touch my skin. A pleasant shiver went through me, but it was nothing compared to what I'd felt with Maxime.

That dance lasted an eternity. An eternity in which Frédéric's scent enveloped me, his fingers wandered over my skin, his breath tickled my neck… An eternity in which my thoughts were far from the dance floor and far from him.

"Can we take a break?" I asked.

Frédéric, ever the gentleman, agreed immediately. I wondered if he was capable of saying "no" or behaving rudely. Although I appreciated the ease of our relationship – he tried to please me, and I let him – I was now expecting a little confrontation. Just to see if he was as tough as Maxime.

"I saw some friends over there, do you want to come?" he asked.

"Um … no! I saw Baptiste and I wanted to talk to him."

My lie went off without a hitch. Once again, Frédéric was accommodating and just nodded. He dropped a tender kiss on my cheek and threaded his way through the crowd, leaving me alone near the bar. Despite the festive atmosphere, the laughter and frenzied dancing, my mood was far from joyous. I felt bad, even torn up. I should have been happy to be here, to party, to have fun with the man I'd liked for months. But instead I was upset, even a little angry.

Once again, Maxime had ruined my evening.

"Hi!"

Anita's voice roused me from my bitter thoughts. I concentrated on wearing a neutral expression and smiling broadly.

"Nice maniacal smile," she commented.

"Sorry … I think I'm a little tired. You came alone?"

"Alone? Good grief, do you know me at all?"

At least Anita got a smile out of me. She handed me a glass of wine and clinked it against her own.

"To men!" she giggled.

"Fictional ones!"

"Certainly not! There's nothing better than a good reality, full of muscles, passion, and testosterone!"

I arched an eyebrow, frankly unconvinced. For me,

men could be summed up in one word: *problem*. Actually, two, if you added *migraine*. I took a swig from my glass, letting my gaze skim over the crowd. I was now dreading the moment when Frédéric would come back and I'd have to return to playing the part of a girl delighted to be here.

Well, the part of a girl delighted to be here *with him*.

"Maybe I should have turned him down," I finally admitted.

"The florist? The one you blush for and dream about?"

"I don't know. Why is it always so complicated? I don't understand him. He's sometimes sweet, then suddenly icy, then he compliments me…"

A smile blossomed on Anita's face. I looked at the situation from every angle, but I couldn't find a solution. I wondered if there even was one.

"What's so funny?"

"You. The situation. It reminds me of an old affair I had with a man. He drove me crazy. We spent our time arguing and bickering. One day, he kissed me and I slapped him. And then I kissed him back…"

"Was this your first marriage?"

"I never married him," she said. "But I can't regret what happened between us."

I contemplated her face tinged with nostalgia. I'd always viewed Anita as enthusiastic and playful by nature. She laughed at everything, including herself, and didn't hesitate to be generous with her time. She surprised me with this story.

"It was during my first marriage," she added with a laugh. "I married a man I'd fantasized about. And I loved another."

"It's a bit more complicated for me," I whispered. "Frédéric is kind and sweet. And pleasant…"

"And probably terrifically boring. You're living in books, Sarah. Maybe you should look up!"

She nodded toward the crowd and I spotted Maxime, strolling along with Damien. Our eyes met and he gave me a knowing smile. His appearance was enough to take my breath away. In ripped jeans and a black shirt, he attracted glances from all the women. A flash of jealousy gripped me but disappeared as soon as he locked eyes with me again.

"See you later, I'm going to dance," said Anita.

I just nodded, fascinated by the way Maxime parted the crowd as if the planet belonged to him. His confident, almost arrogant attitude radiated from him, making him so unlike the Maxime who was shut up in the bookshop.

"You came after all?" I marveled.

"I came with Anita."

I frowned, surprised. I hadn't realized that Maxime and Anita were more than nodding acquaintances. Damien was as surprised as I was, and his eyes darted back and forth from Maxime to me, uncomprehending. He finally kissed me on the cheek.

"You look very pretty," he complimented me.

"Thanks."

I pretended not to notice Maxime's inquisitive look. Damien's words had little effect on me, unlike the eyes of my flatmate, which were fixed on me and bowling me over.

"I don't know what you did to this man, but he apologized to me!"

"You were right," said Maxime. "I couldn't miss a chance to get some air."

"I thought this wasn't your thing?" I asked. "Drinking, laughing, talking…"

"Dancing," he cut in.

His voice was husky and his eyes wandered to my legs. I blushed immediately, almost forgetting Damien was there. The memory of my body molded to Maxime's set me ablaze straightaway. I'd had a chance to feel his hot, muscular body against mine, and I was ready to do anything to repeat the experience and make it last.

"You want to dance?"

It was more of a general question than a proposal, but Maxime nodded and gestured toward the dance floor. He took my hand and drew me into him. My breasts collided with his hard chest and my heart raced.

"I thought I had to keep my distance," I whispered.

"You are. Let's say I'm having trouble keeping mine, then."

His hand was resting politely on my cardigan, which

I now regretted putting on. All around us, the crowd had drawn back a bit, leaving us in our private bubble. I was still trying to interpret his last confession when he changed the conversation.

"Where's your knight in shining armor?"

"Off saying hi to some friends. How was your sandwich?"

"Not bad."

We were two seconds away from talking about the weather or the quality of the sound coming from the speakers. I decided to return our discussion to the subject that interested me the most: him.

"So, apologies to Damien?"

"I owe him for a bunch of things. This evening, my freedom, this dance. You," he added in a lower tone. "That's enough to make me grateful."

He closed the distance between us even more, pressing his rough cheek against mine. My body's embers instantly burst into flame and I shut my eyes, enveloped in his sweet warmth. The music barely reached me, but Maxime kept the rhythm, rocking slowly and gracefully on his feet.

"You're a really good dancer," I complimented him.

"Leftovers from an old movie. I learn a lot of things for movies."

"Like what?"

"I know how to chop a carrot, for example. Knock a

guy out with a glass bottle, weave in and out of traffic, too. Kiss."

"That I noticed."

"I'm not always acting. In any case, not with you."

"And why is that?"

"Because I care about you. And because I also learned to slip away discreetly in my last movie."

I moved away from him, not understanding. For a second, I thought he wanted to run away and take advantage of his free evening to go back to Paris. The prospect frightened me – I didn't care to become an accomplice to a criminal on the lam.

"You have repairs to finish," I noted, hoping to bring him back to earth.

"I wasn't talking about me. Your neighbor is twenty yards away. What do you want to do?"

"What do you mean, 'What do I want to do?'?"

Maxime turned me around and I found Frédéric, his eyes riveted to me, having some semblance of a conversation with another man. He smiled at me, but I still noticed it didn't reach his eyes. Maxime drew me back against him and brought his lips to my ear.

"Well, either we stay here and you end up with the good guy, or you decide to run off with the bad guy."

I pulled away and stared into his eyes. Maxime didn't blink and was even fiercely serious.

"That's what it comes down to? He's the good guy and you're the bad guy?"

"I think so, yes."

"And so, I have to choose between him and you?"

"Almost. You have to choose between a guy who'll show you a pleasant, but dull, evening, and a guy who will show you an unforgettable evening."

"Okay, so, I'm choosing between a nice guy and a conceited one?"

We smiled at each other, but Maxime didn't take the bait as I'd hoped. On the contrary, he got into my game too easily. I glanced over his shoulder. Frédéric was still there, arms crossed, waiting for our dance to end.

"I thought you hadn't realized. But this florist is an unbelievable poser. He's much too smooth – I find it highly suspect."

"This is a real character assassination," I laughed.

"He deserves it. And honestly, he doesn't deserve *you*. This guy doesn't know you, Sarah. He doesn't know you like I do."

His serious expression, almost worried, made me suppress my smile. My joke had taken an unexpected turn. To my eyes, Frédéric was a pleasant, polite, and thoughtful man. If I didn't deserve that kind of man, I wondered what I should expect for myself. I tried to stop our dance, but Maxime was holding me much too closely.

"I think you're mistaken," I murmured, without much conviction.

"No. I know it. And you know it, too. I see it in your eyes."

I stayed silent, trying to find a way to avoid this conversation. Even though I was asking myself a lot of questions about my relationship with Frédéric, I didn't want to talk about it with Maxime.

"You see it?" I said, aiming for sarcasm.

Maxime nodded, then pressed his cheek to mine. I felt his breath on my neck and my heart skipped a beat.

"You see," he murmured, "I would never give you flowers, I'd give you *The Name of the Rose* or *La Dame aux Camélias*. Because I love the gleam of excitement in your eyes when you cross paths with a book."

His beard stubble scraped my skin but I didn't care. Maxime went back to his initial position, facing me. I didn't even have the strength to blush anymore. My energy was concentrated in my trembling legs, which were doing the impossible in keeping me from collapsing to the ground.

"It's your choice," he repeated.

The music stopped and Maxime withdrew his hands from mine. I missed the heat of his body immediately. An icy distance slipped between us and the air seemed to lose a few more degrees when Frédéric rejoined me, wrapping a possessive arm around my waist.

"Everything all right?" he asked.

"Um, yes."

My voice was barely audible. Maxime slipped away,

losing himself in the crowd and abandoning me to my thoughts. I hated that he could unsettle me with just one sentence. At his touch, all my certainties evaporated.

"You want to dance?" offered Frédéric.

"Me first!" interrupted Anita's sing-song voice.

I could have erected a statue to her for that. Anita gave me a conspiratorial wink and grabbed Frédéric's hand without even asking his opinion. I had time to see his annoyed expression as she dragged him far away from me, thus giving me the opportunity to stop holding my breath. I went up on tiptoe, looking for Maxime. I hesitated between going back home to the apartment alone or trying to pull an explanation out of my flatmate.

Eventually I gave up. I wasn't managing to think anyway. I left the tent and took a deep breath as soon as I was out in the open air. The music and chatter reached me mutedly, but I was breathing better. I no longer had that awful sensation of oppression and vertigo.

"You hungry?"

I spun toward Maxime, who was sitting on a bench, offering me his basket of fries. While I was struggling with my emotions, he was perfectly calm and nonchalant. I refused the fries with a shake of my head and crossed my arms over my chest.

"Why are you doing this?" I asked, a bit irritated.

"Why am I doing what?"

"Asking me to keep my distance and then doing your

big dance number and badmouthing my boyfriend. Why are you doing this?"

"I'm not badmouthing him. I'm making an observation. The question is: why are you paying so much attention to what I say?"

He got up from his bench and planted himself in front of me, still munching his fries. Unsettled once more, I stepped back. He was at least right on that point: I was paying far too much attention to what Maxime said to me.

"I'm going home," I announced, to cut things short.

"And giving up the party you sold to me as the society event of the year?"

"Maxime, if you want to fight, I suggest you drive your fist into that tree and stop picking on me."

I was already retreating, moving away from him and the festival. I promised myself I'd leave Frédéric a message, claiming a sudden but terrible migraine. I wavered between anger and annoyance. Maxime had ruined my evening again. That was what annoyed me. That I let him do it was utterly maddening.

To my great surprise, Maxime caught up with me, grabbing my arm to make me face him. He threw his fries into a bin and wiped his greasy hands on a napkin.

"I'm doing it for you," he said finally.

"No, you're doing it for you. You enjoy destroying everything around you, don't you?"

"Basically," he admitted.

"So, you decided to destroy something important to me. It didn't occur to you that I liked Frédéric? That maybe he was my only chance to be happy in this town? In case you haven't noticed, I'm not exactly beating men off with a stick."

Anger was burning me from the inside out, making me lose all my bearings. Maxime only had to stay for a few weeks, and he was making a total mess of my life.

"Because they're all idiots," he said. "And it would be so easy…"

"Easy?"

"… for someone to hurt you," he finished, out of breath.

He ran a nervous hand through his hair, studiously avoiding my gaze. I tried to understand, but Maxime was a real puzzle, and I didn't have all the pieces.

"It's the effect you have on me," he began again, more gently. "Seeing you with him makes me mad."

"You … you're jealous?"

He glanced up at me, incredulous. I couldn't hide my smile – it was so ridiculous. Maxime Maréchal, A-list actor, was jealous. And smitten with me. I didn't know which was the most absurd.

"And what about the whole 'keep your distance' thing?"

"I messed up," he confessed, more relaxed. "I mess up a lot of things in my life. But that led me here, so it's probably not that tragic."

"So, you came to this party just to keep an eye on me? I'll ask Anita how she made you change your mind. I'd love to know."

"It wasn't Anita, it was you. You said you were going dancing, and I wondered what it would feel like to dance with you."

"Was it any good?"

"It was ... better than good. Much, much better."

He smiled and a soft warmth bloomed in my cheeks. My anger had vanished, replaced by a feeling of well-being and sweet satisfaction. Talking with Maxime like this was so rare that I savored every second. The frantic beating of my heart was enough to confirm what I feared: I liked Maxime too much for my own good.

I cleared my throat, hoping to lighten the mood, and asked:

"You want to do it again?"

"You want to go back there?" he marveled. "I thought you wanted to go home and read a book."

"I doubt a book would be more appealing than dancing with you."

Maxime stepped toward me and took my hand in his. His body was much more relaxed, his smile wider. Even his eyes, usually so dark, seemed to have taken on a lighter shade. For the first time since we'd met, Maxime seemed happy.

The idea that it was because of me made my heart

pound so hard that it felt like it would beat out of my chest.

Accompanied by the distant music, we danced in the middle of the street, pressed up against each other, all the other drama fading away.

"Still just as good?" I asked, feeling his hand slide toward the small of my back.

"So good."

The vibration of his warm voice against the skin of my neck made me shiver. His hand slipped under my cardigan and explored my bare back.

"Even better," he whispered.

Another shiver went through me, rolling down my spine to my toes. Dancing had never felt like this before. Eyes closed, I let myself be rocked in his arms. I shoved down the successive waves of guilt, thinking vaguely of Frédéric – my official escort – while I danced with another man. What I felt with Frédéric had nothing to do with what I felt in Maxime's presence. It was like comparing a new book with a used one. The former was smooth and perfect, smelling of fresh ink. While the latter, dog-eared and damaged, had yellowed pages and the intoxicating scent of time. They could have the same text, but the used book also told hidden stories, the ones that fascinated me.

That's exactly what Maxime was. A beautiful second-hand book, beaten up, with secret stories marked on his body.

"You've done it," I said finally.

"Done what?"

"Made the evening unforgettable."

A luminous smile lit his face and I let myself be overcome with joy that eclipsed the last glimmer of guilt. Without realizing it, I'd made a decision: to put an end to my relationship with Frédéric. Not for Maxime. Just … for me, to feel what I was feeling now, to forget myself completely in the arms of a man, to hear my heart beat deafeningly loud.

Maxime's hand pressed against my back, to bring me closer to him.

"Don't I still need to see you weave in and out of traffic, knock a guy out with a bottle, and … chop a carrot?" I teased.

"That's true. Let's start with the easiest."

"Which is?"

"Chopping a carrot. Have dinner with me tomorrow night."

Chapter Eleven

I knew our route by heart. Damien would wait for me every morning in front of the bookshop, checking his laces. We'd run along the square, pass by Baptiste's restaurant, then go up the road that led toward the vineyards. After the first intersection, we'd turn right and run down the little slope to a winding path. We'd cross Damien's vineyards, then his neighbors', and come out in the woods.

I'd been running since I was eighteen, every day, sometimes twice. It gave me a perfect excuse to be out of my parents' house and free to move. I would run until my lungs exploded, until my legs couldn't do it anymore. In Paris, I'd finally had to buy a treadmill. The feeling wasn't the same; my legs were moving, but the scenery – my apartment walls – wasn't enough for me.

Here, things were different yet again. Damien was

always with me and my time was limited. Freedom under constraint. During the first week, I'd asked Damien if he was only running to keep an eye on me. Out of breath, he'd just grunted and given me the finger. So, I'd been right, and I'd snickered with satisfaction.

"Am I that dangerous?" I'd asked.

Damien had stopped running. He was no athlete, and the first few yards had been painful for him. Hands on his knees, trying to catch his second wind, he'd lifted his red, sweat-covered face toward me.

"You're not dangerous. You're out of control."

"I'll take that as a compliment. Nothing's more boring than a predictable guy."

"The league of predictable guys says fuck you," he'd replied.

"Nobody made you save me."

"I'm predictable *and* a masochist. You're welcome, you plonker!"

"I'm just asking a question!" I'd defended myself. "You're the one who loves to say we always have a choice! Why keep bailing me out if it gives you such a headache?"

"Because I was taught not to leave anybody in deep shit, Maxime. Not you, not Sarah."

He'd leaned against a tree and wiped his face on his soccer jersey. His breathing had found its normal rhythm.

"Weird girl, huh?" I'd asked, stretching out the muscles in my shoulders. "Those books, that shop."

"Don't touch her!"

"Not a chance!" I'd sneered. "Not exactly my type!"

"I suppose her jeans aren't tight enough. Or her breasts aren't big enough? Unless it's the size of her brain that scares you?"

He'd then stretched out his calf, hand flat on a tree, all the while grimacing in pain. Sarah wasn't my type. Much too sensible, much too serious, much too *good* for a guy like me.

"Anyway, she'll never be interested in you! Shall we go back?"

Today, we were running the same steep path again. Except this time Damien was ahead of me, his pace much brisker than when I'd arrived. In almost five weeks, he'd lost a little weight and gained muscles and agility. This slope that had made him suffer so much at the beginning now seemed to be a real pleasure.

"Should I sing 'Eye of the Tiger' now or wait a bit?" I laughed.

"In two months, I'm running the Médoc Marathon!"

I didn't dare tell him that his performance was so noteworthy only because mine was so mediocre. I'd been struggling since we left the bookshop, even stumbling on this path I knew by heart.

I joined Damien at the top of the hill, admiring the view of the vineyards and surrounding countryside. Here, despite my ankle monitor, I felt incredibly free. I took a deep breath and checked the time on my watch.

"What's going on?" asked Damien.

"Nothing."

"You keep looking at your watch. And you ran behind me."

"You've got a nice ass."

"Delighted you like it. Now, tell me what's wrong!"

"You're a real pill, do you know that?"

He came up to me and studied my face, looking for a clue that would betray my state of mind.

"I know. You want to have a shouting match, is that it? Say so, it'll be easier!"

He poked his finger into my chest and narrowed his eyes. Despite years of separation, Damien still knew me perfectly. I wasn't the kind of guy who spilled. I mulled. I brooded. But I never wore my heart on my sleeve or confided my deepest, darkest thoughts.

"You're hiding something from me. And if you're hiding it, that means I won't like it."

"Stop carrying on and save your energy for the way back!"

He stared at me again, and suddenly his eyes lit up.

"Is it Sarah?"

"We should go, you're going to make me break the law," I answered, trying to walk around him.

"Believe me, if it's about Sarah, I'm going to make you run so fast that you'll be back before they know it. And then I'll kick your ass."

I knew Damien was like a guard dog around the

people he loved. Here was the proof. He kept a sharp eye on his daughter and acted like an over-protective older brother with Sarah.

"Let's make it simple: yes, it's Sarah. And no, I don't want to talk about it."

"Why not?

"Because! And because I know you'd probably tear me two or three new ones!"

"What's going on with you and Sarah?"

"She's my landlady," I said sarcastically.

"Don't try to be an ass, Maxime. I know you already are one!"

"I'm not. The exact opposite, I want to do things right. Sarah doesn't know anything about me. She doesn't know my past, and believe me, I'm well aware that she deserves better than me."

"But…"

"But I'm failing to keep my distance. She … she's not what I imagined. And I'm probably not the kind of guy she dreams about. I'm shut up in her home, I have a fucking ankle monitor, and I'm not sure I'll ever work again. So yes," I shouted, "I know I'm not the ideal man for her!"

"Good. If you're aware, there's no point in me doing the whole song and dance, or my speech about castrating you with my bare hands if you hurt her!"

I swallowed a bitter laugh. All this carrying on for nothing! I already knew I was risking destroying everything. I was used to it. It struck me that I'd taken great care to destroy a life lots of people dreamed about. Money, fame, movies, accolades, wild parties – I'd had it all, without ever being satisfied.

And now, Sarah. This girl who'd landed in the middle of my car crash and showed me that she wasn't afraid of me. My warnings had been useless. Kissing her had been like walking on the edge of the abyss: simultaneously terrifying and exhilarating.

The very thought of her lips on mine made me crazy. Crazy enough to go to a village festival, crazy enough to ask Anita's help, crazy enough to dance in the middle of the street with her. Damien was right about one thing: I was out of control … especially with her.

"We're having dinner tonight," I said finally.

Damien choked on a mocking laugh. Patiently, I waited for him to calm down.

"I have nothing to worry about, then," he scoffed. "Your cooking will be enough to scare her off!"

"I was counting on you to help me."

"Not a chance. I only cook for my daughter and everything comes out of those wonderful things called … packets. You should try it," he suggested, giving me a pat on the shoulder.

I sighed and broke into a run again. Damien took a few seconds to react, then followed me. I lengthened my stride, hoping he couldn't keep up. But to my great surprise, Damien kept pace with me and was soon beside me.

"Why not have dinner at Baptiste's?"

"Because I only have one hour of freedom in the evening."

And because of some vague story about carrots to chop, I thought with a smile.

"Trying to impress her, huh?"

My only response was a dark look. I now regretted discussing Sarah with Damien. He'd undoubtedly scupper my plan during the play rehearsal, just before my dinner with Sarah. He was capable of ruining everything, before I even had a chance.

Despite my breakneck pace, Damien managed to grab my arm and stop me.

"What?" I said, annoyed.

"I didn't bring you here to destroy your life."

"I know."

I refrained from promising him anything. Since Sarah had entered my life, I was no longer certain of anything, and I was struggling to anticipate my reactions. I swiped a hand across my sweat-soaked forehead, avoiding my friend's eyes.

"I brought you here to keep you out of the nick and make you think about what you have to do, what you have to do for yourself. I've seen your movies, Maxime, and I know you're made for it."

"Obviously. That's why I fired my agent!"

"I can't deny that Sarah is a great girl. I know it. I see it every day. She has such a big heart, and she always sees the best in people. But she lives here and you … you're not from here."

"Are you telling me I have to choose between her and my career?"

"I'm telling you that you have to start trying to salvage things. You should call Mathilde."

"I fired her," I reminded him again.

"I know. Apologies can work! And if you add in a promise or two…"

"I'm not a guy who makes promises. That's the best way to fail at everything."

"So, find a solution, a real one, to get your life back on track. How long do you have left here? Two, three weeks? You're not going to stay here for ever, you're going to have to return to Paris and…"

Damien's voice trailed off. I knew why he was talking about my work. He was probably hoping to divert my attention from Sarah, talk up the Parisian life, its crazy energy, and my dream profession. Except that since I'd encountered Sarah and her unsettling gaze, the whole scene had lost its appeal.

"She comes first."

Damien sighed, arms dropping back to his sides, aware that he'd failed to get me to give up. He looked around the surrounding countryside before speaking again.

"Call Anita, she knows how to cook."

I thanked him with a nod and we resumed our running session. We were late and I covered the last two hundred yards at a sprint. Despite everything, I had time to think about what Damien had said to me. I knew he was right, and I knew I had to do something to save my career.

Upon arriving at the bookshop, I leaped up the stairs as fast as I could. Sarah was in the kitchen, enjoying her morning coffee.

"I'm late," I explained hastily, pulling off my sweaty T-shirt.

"Barely one minute," she reassured me after checking the time on the clock.

Her gaze swept over my body and I shivered as I envisaged her doing it again, later tonight.

"Sleep well?" she asked.

"Not really. Maybe I'm just anxious…"

"About the idea of cooking?"

An impish smile lit up her pretty face. Her eyes sparkled with mischief and I knew she was getting even with me. This little act amused me. Sarah was pretending not to know what was going to happen and I joined the game. But we were both aware that by this time tomorrow, our relationship would have changed.

One way or another, everything would change tonight.

"Apparently my reputation precedes me," I grinned.

"Not only for cooking," continued Sarah, bringing her mug to her lips.

This was new. Sarah – so quiet, so shy, so reserved – was now challenging me, throwing out little barbs. I'd never admit that I loved it, loved seeing her come out of her shell and reveal herself. I moved toward her and she lowered her eyes again.

"We'll take up this conversation again tonight," I assured her. "I have a wall to repaint. And my boss… Let's just say she's demanding."

Even though she was buried in her mug, I could sense her luminous smile. Her hair fell over her face, hiding her blush. I promised myself I'd get back to this subject during our dinner. Making her blush was a pastime I never tired of. I headed for the bathroom, but swung back toward her just before going in.

Sarah's eyes were on me, examining my back. She immediately hid her gaze, but I knew what her eyes had been fixed on: the tattoo on my right shoulder blade.

"I didn't know you had more of them," she murmured.

"You never asked."

"Do you have others?"

"No."

"What does that one mean? I've always been terrible at chemistry," she said coaxingly.

"I'll tell you tonight. Speaking of which, do you have rehearsals tonight?"

"Two hours at least. Also, Anita just sent me a message to say she's sick in bed. We'll have to do it without her."

"Good. I'll come pick you up."

"It's a hundred yards away, I think I'll be all right."

"No! I asked you to dinner, I'm coming to get you. Imagine if you met someone sketchy on the way…"

"Someone like Frédéric?"

"Possibly."

With my T-shirt rolled into a ball, I wiped a droplet of sweat rolling down my chest. I hadn't dared address the subject head-on. But after last night, and especially before this evening, I had hoped Sarah would clarify the situation with Frédéric.

"I broke it off," she admitted shyly.

"I'm not going to pretend to be sorry," I replied with a smile.

"You have a wall to paint."

She finished her coffee in one gulp and got down off her stool. Then she cleared the table and gave me a little wave before opening the door. I watched her hurry down the stairs to the bookshop, hoping the day wouldn't drag on for ever.

As soon as Sarah had left the bookshop to go to the theater, Anita showed up. She'd taken care to do some shopping and already prepared some things. However, my first question had thrown her.

"No carrots?"

After a few seconds of silence, she set down her knife.

"It's a quiche. So, no – no carrots."

"Can we add some?"

"You told her you'd make something with carrots?"

"Sort of. It's not a big deal, we'll do without!" I said with a shrug.

"Shall I break the news to you? She doesn't care about carrots! She doesn't even care about this dinner. Knowing her, she'll be too busy spoon-feeding Baptiste his lines until he can manage three of them together without stammering."

And it was true.

Arriving at the theater, I'd sat down discreetly in the back. On the stage, Sarah was trying to show Élise where she should stand. Damien was droning through an interminable monologue, while Baptiste was struggling with his costume.

She finally met my eyes, and suddenly the tension in the air lessened. I sat through the last thirty minutes of the rehearsal, silently correcting Damien's every mispronounced and forgotten word. Élise finally managed to move around the stage, almost getting close to where she was supposed to be.

With a pang in my heart, I realized that I might not see the play. I'd have to send a written request for a furlough to the police station, and I wasn't very good at making obsequious requests or wading through miles of red tape.

Sarah announced the end of rehearsal on the dot. I couldn't help but smile and raise an eyebrow in her direction. Her false cheeriness and the prompt finishing time betrayed her nerves about our dinner together. To be honest, I was as edgy as she was. She still took the time to clean up the hall, gathering the props in one corner and the chairs in another.

Standing near the door, I waited as patiently as I could.

"Ready?" she asked.

"Ready," I replied, without knowing what exactly we both meant by that.

She locked the door to the theater behind us and we headed for the bookshop.

"That rehearsal was exhausting," she sighed. "Between Élise not knowing where to stand and Damien barely being able to retain four lines."

"Is it like this every year?"

"More or less. Élise knows her lines, she studied it at school. She just has to learn how to move around the *whole* stage."

"That's the advantage of the movies, you can do another take as many times as you want."

"You're not wrong. I'd love to see that someday, a movie shoot. You have to explain to Damien how to learn his lines correctly! You must have some trick, or…"

"I just have an excellent memory."

We reached the bookshop and I opened the door for Sarah. She climbed the stairs and stopped short after opening the door to the apartment.

"Is there a problem?" I asked.

"Uh… Nothing. I just… I suppose I was expecting … something else," she stammered.

I glanced at the apartment, still not understanding what Sarah was talking about. The living room was in the same condition as it was this morning and the kitchen had been meticulously cleaned.

"You didn't set the table…"

Suddenly, it hit me. To seduce Sarah, I'd danced with her. I'd told her a few secrets, and I'd even succeeded in getting rid of Frédéric. But in her world, there was another enemy to combat: everything she'd ever read in books. And I imagined that in the books, for this kind of dinner, you got out the tablecloth, a pink rose, and some candles.

"All those books are working against me," I said, as I headed for the kitchen.

"Maxime, it's not…"

"Don't make me go buy flowers from Frédéric, I could take it as an invitation to take a swing at him!"

She stifled a laugh and held up her hands in a gesture of apology. I finally set out our plates and invited her to sit. I put down the dish I'd prepared with Anita's help and sat down in turn.

"No carrots," I announced.

Sarah smiled at me as I served her. My nervousness had ended up evaporating in favor of a sinking feeling. My conversation with Damien had had the desired effect. We'd been living together here in a bubble, but soon I'd have to face reality. Starting something with Sarah would be unfair; I had nothing to offer her but my debts and ruined career. Our relationship was only ever meant to be a temporary arrangement.

Maybe we should leave it at that.

"So, that tattoo?" she asked eagerly.

She ate a bite of her food, and a brief moan escaped her. She set her fork down and applauded me shyly.

"It's delicious!"

"Thanks. The tattoo is the chemical formula for adrenaline," I said, digging into my plate.

"I should have known. 'The formula for adrenaline.' You'd make a good book title!"

"Is that your hobby? Finding book titles for people?"

"Sometimes."

"Is that how you named the bookshop? 'All you need is books'?"

"All anybody should need is books! You're the only one who prefers adrenaline – and briars."

"I thought you liked that one."

The memory of her index finger tracing my other

tattoo was very fresh in my mind. I'd seen her fascination and voracious curiosity. For the first time in months, I'd felt a burst of adrenaline without the need to fight.

"Sure. But … you're the kind of book that comes in several volumes," she added with a smile.

She looked shyly up at me. A wave of burning desire gripped me. Were there rules about this sort of thing? Like, that I had to wait until she'd at least finished eating before kissing her?

Very quickly, she redirected the conversation to my acting career, asking me about the script I'd received.

"You haven't read it?" she asked, astonished.

"First I want to work things out with Mathilde. Damien thinks I owe her an apology."

"I'm afraid he's right."

I heaved a deep sigh, already close to tearing my hair out about the situation. I'd never made an official apology. Not to anybody. I just took, and left, without ever regretting my choices. Except this time there were too many things at stake: things more important than my career.

"I'll help you," she offered.

"You really want to get rid of me?"

"Well, before eating this, I'd have said yes. But now, I'm having some real doubts!"

"I … I have a gift for you. To say thank you."

I went to my room and got the picture frame I'd bought at the corner minimart. I was dreading Sarah's reaction a little bit. Either she'd sing my praises, or she'd kill me.

"Maxime, you didn't have to do that," she said when I handed her the gift-wrapped package.

"Just a souvenir."

"You think I'd forget you?"

She looked incredulous, but didn't laugh. I was grateful. I appreciated Sarah being serious with me, not bombarding me with unpleasant fake laughter. It made me feel like I was worth something.

"Usually people remember me for the wrong reasons," I pointed out.

I handed her the gift and she pressed her lips together. She delicately pulled back the paper and an excited smile spread across her face.

"It's Perdican's last monologue."

"Yes."

She stroked the glass in the frame with her fingertips, rereading Musset's words about lying men and treacherous women. I moved closer to her, pointing to the frame.

"I was thinking that it could help Damien learn it," I joked. "And it can decorate the bookshop downstairs?"

Even at my first ever audition, I hadn't been so nervous. I'd stammered, yes. But I hadn't felt this level of anxiety. For reasons I didn't understand, Sarah's opinion mattered to me more than anyone else's.

"It's perfect," she said finally.

"Do you really like it? Because, since I had to tear out the page, I was afraid that…"

"Let's say the thought counts more than the vandalism," she reassured me, looking directly into my eyes.

I knew in that moment that my relationship with Sarah wasn't something I could leave behind here when I finished my sentence. It had to be more than a temporary arrangement.

Slowly, I closed the distance between us. Sarah didn't blink, hands clutching her frame. I laid a furtive kiss on her jaw, giving her one last chance to run away. But Sarah hadn't moved an inch. Perched on her stool, she was waiting for my kiss.

So, I gave it to her.

And I did my best to make it perfect.

Chapter Twelve

There were a whole lot of things I'd remember from having Maxime live with me: his early hostility, his ability to make me blush with two words, our nocturnal dance in the middle of the street, the way his eyes lit up when he laughed. All these memories would stay in a corner of my mind, double locked like precious treasures.

On the other hand, his kisses would remain etched on my body, on my lips and the delicate skin of my neck, like scars of joy. I'd only have to brush them to plunge back into what I was feeling now: an intense, uncontrollable heat.

Maxime laid his hand on my cheek and drew me closer to him. His lips moved gently against mine. He was taking his time, titillating me with slowness. He eventually abandoned my mouth to kiss my neck, sucking the skin in between his lips. I tipped my head back and moaned with pleasure. Immediately, Maxime once again took possession of my mouth and slipped his tongue inside. I plunged my fingers into his hair and did my utmost to make our bodies touch. I wanted to feel him and touch him.

While I was still seated on my stool, Maxime thrust himself between my legs, pressing his erection against me. His hands found my hips and abruptly brought me towards him. Surprised, I stifled a cry in his mouth. My rear on the edge of the stool, I teetered and clung to him, my fingers gripping the front of his T-shirt.

He smiled against my mouth, and his warm hands slipped underneath my blouse, tenderly caressing my back.

"I'll have to take this off of you," he warned me.

I pulled away from him, a little panicked.

"Here? But what if someone…"

"Here. I don't think any intruders will make it to the bedroom."

His lips curled into a lascivious smile, full of sensual promise. His hands slid back down the outside of my thighs, before coming back up, torturously slow, toward my crotch. I bit my lips hard enough to hurt myself, while his fingers trailed around my groin. I wriggled in frustration on my stool and was rewarded with another smile.

Maxime leaned over and delicately undid the lowest

button on my blouse. He kissed my stomach, then undid another button, and I got another kiss. He repeated the same gesture, grazing my skin with his breath, ignoring my frantic trembling. When he reached my chest, he laid a kiss on the fabric of my bra, then between my breasts. Finally, the last button gave way and he pushed the fabric off my shoulders. I shivered and immediately covered myself with my arms.

"Stand up."

His voice was a little husky, fiendishly sexy. I obeyed, still intimidated, but burning with unprecedented desire. In taking his time, Maxime knew perfectly well what he was doing; he wanted to soften me up, and I appreciated that attention. He'd immediately understood that my experience was limited. Limited to one bed, my own room, in reassuring darkness. Here, I was in full light, half naked and entirely at his mercy.

He caught my face between his hands and rained kisses onto my cheeks and mouth. Then he pressed his forehead to mine and sank his gaze, dark with desire, into my eyes.

"Do you want to go to your bedroom?"

I shook my head, determined not to flinch in front of him. I wanted to live this experience, free myself of the last barriers with him. To assure him I wasn't going to change my mind, I uncovered myself and seized the bottom of his T-shirt. Maxime encouraged me with a smile and I took his shirt off.

Right from his arrival at the bookshop, his tattoo had fascinated me. The thorny vine. To ward off, to signal danger, to keep anyone who might approach at a distance. Without asking, I resumed my ritual, following the line of ink with the tip of my finger. His breathing sped up, as if he were resisting the urge to push me away. I looked up at him. His face was tense, his jaw clenched, but his eyes burned with uncommon desire. When I reached his shoulder, I placed a light kiss there, then another on his chest. Under my lips, I could feel his heart racing.

"What are you doing to me?" he hissed.

"Do you want me to stop?" I asked, alarmed.

"Definitely not. Never."

I kissed his chin, then went up on tiptoe to regain the taste of his lips, my hands resting on his chest. He was still so gentle, so careful, but now I understood that he was holding back, as if he were afraid of breaking me.

"Turn around," he ordered me, breathless.

I complied that very second, ignoring my stomach, which was twisting in anticipation. Maxime pushed my hair back over one shoulder and caressed my skin with his lips. His index finger slid underneath my bra strap to the hook. He undid it and pushed the straps down over my arms, until the bit of fabric fell at my feet.

With his palms, he caressed my unobstructed naked back, taking care to pass over my ribs without ever touching my chest. I panted, struggling to suppress the successive waves of heat crashing down on me. Although sweet, this agony was unbearable. I rubbed my thighs together, trying to soothe the throbbing ache caused by my desire.

"You're so beautiful."

I was almost happy to have my back to him, my blush was so intense. My legs were trembling, and I was reassured to feel Maxime press against me. His muscular chest fit my body perfectly, and his avid mouth was exploring the delicate skin of my neck.

"I'm going to taste every inch of your skin," he whispered in my ear.

He sucked on the skin of my neck, then his tongue ran over the curve of my shoulder. His hands found my waist and slowly crept up to my chest. A cry of pleasure stuck in my throat the second he brushed the sensitive tips of my breasts. I arched, hoping he'd touch me again, and properly. My chest was tight and I wanted to feel Maxime's rough hands on me.

Forgetting all restraint, I moved my butt against his hard cock. Maxime growled and bit my shoulder. His hands resumed roving over my body, caressing my exposed neck. His finger passed over my mouth, and with the tip of my tongue I played with it.

"Keep that up, Sarah, and I'm going to come in my jeans like a teenager!"

"Would that be so bad?"

"I'd planned on burying myself in you."

Invigorated, I let my hands stray over his thighs and creep up toward his crotch. His cock was forcefully stretching his trousers. I caressed him for a few seconds, before Maxime regained control. He chased away my curious hands and slipped his finger into my mouth again. I'd never felt such excitement, euphoria laced with adrenaline. I was even forgetting my inhibitions.

I licked his finger with pleasure, receiving his little sighs of satisfaction like rewards.

"I can't wait to be inside you," he growled, pressing his cock against my ass.

He pulled his finger out of my mouth, and I protested for form's sake, very quickly distracted by the route his finger was taking. Tracing little circles around my erect nipples, he finally achieved his goal, rolling them between his thumb and index finger.

A first detonation of intense pleasure shook my body. Maxime kissed my shoulder tenderly, to soothe me, before sounding the charge again. He went back to drawing arabesques on my chest, waiting for my breath to be short enough to caress my nipples. I moaned with frustration, but Maxime remained implacable, having fun with my arousal, pulling on my aching nipples, only to leave me panting and unsatisfied.

Finally, Maxime abandoned my chest. His right hand slid down along my stomach and unbuttoned my jeans, then pulled down the zipper.

"I'll help you get these off, okay?"

I nodded, incapable of even speaking. I was too excited, too frustrated, too worn out to say anything. My jeans fell to my ankles, followed by my panties. Behind me, I felt Maxime's fingers tickling along my legs. He went back to his initial position: his strong, muscular chest against my back, while his right arm wrapped around my waist.

"Is that good?"

"Yes."

"Show me…"

His fingers darted to my groin and his hand soon covered my wet pussy. Just that gentle pressure pulled a cry of relief from me. Maxime caressed my crotch while moaning into my neck. My whole body was vibrating and all my blood rushed between my thighs. His middle finger slipped between my labia, and after a furtive caress plunged into me.

Another cry escaped me, between surprise and amazement. I clutched at the counter, knocking over my glass as I did so. His middle finger moved gently in and out, soon accompanied by his index finger.

"Maxime," I murmured, on the edge of implosion.

"Let yourself go. Next time, I want you to do it in front of me!"

He didn't give me time to respond and sped up the rhythm, pushing in and out of me energetically. My body tensed little by little, trying to hold back my orgasm as long as possible. But Maxime wouldn't let up. He always demanded more. He loved to fight and did so mercilessly, just to finish me off.

I arched a little bit more, shots of ecstasy running through my body like so many sparks from a bonfire. I closed my eyes, forgetting myself in his arms. It was there, very close, and I knew it would take me right over the edge.

"I just changed my mind. Next time, it'll be my mouth you feel there!"

He backed up his promise with pressure on my clit, which pushed me to my limits. One final wave of heat engulfed me, and a second later everything I was trying to hold back gave way. My orgasm made my whole body shake and I very nearly collapsed onto the floor. Maxime's arm was all that kept me upright.

"This is the first chapter," he murmured into my neck.

Worn out, I struggled to open an eye. Maxime took my hand in his and led me toward my bedroom.

"Have you got something?" he asked.

"Uh … yes," I replied awkwardly.

"Me too, but I like that you're prepared."

He opened the door to my room and closed it behind me. Then he turned on my bedside lamp. Suddenly conscious of my nudity, I clapped my arms around myself. Maxime sighed in disapproval, then came closer.

"You need to keep your hands busy," he said severely.

My cheeks flushed immediately. I still had his

previous plans in mind. I'd never touched myself, not really. Doing it in front of him was embarrassing and very arousing. Maxime must have understood right away what I was thinking about, because he came over and stroked my cheek with the back of his hand.

"I love that," he said. "The way you blush. Impossible for you to hide a thing."

"Personally, I find it mortifying."

"To get back to your hands, I was actually thinking that you could undress me."

I was not reassured. I'd never had to remove a man's clothes before. That said, I'd never been undressed by a man before, either. Usually – if I can say that, since my relationships could be counted on one hand – we would go into my bedroom, each take off our clothes, and end up underneath the covers. I barely turned on the light.

I'd always considered sex as a sort of obligatory social ritual.

With Maxime, it was unrecognizable. What I felt for him was intense and uncontrollable. But in a good way – not just good, but exhilarating.

"I'm sure you can manage," he encouraged me.

My hands, still trembling, reached for his belt buckle. I grazed his muscular stomach and felt a slight tremor.

"It's rare for someone else to undress me," he explained.

"Oh. A privilege then?"

"Let's find out."

I undid the buttons on his jeans and pulled them down over his thighs. He lifted his feet one at a time to dispense with them totally. I took a deep breath and grabbed his boxers. As with his pants, he got rid of them with a kick and announced while moving toward me:

"Chapter Two."

Though I'd sensed his arousal through his jeans, seeing his erect penis in front of me was impressive, by my previous standards anyway. I backed up toward the bed, until my legs hit the side. Maxime glanced at my bedside table, looking for condoms.

"In the drawer," I panted.

He nodded and erased the distance between our two bodies. I sat down on the mattress, used my forearms to scoot backwards, then lay down completely. Maxime smiled at me and stretched out in turn, hovering above me. His warm body fitted itself to mine, as I parted my thighs to help him get comfortable.

His mouth found mine for a slow, gentle kiss. My hands tangled in his hair again, before sliding to his shoulders and caressing his second tattoo. He moaned against my lips and finally left them for my neck. His hands stayed politely on my hips, keeping me pinned to the bed, a prisoner of his body.

My breasts were still sensitive and heavy with his caresses, too – when his mouth closed on my nipple, a cry of satisfaction escaped me. Despite my first orgasm, the nervous sexual tension running through my body was still there, ready to burst at the slightest contact and tear me into pieces.

Maxime laid kisses on my chest, then traced a burning line to my navel. He brushed my vulva, ignoring the fact that I was squirming beneath him, too excited to contain myself. Then, very slowly, he did the same in reverse, creeping over me like a tiger happy to stare at its prey before finishing it off. His gaze was so dark, I could no longer make out his pupils. I saw only a dark well of hunger and desire that made my heart beat at full tilt.

His smooth, hard cock slammed into my stomach, and for a few seconds that didn't last long enough, he had the audacity to caress my genitals with his. I stifled a curse, hiding my face in the pillow, torn between pleasure and prohibition.

"So, as I was saying … Chapter Two," he announced, reaching for my bedside table.

"Chapter One was a page-turner."

"That's my best weapon: the first impression. Afterward, it goes downhill."

I laid my hand on his cheek, keeping him with me. I hated the image Maxime had of himself. Certainly, there was his anger, his excesses, that hostility he dragged around everywhere. But I now knew there was something else, a crack, a secret badly hidden by that briar wrapping around his arm and his heart.

"You're right. When I get to know you, it's different.

Better. I think Chapter Two will be better than Chapter One."

"Are you talking about sex or me?"

"Both. Together."

I opened my thighs a little more, letting him know I was ready. Maxime dropped a kiss on my lips, then got a condom and slipped it onto his erect penis. Once again, he brushed my wet pussy with his cock, a mischievous smile spreading across his face. He looked directly into my eyes as one of his hands slid down the length of my body, making me shiver with pleasure. At last, he gripped the back of my knee and made me lift it so I could wrap my legs around his waist.

His mouth found my neck, the exact place where my pulse was pounding wildly. I closed my eyes, already breathless, feeling his cock working its way inside me. I moaned heavily, somewhere between relief and pleasure. I tightened my thighs on my lover, letting myself be guided by his slow rhythm and my own sensations.

At each of Maxime's thrusts, I arched a little more. My hips met his naturally, without shame, without embarrassment. My whole body was dancing with him, held tight and bound with his. Too quickly, the first waves of heat and shudders of pleasure surged over me. Maxime sped up his movements, his hand found the small of my back and pulled me firmly against him, our two pelvises perfectly locked together.

"Again?" he asked.

His satisfied smile spoke for him. He delighted in torturing me, taking me right to the breaking point, only to slow down and delay my release. I nodded, desperate to explode the ball of desire nestled in the small of my back.

And very quickly, his rhythm grew unbearable, ripping cries and moans of pleasure from me. Maxime was in control of my body, complementing his domineering thrusts with tender caresses and passionate kisses. My hands clung to his biceps and he pressed his forehead to mine. Our searing breath mingled, his panting melded with mine. Suddenly, my body tensed and started to shake with pleasure. Eyes closed, a strangled cry in my throat, I could still clearly see sparks, while a multitude of little flames seemed to lick at my body. The wave ebbed slowly, leaving me spent and collapsed on my bed. Maxime pushed back the hair on my forehead and came in turn with a grunt of satisfaction.

For several long minutes, his muscular body rested on mine. Both of us were catching our breath. Finally, he withdrew from me and rolled to the side of the bed. In one quick movement, he got rid of his condom and folded the sheet back down over our entwined bodies.

"I'd forgotten you were such a bookworm. Two chapters in such a short time," he joked.

"I can't wait to see what happens next. The beginning is very promising."

He took me in his arms, allowing me to rest my head against his chest. With the tip of my finger, I traced his tattoo yet again, almost sure I could untangle the intermingled briars. Many things about Maxime intrigued me. But I was still missing a piece of the puzzle, a detail that would help me understand that anger just under the surface.

I still hoped to find out one day, and I was counting on using this moment of intimacy to solve the riddle.

"What happens in Chapter Three, exactly?" I asked, very curious.

"We'll improvise. I've always been better at that!"

"I was serious, you know. About Mathilde, about helping you."

I looked up at him, but his hand paused in stroking my back. His face hardened, and he did everything he could to avoid my gaze. In vain, because after a few minutes, I laid a hand on his cheek and forced him to look me in the eye.

"What are you hiding from me?" I asked.

"Nothing," he spat. "Listen, Sarah, I'm not really into pillow talk. So, if you don't mind, I'm going back to my room."

"What?"

I barely had time to sit up before he'd already put his boxers back on and gathered up his things. I wrapped the covers around my chest and sat there in the bed. I had clearly struck a nerve, but what was it?

"So is there something I don't know about you and Mathilde?"

"Listen, I have to—"

"Stop running away. I know you're hiding something from me."

"I'm an ex-con, doing my time at your place," he reminded me. "No mystery, just a shitty situation."

His voice was brittle, and I even sensed a hint of anger. He left my room and I ran after him, trailing my covers and my pride.

"So, that's it? You just wanted sex?"

"Sarah, no. It's… Look, I deal with my problems by myself, especially with Mathilde."

"Especially with Mathilde? Since you've been here, how many phone calls have you gotten? How many letters? How many emails? You're not dealing with anything, you're letting the situation deteriorate."

"So what? You think you can change that?"

"I'm offering you my help. You could call her? Or send her flowers? Or … write to her? That might be the best thing – less confrontational."

"No," he said.

"No to what?"

"To writing to her. To the flowers, to everything," he added after a brief pause. "Leave me alone. Two more weeks, and I'm out of here!"

He crossed the living room, leaving me dazed on the threshold of my bedroom. As I'd developed a habit of doing for the last few days, I replayed our moments together in my mind. The dance, the kiss, our conversations at the bookshop, the renovations, the rehearsals, even the way he could quote Shakespeare without realizing it.

My gaze fell on the little kitchen and the pile of books I had to wrap for blind dates.

"See you tomorrow, Sarah."

"I'll leave a note about … the books."

I felt devastated, but at the same time, my mind was turning over lots of little things that I'd ignored until now. Like the way I would leave him notes to tell him what to do – wrap the books, put them aside, sort them, label them. Invariably, Maxime apologized for not seeing them, before getting down to work as quickly as possible.

His little tricks. His incredible memory. His panicked look in front of the bookshelves. His abandoned script.

I'd finally found the missing piece of the Maxime puzzle.

"You can't read," I said, in shock.

He stopped short and kept his back to me. That was it. He couldn't read. Never. He didn't text, he called. He didn't read my instructions, he asked for them. He didn't read his lines: hearing them twice was enough for him to remember everything.

He turned his head, fists clenched, just letting me catch a glimpse of his profile.

"Is that it? You…"

"I don't read very well," he answered, in a weary voice. "Not well and too slowly."

It wasn't anger, it was shame. A shame so powerful that it frequently overwhelmed him. To keep people from making fun of him, he acted like a bully. He lashed out so no one would know his secret. He lashed out because he didn't have the words.

"But..."

"Mathilde records my lines and I listen until I know them by heart."

"She knows?"

"From the first day. I wouldn't have been able to pass my first audition if she hadn't helped me. She understood right away."

I took a step toward him, simultaneously saddened for him and dismayed to realize he'd put in place a whole defense system to protect himself. The bramble was a true unassailable wall. It protected him and kept away intruders.

"Why didn't you say anything to me?"

He finally turned toward me, face tense with rage. If he wanted to scare me, it was working. But I refused to give him the satisfaction. My feelings toward him hadn't changed. He was still the man who'd drawn me in, with his wit and his dark allure.

"There's something worse than contempt," he said after a short silence. "Pity."

He grimaced and I did my best to keep a neutral

expression. For me, not knowing how to read was the equivalent of hell on earth, and it was hard not to show it.

"I am sorry for you," I admitted. "And I'd like to help you. Maybe I could go over the basics with you and—"

"Anita's doing it," he cut in.

"Anita?"

"She comes here to help me read and write. One day, she asked me about a book and I couldn't find it for her. That's how she figured it out."

Once again, self-hatred twisted his beautiful smile. In that moment, I realized that all that anger was directed as much toward himself as toward others. He hated himself and made sure other people hated him, too.

I took a step toward him again. He was close enough that I could touch him.

"Good night, Sarah."

"Maxime..."

"I told you to keep your distance."

"In case you hadn't noticed, I'm a grown woman."

"I noticed. But obviously you deserve better than an actor whose career is in free fall and who can barely write a shopping list."

"I don't care about your career. And I never make shopping lists, either. I'm happy that you told me, and I promise, it doesn't change anything for me."

"Obviously it changes everything! What would you do with a guy like me?"

"You mean … what *wouldn't* I do?"

I pressed my body against his, trying to use all my powers of seduction. I hadn't got far with my powers of persuasion. But I didn't feel confident of either. Wrapped in my sheet, with my hair all tangled, I probably looked more like a hungover student than the sirens he was used to kissing on screen – and off it, too.

A slight smile touched Maxime's lips. Either I'd succeeded or I was being truly ridiculous. I decided to try my luck to the end.

"We could skim through Chapter Three together, couldn't we?"

His smile transformed into a little laugh and he brushed my cheek with his fingertips.

"It changes nothing for me," I said with conviction.

With my hand, I covered the tattoo hiding his heartbeat. I began again:

"I like the person I am when I'm with you, I like it that you make me feel new things. Who cares about the rest? I'm going back to my room; you do what you want."

I hoisted the covers back up around me and headed for my bedroom. I didn't have a chance to cross the threshold before I felt Maxime's arm encircle my waist and pull me against him.

"All right, then. Chapter Three," he murmured in my ear.

He pushed the covers away, tossed his clothes into a

corner, and laid me down on the bed. The next moment, his body was covering mine. Somewhere, buried in his clothes, Maxime's phone vibrated. He protested, but I encouraged him to get up. A call at this late hour was never a good sign.

"It's Mathilde," he said, retrieving his phone. "She can wait."

Chapter Thirteen

More than once in my life, and especially in my life as an actor, I'd had the opportunity to find myself in bed with a woman.

This wasn't a novelty or an achievement.

And yet, with Sarah, everything was different. Before that night, I had never set foot in her bedroom. Now we were in her territory, covered with a flowered quilt. She was still sleeping, naked and on her stomach, hands stuffed under the pillow, with that adorable pout on her face. I had no desire to see her wake up and get out as soon as possible, as I had with previous girls. On the contrary, watching her body rise with each breath was hypnotic.

Sarah had this inexplicable power over me: she calmed me, as if the tumultuous elements of my life – my career, my troubles with the law, my dark secrets, and my anger always bubbling just under the surface – had frozen, to give me a break.

A break. That was exactly what I'd found here. I was no longer on a treadmill of movie shoots, celebrity, and interviews. I wasn't trying to impress an audience, nor hide my feelings. I'd finally realized that my universe was not populated exclusively by enemies, and I could count on people other than Simon and Mathilde.

Here, at Sarah's place and, above all, among the books, I'd realized that I couldn't pretend anymore. Anita had noticed that I was virtually incapable of reading a sentence without stumbling over every word. Worse, sometimes I read words without grasping the meaning. So, she'd helped me. Just like that, without asking my opinion or claiming any compensation. As soon as she could, while Sarah was busy with rehearsals, Anita had come to help me. I would take advantage of my hostess's absence – her garage sales or dinners at Baptiste's – to do my lessons.

The humiliation of the first sessions had given way to a kind of satisfaction. It wasn't perfect, but now I could write a list of words without too many mistakes.

As the first rays of sunlight filtered through the shutters, I took a good look at Sarah's bedroom. Books, as always, in all four corners, piled dangerously on top of each other. The few bookcases attached to the wall were so full that the shelves were bending under the weight.

The wallpaper was a bit faded, and Sarah had built a window seat so she could sit there comfortably.

"What are you thinking?" said the sleepy voice beside me.

She pushed her disheveled hair out of her face and laid her head on my chest, eyes fixed on my tattoo. A brief smile drifted over her lips and I surprised myself by wrapping my arm around her and letting my fingers caress her back.

"That you need some new bookshelves. Or fewer books."

"New bookshelves, definitely. I was hoping you were thinking about bringing me breakfast in bed."

"Let's make one thing clear: I will never measure up to what you read. Even if it's set after the 1960s."

Her fingers wandered over the design on my skin, moving up along my arm, tickling my shoulder, before ending up at my heart. In silence, she rested her hand against my chest. I knew she was feeling my heartbeat. It was always fast in her presence.

"Why wouldn't you measure up?" she asked me.

"I'm the bad guy, remember?"

"You danced with me in the middle of the street, that was pretty romantic."

"Can you feel my foot?" I asked.

"What?"

"Can you feel my foot?"

I deliberately jostled hers. Then she did exactly what I

expected of her. Her foot touched mine, brushed my ankle, and slid up along my calf. Sarah grinned at me, nearly proud of this sensual caress.

"Back down," I ordered.

"Okay."

Her foot reversed course. She bumped into my ankle monitor and I took advantage of this momentary distraction to grab her wrists and tip her onto her back onto the mattress. She cried out in surprise before bursting out laughing. I covered her with my body, pressing my crotch against hers.

"I have an ankle monitor! That's the very definition of a bad guy."

I captured her lips for a somewhat rough kiss, leaving her breathless. When I drew back, Sarah pressed her lips together, as if savoring the last crumbs of a fabulous dessert. My penis immediately got hard, ready to pursue this interesting morning chat.

"Girls prefer bad guys," she commented. "Especially when they dance!"

I resumed my initial position, and Sarah curled back into me. I wasn't sure I liked the idea of her thinking so well of me. Though my stay here had been so much better than I'd anticipated – pretty magical in fact – I also knew it wasn't permanent. Sooner or later, I would have to get back to my life – what was left of it – and face up to the mess I'd made of things.

Spending two months with her, possibly several nights… None of that would change me, or the way I was. One way or another, I'd end up destroying what we had.

"For a long time, I thought this tattoo was a warning," she murmured. "Something that said 'Stay away.'"

"That's the idea."

"And then I thought you were protecting yourself, pushing people away because you wanted to be alone."

"Sarah…"

"But that wasn't it. It's ink. Like in books. It tells your story, it's like … a map showing the way."

"I think your vision is a little too novelistic. When I was fifteen, I was in a fight with a guy and got this scar on my eyebrow from a piece of broken glass. When I was eighteen, I thought it would be clever to swipe my dad's car and crash it into a tree."

"Chipped tooth?"

"Yep. When I was twenty, for no particular reason, I beat a guy up so hard that I broke my thumb. I'm not a story worth reading, Sarah. I'm barely worth the ink on my body."

"Works for me," she smiled. "Ink is the essence of a book. Otherwise it's just blank paper."

She laid a kiss on my heart, then on my lips. I didn't really agree with her but didn't have the strength to argue. I lifted my head slightly to check the time on her clock radio. I'd missed my time slot for freedom. I hoped Damien wouldn't be too angry at me.

Sarah's phone rang near her. She grimaced and quickly explained that she had to take this call.

"I put out an ad for salvaging books. It's probably that!"

She grabbed her dressing gown off a chair and got out of bed while answering the call. I took the opportunity to extricate myself from the bed as well, slip on my boxers, and get my phone. Mathilde's late-night call resurfaced in my memory, but my battery had given up the ghost. Out of the corner of my eye, I saw Sarah enthusiastically come alive. She'd probably managed to negotiate emptying out the equivalent of the National Library.

I gave her a little wave, silently indicating that I was going back to my room. I slipped on a T-shirt and plugged in my phone. From here, I could still hear Sarah talking and laughing, proving that her transaction was on the right track and this conversation was going to last for ever. I made for the bathroom and got in the shower, hoping to wake myself up for good. Thinking back on my night with Sarah was not helping me get out of sleep limbo. On the contrary, remembering the lustful movement of her body against mine, her panting breaths, and her face shining with pleasure was leading me easily toward new … chapters.

I had time to get out of the shower, make some coffee,

and get dressed before Sarah reappeared. From her smile, I knew her negotiation had been fruitful.

"Good news?"

"Excellent. An attic full of books. I'm sure not everything is in good condition, but it'll let me fill the bookshop."

"You do realize that it's pretty full already, right?"

Sarah tilted her head and gave me a knowing smile. Yes, she knew. But that didn't stop her. I wondered vaguely if anything would stop her. Damien had told me about her chaotic childhood and her difficulties with the bookshop; she'd uncovered my heavy secret. And yet here she was, all smiles, hair tousled, dressed in jeans that were a size too big and a worn-out T-shirt, utterly desirable.

"Never too many," I answered for her.

"Never too many. You made coffee!" she enthused, rushing toward the coffee pot.

"I'm going to open up and put out the tables."

Sarah's nose was already in her mug. I opened the door to the stairs, ready to descend. I immediately changed my mind, deciding to check if Sarah was really ready for anything.

"Are we having dinner together tonight?"

"I…"

"I'll ask Baptiste to send over something," I assured her.

"It's just, I might finish with rehearsal pretty late.

We're doing the costumes tonight and I wouldn't want..."

"I'll wait. Anita is making me work on grammar."

It was such a relief not to be carrying that secret alone anymore, to no longer have the weight that I'd dragged behind me as solidly as my anger for years. As usual, Sarah had blown me away: she hadn't looked at me with pity or a "Poor you" pout. She'd taken it in and declared that it changed nothing.

For her, maybe.

For me, definitely not.

"Tell her that she has to try on her costume, too, and that her theory of 'everything suits me' will not be appropriate on the day of the show."

"I'll let her know."

I approached Sarah and she followed me with her eyes, between worry and surprise. She took refuge in her mug again, but I managed to take it out of her hands. I set it down on the counter then gripped Sarah's hips. She tensed up and clung to the furniture behind her. I let my lips brush against the skin of her neck, followed the line of her jaw, and ended above her mouth.

"Are we still counting in chapters?"

She shook her head, eyes almost closed, breathing shallow. It was intoxicating to have so much influence over her.

"In volumes," she suggested in a low voice.

"Fine. Then, Volume Two. The Return."

She clamped her lips together and her laugh stayed stuck in her throat. I took the opportunity to press my mouth against hers and steal a kiss. Kissing Sarah had become a real addiction. I could already recognize her first seconds of hesitation, then the incredible moment when she let herself go, before getting the upper hand by wrapping her arms around the back of my neck.

I kissed her for a long moment, trying in vain to find the necessary motivation to go open the bookshop. Now I regretted letting Sarah take her call. We should have stayed in bed. My gaze plunged into hers, and I finally moved away.

"Just let me take a shower and I'll join you."

"Okay."

She edged past me and went back to her room. I got my phone and decided to go downstairs. I unlocked the bookshop door and started bringing out the tables and chairs. In the pocket of my jeans, I felt my phone vibrate against my thigh.

During the night, Mathilde had tried to reach me several times, to no avail. Damien had also probably tried his luck this morning, hoping I'd come run with him. But he could still run: I hadn't slept that well in months. Most notably, without having a drop to drink.

I brought out several bookcases, and after checking the weather placed some books on the tables. The florist picked that moment to come out of his shop. He gave me a stiff smile and I suppressed the intense desire to flip him the finger in return.

"Nice and sunny, huh?" he said as he approached me, flowers in hand.

"Beautiful, yes."

"Is Sarah up?"

"She's taking a shower."

The florist stared at me, as if trying to figure out whether Sarah and I had spent the night together. I was burning with the desire to tell him, to wipe that smirk off his smug face. I reached a hand toward the flowers and said:

"I'll give them to her, if you want."

"Oh. I wanted to talk to her. About last night, she… Let's say she left kind of quickly."

He rubbed the back of his head, looking awkward. I wasn't. Not at all. I didn't care about this guy. He didn't deserve Sarah. Not that I deserved her, either, but I'd rather get run over by Damien's truck than see this idiot with her.

"I walked her home," I informed him.

"Oh. Good. Will you be here for long?"

"Here or with her?"

"Isn't it the same thing?" he said, sulky.

I just smiled, that famous, arrogant, predatory smile I saved for reporters and women. For a brief second, I almost found it reassuring: Sarah hadn't changed me on that front. I was still able to act like a total bastard when the occasion arose. The only difference was that for the moment, I didn't feel like knocking out his teeth one by one.

"That doesn't answer my question," he said, uncertain.

"As far as my presence here, a little less than two weeks."

His hands tightened on his flowers, while he stared at the entrance to the bookshop. He was obviously waiting for Sarah to appear in hopes of salvaging something with her.

"I'll keep them if you want, it might be a while before she comes down."

His annoyance increased until he finally threw me the bouquet of purple and white flowers he'd been holding.

"The sooner you're out of here, the better for all of us," he snapped.

His tantrum didn't bother me, though. I set the flowers down on the one of the tables while Frédéric headed off in the direction of his shop.

"Have a good day!" I called after him.

I was setting up the last chairs presentably when my phone vibrated again. Mathilde's face appeared, and sitting down in the sun, I steeled myself for what was to come.

"For God's sake, you never answer your phone!" said Mathilde, annoyed.

"I'm really sorry. I was sleeping." I wondered

whether to apologize further, for everything else, but that was going to take hours and it sounded as if she had something else on her mind. "Why were you calling at night? Was it so urgent?"

"Um. Yes."

From her tone of voice, I knew it was serious. I was used to Mathilde yelling at me. Especially when I didn't answer her calls. But this was different. Her voice was tense with urgency and worry, the polar opposite of her usual upbeat tones.

"Listen, if this is about the script, I haven't had time to—"

"No, Maxime. It's something else. In any case, I knew you wouldn't read it right away. It's not like anyone there could help you…"

"Sarah could. She knows."

"Sarah, the bookshop owner? But how … *why* did you tell her?"

"She guessed. I know she won't say anything, Mathilde. She's not like that. She's – she's different."

On the other end of the line, I heard Mathilde sigh. I could make out hustle and bustle, papers moving around, the sound of a keyboard being mistreated. I was already imagining Mathilde in her office nook, filled with files and her kid's drawings. I realized now that I'd been unfair to her. Unfair and ungrateful. She'd always helped me, and I'd done nothing but push her away.

Like everyone else.

"Sounds like this trip has been successful for you," she said.

"Yes. You're right, actually."

There was a short silence, during which Sarah finally appeared on the threshold to the bookshop. Hair still wet, she had her phone glued to her ear and was staring at me, an alarmed look on her face.

"Maxime, I'm calling you about Simon."

I sat up, suddenly worried. I hadn't heard from him since our last call. The wind picked up and Sarah came over to me, pale and worried. The moment she squeezed my shoulder with her hand, I realized this conversation had nothing to do with my career or my life. Through the fog enveloping me, I could barely hear Mathilde's voice.

But I knew those few words – the last ones before my phone crashed to the ground – were going to haunt me for months.

"They found him dead, last night. He took his own life."

Sarah's hand gripped my shoulder a little harder, but not enough to keep me in my chair. I dropped the phone and stood up, feeling my anger and rage surging violently. Unleashed by pain, they were imploding everywhere in my body. In the space of a second, everything become unbearable.

The sun, the wind, the tables, the bouquet of flowers, the books, my life, Sarah. Everything. The whole universe seemed to be turning against me, as if to punish me for all I'd done in my life.

"Maxime," said Sarah.

"Leave me alone!"

"Maxime, we can find a solution. We can ask for a furlough, to go to Paris and…"

"Leave me *alone.*"

She tried to grab my hand to hold me back and guide me, but I pushed her away again. I didn't need her. I was trapped here and Simon … Simon wasn't there anymore. And I hadn't seen or felt anything. Too obsessed with my own life, eaten up by my anger, furious with the world, I hadn't sensed his distress.

"Please, Maxime. Stay here," Sarah advised me as I paced the little square like a lion in a cage, ready to jump on the first prey I saw.

"Fucking hell, which part of 'leave me alone' don't you understand!"

She recoiled, staring at me with a mixture of fear and incomprehension. Sarah had never seen me like this, she'd never witnessed these out-of-control moments when my fury took precedence over everything else.

I replayed my conversation with Mathilde on a loop. The missed calls, her voice hoarse with emotion, her unusual nervousness. And then, Simon's death. The ideal son-in-law, good as gold, the one the directors praised to the skies, the guy who made women dream and, with his good manners, held the door for them.

The guy who had invited me to his parents' house last Christmas, declaring that being alone during the holidays was untenable.

I hadn't seen anything. That was what was unbearable. This wasn't the stabbing pain of loss, or the terrifying sensation of being on the edge of the abyss. No. The most awful thing was this suffocating guilt, this shrill little voice crowing that it was my fault, that I didn't deserve to be his friend, that it should have been me.

That I should have died a hundred times at least: between my drunken evenings and my pathological tendency toward destruction. That was the goal of my life: to destroy others and my own life, conscientiously, piece by piece: Mathilde, my career, Simon.

And Sarah would end up that way, too.

"Is everything okay?"

Alerted by my shouts and erratic behavior, Frédéric had come out of his shop, pruning shears in hand. His eyes slid from Sarah to me, before going back to Sarah.

"Everything's all right," she assured him.

She could certainly try to reassure him. The fact that she was crying wrecked her efforts. I would have liked to have the strength to comfort her, but I was too broken and angry to make even a token gesture.

"It doesn't seem like it. Do you want to come to the shop for a few minutes?" he offered.

He shot me an angry look. I frowned and stuck my

fists in my pockets. With a little luck, Frédéric wouldn't be collateral damage. I went over to him, ready to demand that he fuck off and stay in his corner, with his flowers.

"She's fine," I said, teeth clenched.

"She's not fine. What have you done to her?" he replied.

He came right up to me, looking menacing. Normally, I would have grabbed him by the collar to flatten him against the first available wall. But I was still aware that I was on probation and Frédéric would have no qualms about provoking me.

"Go home," I said, grinding my teeth.

"Or else what? If you hurt her…"

"He hasn't done anything," Sarah intervened.

She slipped a hand in between us, before edging her body between me and Frédéric to separate us. Facing me, she laid her hand against my chest, silently encouraging me to back up.

I did so, still angry with him.

"You scumbag," he hissed. "With parents like yours, it's no surprise how you turned out."

With an abrupt arm movement, I removed Sarah from my path and seized Frédéric's T-shirt in my fist. He slapped with his hands and could barely touch the ground when I lifted him. Behind me, I could hear Sarah shouting, imploring me to stop. But it was too late.

Frédéric struggled in my hands, but I was much too

strong. His shears fell to the ground, while I threw him into the flower buckets filled with bouquets he'd just displayed on the square. He crashed against the cobblestones, soaked and shaking with rage.

"Maybe I should have said 'immature bully'?" he spat.

Before he could catch his breath, my fist found the corner of his mouth. He choked with terror and I hit a second time, to knock him out for good. A trickle of blood ran from his lips to his chin. I backed up and gave a kick to one of the buckets, which ended up in the display window.

A small point of impact appeared, then a crack ran all the way to the opposite corner. Frédéric wiped his lip with his hand and shot me a dirty look.

On my left, I heard footsteps and found Damien running in my direction.

"Stop, for God's sake! Have you lost your mind?"

I swiveled toward Sarah, who seemed to have paled to the point of transparency and was staring at the square without really seeing it. I was glued to the spot, exhausted by my own rage and excesses. Now that I'd let it out, I realized what I'd done.

"Sorry!" I said to Frédéric. "I'll pay for the damage!"

"You're a madman who should be locked up!" he screamed, hysterical.

"He's not wrong," commented Damien.

"I don't want him to come near her," I hissed.

I glanced toward Sarah again. She'd gotten up and was heading slowly for the bookshop. A shower of apologies wouldn't be enough to redeem me. I'd have to hope she'd show her usual understanding.

I doubted it, though.

"She's going to pack a bag."

"She's kicking me out, I imagine?"

"No, she's coming with you. I just came from the police station. I've been negotiating your furlough since last night," Damien explained, extricating it from the pocket of his jeans.

He glanced briefly at the flower shop I'd just ravaged. By acting without thinking, I was going to sink into even more problems. I was aware of that now.

"I'm going to help him clean up and make sure he doesn't file a complaint," said Damien.

"Thanks," I whispered.

"You have two days. Then, you'll have, what … one more week?"

"Eight days," I replied.

"Don't screw around! I like having you here, but I don't want to keep bailing you out every time you mess up."

"I know. And what do I do about Sarah? She must be disgusted with me."

Damien slapped my furlough pass firmly against my chest. He smiled at me, then said:

"We'll see about that later. One thing at a time! Let the storm pass and take the keys to my truck."

"Your truck?" I said.

I knew I wasn't in a position to choose, but Damien's filthy truck went at a snail's pace. Getting back to Paris was going to take for ever. Even longer if Sarah gave me the silent treatment to make me pay – rightly – for my fit of madness.

"It's that or nothing!"

He stuck his keys in my hand, not leaving me time to think. I thanked him with a nod before going back toward the bookshop. I heard Damien offering Frédéric his help, which he accepted with a grunt. I thought about what my friend had said. He was right about one thing: he wouldn't always be there to save me.

I had to learn to control myself.

Even better, I had to learn to make amends.

When I entered the bookshop, two suitcases were sitting by the door. Sarah was drafting a note in felt-tip marker, indicating she'd be away and so the bookshop was closed.

"You don't have to do that."

"What?"

"Close your shop, disrupt your plans, endure Damien's truck … or come with me."

"I'm not doing it because I have to."

I scrutinized her beautiful face, free from animosity. She wasn't smiling, but her warm eyes reassured me. In the ruins of my life, Sarah was a breath of hope. She was holding on where everyone else had given up.

"It's what people do when they love someone," she continued. "Support, help, hand-hold, when the other person needs it."

She stuck her sign on the door and passed close by me. I caught her wrist and pulled Sarah against me. I needed to feel her warm body against mine, to realize that I wasn't alone. After a brief moment of surprise, she let me do it, wrapping her arms around my waist as she buried her face in my chest.

"Thank you," I murmured.

"Shall we? We don't have any time to waste."

She got her suitcase, leaving me to take care of locking the bookshop behind us. Watching her walk away, I couldn't help thinking about what she'd just said.

We didn't have any time to waste.

And I loved her too.

Chapter Fourteen

The drive took hours. Maxime, hands on the wheel, had cursed Damien and his too-slow truck over a hundred times. He'd even sworn to buy him a new car as soon as possible.

That aside, Maxime hardly spoke, and I did nothing to encourage him. His anger was still very much present, and in this confined space I didn't want to provoke another crisis. The way he'd lifted Frédéric had terrified me. I now understood what he'd tried to explain to me, about how he could destroy everything around him in a few seconds.

Damien had called me in a panic to explain the situation.

"Simon committed suicide," he'd said in a rush. "In his bedroom. Mathilde has to notify Maxime, but I'm warning you, he may take it badly."

So I'd jumped into the first clothes I'd found, my hair still wet, and run down the stairs. I'd hoped to be the one to tell him so I could break the news gently, hold his hand. But I'd arrived too late, and my presence hadn't been enough. I'd been an impotent witness to his explosion. In an instant, the puzzle was pulled apart once more, with new, warped pieces to put back.

Me going with him had seemed obvious. I knew it would end up that way as soon as Damien had told me about the situation. I couldn't see myself letting Maxime go alone, at the mercy of his old demons. Protecting him had become a sort of automatic reflex.

He'd entrusted me with his secret, and I had to support him.

Even though it was only for a few days, I wanted to make sure he was okay.

Even though it was only for a few days, I wanted to spend time with him.

I was far from being taken in by the situation. Away from his work, Maxime was proving himself thoughtful and lovable. Of course, as he'd said, he was far from resembling a hero from a book. He was better than those heroes. More fragile, more distant, more damaged. Less simple.

I took advantage of a red light to look at his face. Even angry, even sad, Maxime maintained his magnetism. The sharp line of his jaw, his dark gaze, that enigmatic little scar on his eyebrow. I didn't know if I should feel happy or pathetic to have fallen in love with a man who would leave me without batting an eye a week from now.

"We're here," announced Maxime, pulling me from my thoughts.

My eyes ran over the streets, lined with Haussmann-style buildings. Maxime lived on a private cul-de-sac looking out over the Parc Monceau, a bubble of calm in the middle of city life.

On arriving in Paris, I'd been struck by the constant bustle that reigned there. The streets were swarming with people, the vehicles nearly touching each other. The city seemed to be in a constant buzz, driven by frenetic energy. I'd finally understood what Maxime felt while living here: the excitement, that incredible sensation that made anything possible.

He entered a code, and a wide garage door opened. We rushed into the basement and Maxime parked in the space furthest from the entrance.

"The best thing about this truck is that no one will know it's mine," he said sarcastically.

He got our two suitcases and I followed him to the elevator. Within a few seconds, we reached his apartment. The living room was so big my entire apartment could have fit inside. I looked up toward the ceiling, adorned with moldings and decorated with an impressive chandelier. At my feet, the solid wood parquet floor was perfectly waxed. Reflexively, I took off my shoes and walked with care.

"Make yourself at home," he encouraged me. "I'm going to put the suitcases in my bedroom."

"Okay."

I paced curiously around the room. Despite the furnishings and decoration, the living room was icy. There was no trace of Maxime: no photos, no personal touches. It looked more like a show home than a place to live.

Taken aback, even a little in awe, I stopped in front of a bookcase lined with books. It was impeccable: no trace of dust… and above all, no trace of fingerprints on the glass shelves. I glanced at the titles, touching the books and smiling. There wasn't any order here. Poetry, stage plays and novels were all lined up at random.

"They're just there to look pretty," explained Maxime, back in the living room.

He came over to me and stared at the books in turn. He took one at random and opened it.

"Simon gave me this one."

He showed me a note inscribed on the first page. With a weary sigh, he admitted that he'd never been able to decipher it.

"How did no one ever notice?" I asked.

"I have tricks. Like, I forgot my glasses. Or I'll look at

it later. Sometimes Mathilde helps me. Honestly, it's pretty easy when you don't get attached to people."

"So that's your greatest trick, not getting attached to people?"

I reflected bitterly that it must be so easy for him. He passed through people's lives, without ever remaining there. He'd just smile, joke, or sometimes fight, then escape. I now understood that he wouldn't change his ways for me. On the contrary, the distance between Paris and Chateaurenard was going to make things even easier for him.

"That's my trick, yep. In the same way as destroying everything around me."

"You shouldn't have hit Frédéric, but – he'll be okay. He did provoke you."

"It's still no excuse." He shook his head. "Can you read me what he wrote?"

He handed me the book Simon had given him, an old edition of a Molière play. I couldn't help caressing the thick, heavy cover, on which the title of the play was engraved.

"*The Misanthrope*," I said with a smile.

"Yes, he told me that. He thought it was appropriate."

"It is not! You're anything but a misanthrope. And even the misanthrope ended up having a softer side."

"Really?"

"Really. He hates men, but he loves a woman."

Without asking, Maxime moved behind me and wrapped his arms around my waist. I was torn between relief and despair. No matter what I said, or did, I knew our relationship was doomed to be brief. After his last week at the bookshop, he would disappear.

And because he was used to it, he'd do it easily, forgetting me before he even got back to Paris.

He laid a kiss on my shoulder and I opened the book to see Simon's note.

"His mother was a teacher," he informed me.

"Hence the handwriting. Lovely capital letters."

I read the note silently and my throat tightened. I'd been expecting a vague birthday greeting, some little joke. Now, it took on a whole new meaning. I could have easily lied to Maxime. But that would have been unfair, especially today.

I cleared my throat and tried not to get emotional.

"It says… 'Happy birthday, Max. Keep this book, with my signature, until I die: it'll pay you back for at least two or three nights out.'"

Behind me, I could feel Maxime's body, tense as a bow. In spite of myself and in spite of the fact that I didn't know Simon, I felt a tear roll down my cheek. I knew what it was like to lose someone close to you, to feel alone, to struggle against the urge to scream.

I heard Maxime sniff and he buried his head in my neck.

"Arrogant bastard. It would barely pay for one," he said against my skin.

I laughed, too, and we stayed in front of that bookcase for several long minutes, halfway between laughter and tears.

"Shall we eat something? I'm going to order in."

That evening, we ate in front of one of Simon's movies, rebroadcast on television. Maxime told me about how they met, their nights out, their movie shoots. I admired his face, which lit up at each happy memory. But I was dreading the next day, when he'd have to face the present.

That night, I fell asleep in Maxime's arms. But around two o'clock in the morning I woke up alone. I found Maxime, dressed only in his boxers, in his kitchen, a glass in hand. I could tell this wasn't the first time he'd spent a night like this.

"Are you okay?"

"No. Go back to sleep, I'll rejoin you shortly."

I went over to him. His eyes were reddened. My impulse was to take him in my arms. But Maxime had shown me several times that he didn't act like other people. There was a chance he'd push me away and retreat even further into his silence.

"I should have helped him," he finally whispered.

"You don't have to feel responsible for this, Maxime. We all have our demons, don't we?"

He swallowed a laugh and took a swig of what I assumed was vodka.

"I don't think you do."

"Before you arrived at the bookshop, I was on the verge of putting it up for sale. I'm broke, or nearly. And without that bookshop, I'd really have nothing else. Without that bookshop, I wouldn't be much. I don't know how to do anything else. My family is – a mess. My parents left me with my grandmother because I wasn't their priority."

"You can't say my parents were shining stars, either. But him… I don't know, he had everything. Family, friends, career, money. I can't believe I missed the signs. I wasn't a good enough friend," he concluded, tipping a glass over.

"It's not your fault, Maxime."

He gave me a look. I could have repeated that to him ad infinitum, but he'd never have believed it. Guilt and anger ran deep in him. I now feared that Simon's death would lead him into a very dark place.

I laid my hand on his chest, where his heart was beating too fast, and said again:

"It's not your fault, Maxime."

He stared at me, as if gauging my sincerity. I'd put all my conviction into those words, all my strength. Now I wondered if anyone had ever spoken to Maxime like this. His inner circle was limited and very tied to his profession. Who'd worried about his personal life? Who'd told him where his responsibilities started – and where they stopped?

He drained his glass in one gulp and swiped a hand across his tired face before covering mine, still over his heart. He squeezed it and pulled me against him.

"Maybe I should have screwed up much sooner. Then I could've met you before all this mess."

"You don't have anything to feel guilty about."

"Oh, yes, I do," he said.

He lifted me and a cry of surprise escaped me. I found myself sitting on his kitchen island, knocking over his spice jars and the toaster. Before I could apologize, Maxime swept the rest away with his arm, sending his almost empty bottle and an array of brand-new pans flying.

"I'm going to do something very bad in the next few seconds. And I'm going to do it with you. Which should normally clear my head a bit."

He gave me a smile that made me forget everything I feared: our coming separation, his consuming guilt, my life after him. I laid my hands on his cheeks, trying to memorize every detail of his face. His beard stubble pricked my palms, but his eyes, dark with desire, made me forget that sensation.

He pressed his mouth against mine and his hands grabbed my T-shirt to pull it off of me. The next moment, his mouth was caressing my body, finding the tips of my breasts. I let myself go, giving Maxime permission to take possession of my body in his kitchen.

"My condoms are in the bathroom," he panted, as I was trying to pull off his boxers.

"I don't have anything against taking a shower," I murmured.

"I repeat: I really should have screwed up before!"

His smile could have melted Antarctica. He slipped his hands under my thighs and I clung to his hips. I wrapped my arms around his neck and he carried me through his apartment to the black-marble bathroom.

Maxime forgot his grief and guilt while making love to me with a new tenderness, as if he was afraid of hurting me. We made it back to the bedroom at dawn, where Maxime fell asleep at once, his face finally relaxed.

The funeral mass lasted an hour. Simon's parents had succeeded in preserving their privacy, and the reporters were kept away. Even so, some of them didn't hesitate to take photos while calling out to Maxime.

I supposed the fact that I was holding his hand wasn't totally irrelevant to their interest.

"Why are there gossip magazines here?" I'd asked Maxime while we were drinking our coffees.

"Mathilde brings them to me. She likes to know who I'm sleeping with or not."

"And?"

"It's false, most of the time. I avoid sleeping with potential co-workers. I make do with normal girls, who don't pick at their salad, eat fries, and aren't focused on their navel."

"Should I take that as a compliment?"

"Absolutely. On top of that, you put sugar in your coffee."

That had been our mid-morning five minutes of relaxation. Everything came after that, between retying Maxime's tie and helping him learn a speech he would have to recite from memory at the church. I knew he was distressed but he didn't let anything show. I'd sought, in vain, for a good portion of the night, to find a way to restore Maxime's confidence, to make him understand that he was loved for who he was. Even with his imperfections and his anger.

The service consisted of a litany of anecdotes, each more glowing than the last. In front of us, Simon's mother wept silently, facing the smiling portrait of her son. Maxime squeezed my hand so hard that my fingers grew stiff.

"It's your turn," I whispered.

I encouraged him with a kiss on the back of his hand. He stood up, smoothed his jacket, and headed for the lectern. He barely dared to glance at the casket sitting in the center. His hands found the edges of the lectern, and after a brief look at Simon's family he began.

"I… I met Simon at one of my first shoots. He had experience in showbiz, while I was just starting out. We talked, about ourselves, our profession. In that world, to tell the truth, there aren't really many good guys. Except him. One time, when a review got me down, he showed up at my house with some food his mum had made. Beef bourguignon, I think."

He hazarded a smile and I saw Simon's mother straighten up with a remnant of maternal pride.

"*Madame*, it was delicious. One of the best meals of my life, with the best guy on this planet."

The audience relaxed and I heard a few laughs in the church. I stared at Maxime who, fists clenched, was trying to control his emotions. Despite his assertive delivery, I could detect low, hoarse tones.

"I made fun of him a lot. He went grocery shopping for his neighbor, he checked in on his concierge, he paid for music lessons for a kid who didn't have a cent. That guy was … probably sent to Earth to do good. But I won't forget that he swore like a sailor, was late to everything and lied on his résumé about having a black belt in judo."

Another laugh shook the crowd. I smiled at Maxime, encouraging him to go on.

"I've never … I've never been the kind of guy to make grand statements. As you know, I talk with … my fists. Simon never judged me for that, but he'd warn me about what I was risking. That's what I appreciated about him, his ability to listen, to give you advice, without ever lecturing you. I've never met a guy as funny and brilliant as him. The kind of guy who talks with the same passion about an inter-war Russian movie and his mother's cooking."

A tear rolled down his cheek and Maxime took a deep breath.

"This is what I'd say to him today, if I could. I'd tell him that he really fucked up, doing what he did. I'd tell him that I'm really going to miss him. I'd thank him for being there on lonely Sunday evenings, as well as party nights. And I'd tell him that I love him," he choked out, exhausted.

Maxime went down a few steps and stopped in front of the closed casket. Masses of flowers surrounded it and Maxime pulled out a lily to lay near the plaque where Simon's name and date of birth were engraved.

He took his seat again and refused the handkerchief I handed him. Instead, he put the sunglasses he'd removed upon entering the church back on and stayed silent until the priest invited us to leave.

At the cemetery, Simon's parents had wanted to limit attendance to family and close friends. I felt like even more of an interloper attending the interment. Maxime, jaws clenched, just stared at a point on the horizon. Across from me, a beautiful dark-haired woman, hidden behind luxury sunglasses, gave me the unpleasant sensation of being spied on.

After laying Simon to rest with one last prayer, the little crowd of a dozen people dispersed.

"I'm going to talk to his parents, okay?" Maxime asked, as he released my hand.

I moved off toward the exit, but was quickly overtaken by the dark-haired woman who'd been staring at me.

"Hello, I… We don't know each other, I think. I'm Maxime's agent. Well, his ex-agent."

She pulled off her glasses, revealing eyes reddened by tears and a deathly pale complexion. She tried to smile but, like Maxime, she seemed exhausted, devastated by Simon's death.

"You must be Sarah, right?"

"Yes. Um… Sorry, I feel a little superfluous here. Do you think we could get out of this place for some air?"

"No, of course. I wanted to thank you for what you're doing for him. I saw that he was holding your hand… Are you—"

"Let's say yes, to avoid a very long explanation," I cut her off. "For the moment, anyway. In a week he's coming back to Paris."

I already knew how this was going to end. And I also knew that I had to take the initiative to avoid being the one who suffered the most. On our return to Chateaurenard, I would have to manage this conversation for both of us. He'd resume his life here, and I'd try to save my bookshop. Even if he wanted them, there weren't any other possibilities.

"Good grief, it went by so quickly. And this thing with Simon. It's terrible. I feel responsible."

"Maxime, too. He feels guilty."

I stared at my feet and traced a line in the gravel with my toe. I had nothing in common with Mathilde – except Maxime – and I didn't have much to say to her. The location wasn't helping our conversation, either.

"He shouldn't. Simon had gambling debts. Huge ones. I think he was overwhelmed."

There was a long silence as we walked up the cobbled street outside the cemetery. After this afternoon's interlude, life in Paris was going on as before. The same hustle and bustle, the same energy, the same momentum. Nothing had really changed.

"I told Maxime he should rehire you. Are you going to give him a chance?"

"I'd never considered that the conversation we had at the police station was real. Maxime is like that: a real hot-head. That's what makes him talented. His emotions are right on the surface."

"Of course," I agreed.

This conversation, though trivial, was only confirming what I'd been thinking on the way to Paris. There was no future for me and Maxime. He had to act, make movies, and accept breathtaking roles. He had to resume his journey and I had to resume mine.

"Did you come to tell me something?" I asked, holding back my irritation.

"No. Maxime has always known how to surprise me. I don't doubt he'll do it again."

"With or without me?"

"That's not for me to say. Let's say that I see how he's changed with you, but I also know that a long-distance relationship, with an actor and especially with him, can be ... complicated."

"I know."

My heart was still heavy, but I was a little reassured. Reassured to know that Mathilde was friendly, reassured that Maxime had at least one trustworthy woman around him. I spotted a café and suggested to Mathilde that we go have a drink.

Behind us, I heard footsteps. When I turned around, I found Maxime, running with long strides in our direction. When he reached us, he took my hand and laid a kiss on my forehead.

"I'm buying, girls. We'll drink a toast to Simon."

"Good idea," I agreed.

"Speaking of... Mathilde, get me the contact info for that kid Simon helped. I want to pay for his lessons. And make sure his neighbor has someone to do her shopping."

Mathilde gaped for a few seconds, then nodded. We

entered the café and settled in at the back of the room, hoping no one would recognize Maxime. As if the situation was normal, he wrapped his arm around my shoulders and pulled me against him.

"We're going back tomorrow," he reminded me. "Sarah is putting on a play next week. She's overseeing the last rehearsals," he explained to Mathilde.

"It's a community theater production," I clarified.

"You should come, Mathilde, it's going to be amazing! I'm going to order our drinks."

Another kiss on the forehead, a ritual I was getting used to much too fast. I watched Maxime go, then transferred my attention to Mathilde. Maxime was in overdrive. Probably to compensate for all his guilt. Suddenly, I knew at last what I should do for him, so he'd feel better, so he'd understand that, in spite of his mistakes, he was a good guy.

"Mathilde, I have a favor to ask you."

The next day at dawn, we were back on the road, and I had the pleasure of being with Maxime and hearing him swear at Damien's truck again. He had succeeded in suppressing his sorrow. At least, that's what he wanted me to believe. But I could see that he was lost in his thoughts and walled up in his pain. I decided not to talk either. You couldn't force a confidence from someone.

He'd eventually come to terms with it. In time. When my grandmother died, my passion for books had saved me from a reality that was too hard to take. I'd fallen in love with fictional men, dreamed of an ideal family, led investigations with great detectives. Anything that let me avoid facing my life suited me. Obviously, Maxime needed a different solution.

Talking.

Hitting a punching bag.

Repainting all the shelves in the bookshop.

Doing his reading lessons.

It was all good. The only problem was time. I was out of it. We were out of it. But we had a week left; I would make the most of it.

"Here we are!"

Maxime stroked my cheek with the back of his hand, waking me from my doze. This express round trip to Paris had done me in. Simon's funeral had been hard, and keeping an eye on Maxime, who swung between grief and boundless energy, was tiring. Moreover, I'd looked at our situation from every angle, searching for a solution, in vain.

"I'm going to bring the tables out," Maxime announced. "Will you make us coffee?"

This sweet routine elicited a smile from me. I was about to get out of the car when Maxime held me back by grabbing my wrist.

"Thanks for coming with me."

"You're welcome. Given the circumstances, it was the right thing to do."

"For you, maybe. For me, it was ... different. I'm not used to it."

He indicated the space between us, looking vaguely embarrassed. Since he arrived here, this was the first time I'd seen Maxime at a loss for words. I caught his eye and my heart raced. Maxime was looking at me like I was the rarest and most precious thing in the world. I no longer saw the anger or the frustration. On the contrary, Maxime's dark eyes were soft and attentive.

"Not used to what?" I asked, cheeks burning.

"I don't know. You know, I've always wondered why you agreed to host me. I'm not talking about money," he interjected as I prepared to justify myself.

"Maxime..."

"Actually, I've given up understanding. I don't know why you did it. I don't know why Anita is helping me, or even why Damien lent me his jalopy. I don't know, and I think I don't really give a crap. All I know... All I know is that I've fallen in love with all this."

"This?" I teased him.

"I've fallen in love with you."

His confession took my breath away and I felt my smile widen across my face. I didn't know how Maxime did it, but just one look made me forget all my doubts and hesitations.

It was the first time a man had confessed his feelings to me.

And it was the first time I was feeling the same thing.

So, despite our time slipping away and our future looking so hopeless, I answered him with what I'd been burning to say since our night together.

"I love you, too."

Chapter Fifteen

I was standing in front of the last place I thought I'd visit in Chateaurenard. For a brief moment, I was almost tempted to create a scandal to prolong my stay here. In three days, my sentence would be officially over. And I'd return to Paris.

Frédéric's shop was narrow and his décor a bit old-fashioned. The florist barely looked at me when I entered; his upper lip was still swollen from our last encounter. But his eyes were glistening with contempt. For him, I was at best an actor, at worst … a failure. I leaned toward the latter. But I was going to ignore all that, for Sarah's sake.

"I haven't come to fight. I've come here to apologize – and to shop. I need some flowers," I explained.

I ignored Frédéric's arched eyebrow, which seemed to

congratulate me on my perceptiveness. I was not going to miss this guy, and the feeling was mutual.

"Lots of flowers," I clarified.

His contempt changed into vague financial interest. I scanned the shop, stopped in front of the bouquets, then the plants. Buying flowers was Anita's idea. According to her, it was better than a long explanation.

"I need a bouquet for my agent."

"In Paris? A large one?" he asked, a little worried.

He was probably afraid I'd steal something while his back was turned to make it.

"Yes. You make deliveries, right?"

I pointed at the price chart on the wall behind him. Deliveries were broken down into three zones: Chateaurenard, within six miles … and out-of-area. For Paris, I suspected I was going to have to pay the highest rate. But it was a way to make amends for my recent lack of restraint.

"Uh, yes. How many stems?" he sighed, getting out his notepad.

"A couple dozen. Next, I'd like a bouquet of white flowers. For tomorrow as well."

"Any special occasion?"

"Flowers for a grave. I care about this, so do it well. Okay?"

He nodded, all while furiously writing notes. My few orders were going to take him all day and clear out his stock.

"Next, the largest possible bouquet for Anita. Delivery by tomorrow, and then one per week."

"For how long?"

I shrugged. With a little luck, Anita still had many long years ahead of her. Having flowers delivered to her once a week seemed like very little in comparison with what she'd given me. I wasn't reading or writing perfectly yet, but she was going to refer me to someone in Paris for further help.

"Let's start with five years. And finally, a bouquet of roses. Red, if possible."

"All of them, I presume?"

"How many do you have in stock?"

"Around seventy."

"All of them, then. I'll need them for the night of the play, in two days."

"Fine. Anything else?"

"I don't think so."

I unsheathed my debit card, ready to pay for my favorite enemy's entire stock. I hadn't bought flowers in a good long time. The last time had been for my mother's birthday. I didn't even know if she got them. I suspected my father of having done all he could, until her death, to keep her from talking to me.

I still remembered those icy words in the cemetery.

"She died of grief," he'd said, shooting me an angry look.

I shook my head, coming back to reality. I wasn't

surprised at the four-figure sum Frédéric announced. I was shocked, however, that he was holding out his hand for me to shake.

"Really?" I said.

"Really. A man who buys flowers can't really be such a bastard, can he?"

"You'd be surprised!"

"I shouldn't have provoked you or mentioned your family – I apologize too."

After a moment of hesitation, I took his hand in mine and shook it. This guy would certainly never be my friend. He'd now realized that he wouldn't get another chance with Sarah. But he lived across from Sarah, and with him there, I knew there'd at least be someone to look out for her.

Because soon I wouldn't be there to do it anymore. And I hadn't managed to solve the problem of our relationship. Maybe there was no solution. Actually, yes. There was one. But none of it seemed good enough for her. I knew we were on borrowed time; the end of my sentence would mark a turning point in our story. Still, I was sure we could do it.

Her here, me in Paris. It wasn't ideal, but it was doable. I could make trips, come back for holidays, limit my movie shoots. I just had to find a moment to talk to Sarah about it. Since our return from Paris, she'd been alternating between play rehearsals and outside appointments. During that time, I'd struggled to empty the boxes and find spots for the latest arrivals. When I had a free moment, Anita showed up, ready for another reading lesson.

This last week was going by way too fast and I got the unpleasant sensation that Sarah was avoiding me. Sure, we came together at night, but she was getting up at dawn and barely touching her food. I didn't blame her. I confronted reality with my fists, but Sarah preferred to run away from it.

After my visit to Frédéric, I went over to the play rehearsal. The troupe of volunteers had made progress, and the set was now in place. Damien was rehearsing his final monologue, while Élise was trying to adjust her impressive dress. Anita was roaring with laughter with Baptiste, who gave me a nod upon spotting me at the back of the hall.

Sarah and I had our routine. She would look for me at the back of the hall, watching for the hour that marked the end of my curfew. Five minutes prior, I would stand up and give her a little signal. She would announce the end of the session, and we'd go home together, hand in hand, to the apartment. We'd have dinner, and sometimes I managed to wait for dessert before drawing Sarah into her bedroom – or the shower, or the living room – to make love to her.

I listened to the rehearsal for close to forty-five minutes and got up a few minutes before the fateful hour. Sarah checked the time on her watch and turned toward me with a little smile on her lips.

"That's enough for tonight," she announced. "Tomorrow, around two o'clock, we'll do one last dress rehearsal. Damien, reread your monologue, okay? Élise, you have to be … more upset in the last scene. Camille loses her dreams and true love in a few sentences, okay?"

"I've already lost my dreams," she griped as she got off the stage. "Hi, Maxime!" she called with a sweet smile.

I gave her a little wave before thrusting my hands into the pockets of my jeans. Sarah closed her notebook and slipped it into her bag before giving me a luminous smile, with that typical little blush in her cheeks. Our relationship wasn't really a secret – at least not for the people in this room – but Sarah acted like we'd embarked on something clandestine. I had nothing against it; I was used to my whole life being paraded in front of the entire planet – even if, most of the time, it was only half-truths.

But Sarah was right about one thing: I would have liked to keep her all to myself. She was too precious to be fodder for the press.

"Good rehearsal?" I asked, opening the door for her.

"Stressful. I don't know why I inflict this on myself every year!"

"Because you like a challenge?"

Outside, a fine summer rain was dampening the

pavement. I pulled Sarah against me and lifted my jacket to give us cover. To my great surprise, Sarah moved away and lifted her face to the sky.

"It's raining!" I protested.

"I don't care! Come on!"

Within three minutes, we were soaked. Sarah was radiating joy. I took her hand in mine and pulled her against me. Kissing Sarah had become a new addiction, the kind that didn't hurt anybody. Except me, when I asked myself what we were going to do at the end of this week. Sarah pressed her damp body against mine and I felt her smile into my mouth.

"I did this when I was little."

"Kiss men in the street?"

"Go out in the rain. It makes you feel free. Don't you think?"

"Apart from making us catch our death, I don't really see the attraction!"

I shoved back a lock of hair dripping down my forehead. I was lying. Seeing Sarah, so radiant in the rain, soaked to the skin, would remain an enduring memory. I often wondered how Sarah, so different, so shy, so sweet, so my opposite, had been able to take up such an important place in my world. Little by little, patiently, she'd pushed back the dark veil obscuring my life. She'd refused to let me keep my distance.

Sarah had waged her own personal little war against me, running into a wall but finding new ways to bypass it, before finally pulling it down and laying me bare.

I hadn't fallen in love – I'd laid down my weapons. I'd let this woman win against me.

I found myself smiling. Sarah was my biggest and most beautiful defeat, the one I was most proud of.

"What are you laughing at?" she asked, wrapping her arms around my neck.

"You. Or me, I don't know."

"Always so mysterious."

She laid a kiss on my lips and I finally understood the attraction of this stroll through the rain. I lifted her up and tipped her over my shoulder, her delectable rear end close at hand.

"May I ask what you're doing?" she shouted.

"I'm seeing an upside in this little weather ritual."

"Oh. And what is that?"

"Taking a bath."

Sarah was wrapped in her fluffy bathrobe, while I tried to reheat Baptiste's veal with olives. We'd found the dish on one of the window ledges, with a card wishing us a good evening.

"You're going to have to find a movie where you learn to cook," commented Sarah, standing near me.

"I definitely will," I chuckled. "Get back to your play!"

Sarah had retrieved her notebook – miraculously dry – and was listing off what she had to do the next day. Unfortunately, I couldn't come to those rehearsals, but Sarah and Damien had still managed to find a solution so I could attend the play.

"What kind of pressure do you put on the cops to always get your way?"

"Bribery and a touch of blackmail," replied Sarah, without looking up from her notebook.

"That's what I thought!"

"Damien makes a charitable donation. And the daughter of the chief warrant officer is … a big fan of yours! She comes to the bookshop pretty regularly. You must have seen her: a teenage girl, dark-haired, blue eyes, too much makeup, thinks Stephen King is something to do with burgers."

I stifled a laugh, before identifying the young girl in question. Indeed, she'd shown herself to be rather forward with me, quizzing me on my taste in literature. There was no chance I'd be interested in her, even if she was ten years older.

"I see," I said with a smile. "Is your list still long?"

"It seems endless," she sighed, running a hand through her damp hair. "And next week, I'm getting more books."

"Do you never take a holiday?"

"A what? I have no idea what you're talking about."

"Holiday. That thing where you sit on a deckchair and stare at your toes. It must have happened to you at least once in your life, right?"

"Yeah. Five years ago, I closed the bookshop for a week. When I got back, the electricity had gone out, and honestly, I was so bored."

"Really?"

"Really! Anita had rented me a bungalow on some beach. Turquoise water, white sand, radiant sun."

I frowned; that sort of holiday sounded like what most people dreamed of. And then suddenly, I understood. Sarah didn't dream about that type of holiday. She was barely even familiar with the word *holiday*.

"No bookshops around?" I guessed.

"Not one," she moaned. "I thought I would die of boredom."

I burst out laughing, imagining Sarah wandering on her beach cursing humanity. I deposited our plates on either side of the counter and sat on one of the stools. Sarah pushed away her notebook and sniffed her dinner.

"I'm starving! What about you, how was your day?" she asked.

"Books. Lots of books."

Sarah dove into her plate, hiding yet another blush. I swallowed a mouthful of steak, then took her hand to reassure her.

"I had some coffee. Lots of coffee. And I ordered some shelves for the wall in back."

"Maxime, I can't afford…"

"Think of it as a parting gift."

"You're the one leaving, you should get a gift!"

A short silence fell. Without meaning to, we'd started the conversation that we'd both tried to avoid. My departure was no mystery. Our future, however, was.

"That's true, I'm the one leaving," I replied, toying with a piece of steak.

"Monday, right?"

"Damien is taking me back to Paris."

Sarah nodded. I knew what was bothering her. I'd vaguely hoped she would bring up the subject. I wasn't comfortable with romantic notions, grand declarations, and promises about the future. I lacked experience and I didn't trust myself not to mess it up. I knew that Sarah had been brought up on perfect heroes and I was just – me. I was flawed and imperfect, you could even say a mess. In the face of her silence, I forced myself to get a grip on the subject. No matter how bad I was at this, we only had two days to sort it out.

"We should talk about it," I suggested.

"Paris?"

"Paris, here, you. What we're going to do."

She looked up toward me, but did everything she could to avoid my gaze. With her lips pressed together and looking a little shy, she pushed her plate away. She took a deep breath, and when her eyes finally found mine, I saw a touch of sadness.

"We're not going to do anything," she said at last. "There is no 'we', actually."

"'We' just took a bath together. A bath where 'we' made love. There is a 'we', Sarah."

"Tonight, yes. Tomorrow, maybe. But … not Monday."

I'd taken quite a few hits in my life. I'd had my nose broken and my shoulder dislocated. But none of those injuries hurt as much as Sarah's words.

She was dumping me.

She was leaving me.

Coldly. Easily. While I was trying to find a solution for both of us, she was ending our relationship with a pragmatism and rationality that I didn't know she had.

Where was the sensitive girl I'd met? Where was the girl who made me dance in the middle of the street? Abruptly, right in front of me, she was gone.

I scrutinized her face, whose expression wavered between worry and disbelief.

"It's not sustainable," she said finally. "No matter what… Listen, I've thought about the situation and there's no solution."

I had been stunned by her announcement, but this new blow woke me up. She was pushing me away. And she was doing it without even consulting me. As easily as she'd opened the bookshop doors to me, she was shutting them again and pushing me out. Bitterly, I realized that she was only mirroring what I'd done for years. I'd deliberately pushed people away. I'd kept my loved ones at a distance and alienated anybody who'd tried to make a connection.

She was destroying us and it hurt like hell.

"I thought we'd think about it together..."

"Well, let's do it!" she said, annoyed in turn. "Let's think together about this twisted situation where you live in Paris and I live here. Huh? Three hundred miles."

"Plenty of people have long-distance relationships!"

"It's not about the distance, Maxime. It's... How many worlds are there between us exactly? You like acting, you like Paris. Your life is there. Meanwhile I have the bookshop, my whole life is here. My friends, my customers. Everything."

"*Almost* everything."

I clenched my fists, holding back my growing anger. Listening to Sarah was like taking a punch to the gut, the kind that left you breathless and shocked. I was so used to facing Sarah's shyness that her sudden inflexibility astounded me.

Avoiding my gaze, she dealt me another blow:

"*Everything*."

The blade, as painful as an icy wind, pierced me again. This time, disappointment was stronger than anger.

"You'd wind up resenting me," she said.

"For making my life a little bit more … pleasant?"

"For reining you in. For holding you back. I've seen your movies, Maxime. I know what you're worth. It wouldn't be fair for you to stay here, when everything is waiting for you there."

"No one's waiting for me."

"That's not what Mathilde says."

"Officially, Mathilde isn't my agent anymore."

Sarah bowed her head and I ran a hand over my face. I was tired. We were in the middle of dinner, and this conversation had taken much too dark a turn. I had just wanted to talk … and now, we were breaking up. This wasn't how I'd pictured things. I'd naively believed Sarah would agree to a compromise.

"You know very well that's not true," she sighed. "And even if it was, it doesn't change anything between us. You can't stay holed up here, and I can't be there. I'd go so far as to say that you *have* to be there and I have to stay here."

"So, you want … to just stop?"

"I want us to live dangerously, by becoming friends."

She gave me one of her luminous smiles, but it wasn't enough to erase what she'd just said to me. My usual rage came back, roaming the surface of my skin and ready to jump out. I felt like sending the plates flying, hitting a wall as hard as I could.

"I don't want to be friends," I rasped.

"But…"

"I don't. I don't want to pretend nothing happened. I don't want to help you soothe your conscience by becoming friends. I don't see how the fact that you live here is incompatible with my life there! It's bullshit, Sarah! Nothing but bullshit."

"That's not how I picture a relationship," she answered, very serious.

"And what do you know about relationships? What they say in books? You think that kind of bullshit is realistic? Goddammit, Sarah, open your eyes!"

My hand crashed into a pile of books, which collapsed to the floor. She jumped off her stool, frightened. That simple gesture helped me push back the wave of anger threatening to overwhelm me.

"I'm sorry," I said immediately.

"Maxime, it's not…"

"Not what? An ideal world? A perfect relationship? Sarah, all these books," I explained, pointing at them, "are nothing but a bunch of bullshit, made for girls like you."

"Girls like me?"

"Dreamy, romantic, divorced from reality. Sometimes life is complicated. And sometimes, yes, you have to confront reality and find solutions. Make compromises."

"That's what I'm doing," she objected, teeth clenched. "Being in a relationship means thinking about the other person."

I stared at her, stunned. Sarah was so calm that I

wondered if she'd planned this conversation. I thought she was avoiding it, but now I realized that she'd honed her arguments and prepared to face my anger.

"And you think by deciding for both of us you're thinking of me?"

"That's all I've done since the beginning," she retorted.

"The beginning? And when was that?"

"The day when … when you let me touch your tattoo."

"So, since that moment, you've been thinking about this conversation?"

"I thought about how I'm going to manage without you," she admitted, voice hoarse. "How to make you understand that your life isn't here. I saw your apartment, Maxime. And I know mine, there's no comparison. I talked to Mathilde, I realized what your life was."

"'Was', yes. I don't intend…"

"I read the script, Maxime. It was really good. Aside from you, I don't know who could play the main character."

Cautiously, she walked around the counter and approached me. Though Sarah showed determination in the bookshop, usually when we were together she was much more hesitant and doubtful. But tonight, I was talking to bookshop Sarah, the one who wouldn't change her mind.

"You're an actor, Maxime. I've seen it. Mathilde sees it, too."

She was trying to win me over, but I was too outraged to let her. I held up a hand in front of me, silently ordering her not to come closer. I took a deep breath and closed my eyes. The anger slowly drained away, leaving behind a sort of weariness.

I'd always lived my life this way. I pushed people away, warned them off. Sarah hadn't heeded my warnings and I'd let her enter my life. And now, she was leaving it.

Someone leaving me was nothing new. My mother, Simon, Mathilde, Sarah. But it was the first time that it hurt so much, an icy pain, fracturing my body like a blade of ice. A hailstorm of blows wouldn't have hurt as much.

"I'm going to sleep. You have a play to get ready for, don't you."

I headed for my room, more bitter than ever. Before this dinner, I was cursing time for passing too quickly. Now, I couldn't wait to leave this place.

"Maxime…"

"Good night, Sarah."

I escaped to my room and closed the door behind me. Then I stuck all my things in my suitcase, only leaving out exactly what I needed for the next two days.

On the other side of the door, I could make out the sounds of dishes. I vaguely hoped Sarah would knock on my door, that she'd do what she'd always done in refusing to let me always run away. But she did nothing. After a few minutes, there was only silence.

I stretched out on my bed, replaying our conversation and wondering what had gone wrong. When, exactly, had I lost control of my life?

"I do so enjoy our little chats," cooed Anita, as she wrapped her arm around mine.

"I'm leaving the day after tomorrow," I reminded her.

We exited the bookshop and I locked the door behind us. Anita had given me one last refresher lesson. I still wasn't a good reader, but if I took my time, I could decipher a menu in a restaurant. I'd even managed to write a card for Simon's parents. True, it was just a few words and my signature, but it was more than I could have imagined just a few months ago.

"I suggest we not talk about unpleasant things this evening!" said Anita.

"Absolutely. I had my fill last night."

Anita gave me a sideways glance. She'd gotten Sarah's version that morning, then mine tonight. Even so, she hadn't been able to mediate. According to her, we were both wrong.

"She'll eventually understand," she reassured me. "And you'll also eventually understand *her*."

"I doubt it. I'm just going to leave on Monday morning. Do you know your lines?" I asked, changing the subject.

"Like the back of my hand. Look at this crowd!"

Outside the theater, dozens of people were waiting. For this little village, it was the social highlight that also marked the end of summer. Within a few days, the tourists would leave their second homes and get back to their normal lives, like me.

"We'll go in through the wings," Anita said, walking around the village hall.

I followed her silently, through the hall's maze of corridors. I picked up on a sort of restlessness, between the costumes being altered and the lighting being adjusted. Sarah was on stage, fine-tuning the last details of the set to perfection. I watched her for several long moments, almost reassured to find her hollow-eyed and sad. In spite of all her preparation, she was taking our separation as badly as I was.

She finally felt my gaze on her and raised a hand to wave. I didn't bother to respond. If we weren't together, we might as well cut all ties. Being friends wasn't – and would never be – an acceptable compromise. I backed away and found Anita and Élise in makeup.

We joked around for a while. Élise wasn't thrilled to be going back to Paris and starting classes again. I suggested she come help me and take up Anita's torch.

"Obviously, I'll pay you. Think of how much more comfortable your life as a student would be!"

"You mean I'll be able to abandon my exciting career as a telemarketer?"

"Let's say I can definitely help you find something better."

"Good grief, Élise, haven't you finished with your hair yet?" Sarah interrupted, on edge.

"Just two more minutes! Calm down, it'll be fine!"

"If Damien ever shows up, yes!"

"Did you call him?" asked Anita.

"A billion times, yes."

In the next second, she took her phone out of her pocket and dialed Damien's number. Anita shot me a worried look, then checked the time on her watch. Without Damien, the play couldn't go on.

"Finally! For heaven's sake, where are you?" she cried. "The curtain goes up in fifteen minutes!"

I could make out Damien's agitated voice and saw Sarah grow pale. Her face sagged, and for a brief moment, I thought she was going to faint.

"Oh no. I'm so sorry… Keep me posted, okay?"

She tossed her phone onto the makeup table and collapsed into a chair near Anita, looking full of despair.

"His daughter's got appendicitis."

Anita and Élise exchanged worried glances. The latter put down the hairpins she was holding and swiveled toward Sarah.

"And what are we going to do?"

"Cancel," replied Sarah tersely.

Immediately, the commotion in the wings ceased. The volunteers and actors stopped and turned to Sarah. The unease and disappointment were palpable. This production had required so much energy and time. To see it all go up in smoke was devastating.

"Perdican is in almost every scene, I can't do it without him."

"Who said anything about doing it without him?"

Anita's intervention plunged the little troupe into confusion. She turned to Sarah and dropped a bomb I hadn't seen coming:

"Maxime knows Damien's lines, he'll play Perdican."

"What?"

Sarah and I had shouted in unison. There was no way. I'd never been in a play in my entire life. And I was still reeling from my last conversation with Sarah, and angry: not exactly in the right condition to play a spurned lover who seduced one girl to make another one jealous.

"I don't think that's a good idea," I murmured.

"On the contrary, it's perfect! You can act and you know the lines!" Anita enthused.

"I… No, not really."

"No, she's right," Sarah chimed in. "You know the lines like the back of your hand. And we'll be able to help you between scenes if need be."

"Sarah, I really don't…" But the hope in her eyes

made resistance useless. I couldn't refuse her this. She had broken my heart, but I wasn't about to shatter her dreams. "Fine," I said. "I'll do it."

"Baptiste, get Damien's costume! It should fit him!"

And the backstage commotion resumed, as if nothing had happened. Two volunteers ran to a dressing room while Sarah caught her breath, worn out by emotion. We exchanged a sad look. Despite all our efforts, fate had conspired to bring us together yet again.

"Thank you," she murmured, on the verge of tears.

"It's not like anybody asked my opinion."

"Briars and adrenaline. You're going to like the theater!"

She stood up and I realized that I was letting a chance to plead my case get away. Or rather, our case. Anita suddenly appeared with my costume and made me pull off my T-shirt in front of everyone. Sarah vanished in the direction of the stage, her notebook clutched against her.

"We'll practice during the first two scenes," Élise proposed.

I nodded, lost and a little dumbfounded. I had no idea what to do and would have to rely on my memories of the rehearsals for the blocking.

"It'll all be fine," she added.

Most probably she wanted to reassure herself more than comfort me. The spectators' applause could be heard, and the whole cast were huddled together for a group hug.

"Join us," Anita encouraged me.

This woman made me do the craziest things: teaching me to read again, roping me into a stage play, making me order flowers. Someday, I promised myself, I'd pay her back.

And now, I found myself in the arms of the other volunteers, cheering each other on for this single performance. They slapped me on the back, tousled my hair, and wished me luck in a way that made me feel as if I had the fate of humanity in my hands.

"Shall we?" said Élise. "We'll try to do it quickly … and well. My goodness, I can't believe I'm going to help Maxime Maréchal run his lines!"

The curtain went up and Anita made her entrance, in the guise of her character, the nosy nanny.

Élise helped me with my first scene by rereading it with me; Sarah and Anita were right – the lines came back to me easily.

"Ready?" Sarah asked as I was waiting to go on.

"Now you ask my opinion?"

"Not really. Just making conversation," she said with a smile.

The next instant, I was on stage, to the amazement of the audience. There was a long burst of applause, which gave me goosebumps and had the virtue of making me forget, for a few seconds, both my heartbreak and my nerves. I just smiled, hoping to remain sufficiently in character so as not to wreck Sarah's work.

As my gaze swept over the audience with a gratitude that had never gripped me so tightly before, I recognized some familiar faces.

Claude.

Mathilde.

And my father.

All three, side by side, in the third row. My father was dressed in his best outfit: a thick plaid shirt and a threadbare jacket. He nodded in my direction and a brief smile lit his face. I could count my father's smiles on one hand. Like he was saving them just to bring them out on special occasions. The last time, I'd been twelve and had cut wood for an entire afternoon.

The applause trailed off, indicating that I had to start. I smiled at my father, and with sudden pride and not a trace of nerves, launched into my first line.

"Good morning, Father; and my dearest sister. How wonderful! I'm so happy!"

At the end of the play, I spotted Sarah weeping with joy. I'd seen lots of actresses cry before, especially at awards ceremonies. But it was different with Sarah; she was crying from joy mixed with pride. She was crying for all of us, for the work we accomplished, for the end of summer, for all the advice she'd given us and that we'd listened to.

As the audience applauded wildly, Frédéric suddenly appeared, a gigantic bouquet of roses in hand. Sarah's tears intensified and the red petals barely outshone her burning cheeks. Hand in hand, the whole cast saluted the crowd and the curtain fell.

"Were you the one who got the flowers?" Sarah asked.

"Yes. Were you the one who got my father to come?"

"Yes. Mathilde helped me. I didn't know you would perform tonight, I just wanted the two of you to … talk. I'll let you go, he's behind you."

Though the first words we exchanged were hesitant, my father's presence touched me even more than his awkward praise. He waited at the theater exit for me to change and then I bought him dinner at Baptiste's. On the square, I saw Sarah going home to the apartment, her flowers clutched against her. She gave me a little wave, and a slight smile played over her lips.

This time, I waved back. Then I saw the cast and crew surge up behind her and burst out laughing as they surrounded her. For a time, I'd imagined convincing her to come to Paris with me. But I now understood what kept her here. I was even grasping why she refused to have a long-distance relationship: no conversation could ever have recreated the emotion of this evening.

"Ready?"

A mug of coffee in his hand, Damien was waiting patiently for me to load his truck. Sarah was chatting with him, wrapping books for her mystery parcels. She'd spent her Sunday at yard sales, amassing as many books as possible. They were waiting in boxes, ready to experience a new life.

"We can go now!" I yelled, tossing a last bag onto the passenger seat.

Damien drained his mug in one gulp. His daughter was still in the hospital, and Anita was looking after her for the day. He joined me at the truck and shot me a severe look.

"She at least deserves a proper goodbye!"

"We don't have much left to say to each other."

"Stop being a bungling idiot and go say your goodbyes! In any case, we're not moving from this spot unless I've seen you thank that girl for saving your ass."

I grumbled for form's sake. I knew Damien was right. But I also knew that thanking her would never be enough. She'd managed to open my eyes to my life and make me realize that I was headed for disaster. For all that, she'd also broken my heart into such tiny pieces that I doubted I'd ever be able to glue them back together.

I joined Sarah in the bookshop, closed the door behind me, and locked it. I didn't want us to be interrupted.

"It's the big day," said Sarah, piling up books in front of her.

"Yes. Damien threatened to fake car trouble if I didn't come to thank you. So, thank you."

"You're welcome. Thanks for the play, it was the best. You're … you're a really great actor, Maxime."

"I know. That's why you broke up with me."

I couldn't help it. I was still hoping she'd change her mind. Failing that, I wanted her to feel just a little of my pain. I refused to be the only one suffering.

"I hope things are better between you and your father."

"It'll take more than a dinner. It's pretty hard to put years of resentment behind you."

There was a heavy silence. I should have left immediately and gone back to Paris to forget her. But my body refused to obey.

I would have liked to take her in my arms and feel the warmth of her body against mine.

I would have liked to make her blush, one last time.

I would have liked to tell her I loved her again. Because I was thinking it, and a few days earlier, just that thought was enough to make me happy.

I would have liked to be Maxime. Not the actor, not the convicted felon, not the arrogant guy who'd arrived here. Just myself, the guy who was taking back his life and who was now going to miss the sight of all these books.

"I ordered you two more batches of shelves," I admitted finally.

"You shouldn't have!"

"You could put them under the stairs or on the wall at the back."

"I'll be sure to."

Her voice faltered, betraying her emotions. That reassured me. I wasn't the only one destroyed by the idea of leaving. Damien honked his horn, breaking another agonizing silence.

"Thank you, Sarah."

To my great surprise, she dove into my arms and hugged me tightly. My broken heart found the strength to beat faster, while I breathed in her scent.

"Take care of yourself, okay?" she asked, backing away.

"I'm going to try. If I ever screw up, I'll make sure to end up back here."

"You can come back without screwing up. Especially without screwing up," she laughed.

"And don't let just anybody get close to you, okay? You deserve… Honestly, you deserve a love story out of a novel. You know the ones I mean."

She nodded and I unlocked the door. I went out onto the square, able to breathe again.

As I was settling into the truck next to Damien, I glanced over at the bookshop window. Just like the day I arrived, Sarah came out of her shop in those same old shapeless jeans. As usual, she gave us a little wave.

Damien started the truck, and I promised myself I'd never go through this again. I'd never again endure her presence if we weren't together.

Chapter Sixteen

Three weeks later

"But are you going to celebrate it anyway? A drink? Or dinner?" Anita fumed, setting her book back down on the coffee table.

"It's not a major event, though!"

"Sarah, I'm old, every opportunity for a party is a good one. So, your birthday is a perfect excuse."

"Anita…"

"We could go to Baptiste's? He'd make you your favorite meal. Do you still like braised lamb?"

"Why wouldn't I like it anymore?"

"I don't know. Sometimes things change. And sometimes, you change your mind about decisions you may have made."

Book club had been over for a good hour, but Anita had offered to help me put away a box of books that had arrived during the day. The subject of my birthday had come up in between a 1950s detective novel and a historical romance. Now I was doing all I could to divert my friend's attention.

"So, I still like braised lamb, and I still don't want to celebrate my birthday," I summarized.

"But why?"

"Because I'm not... Because I have work. And I'm really tired. If you want, I'll just finish this box tomorrow."

But Anita completely ignored my offer. Instead, she got out a pile of books and set them down near her for sorting. I heaved a weary sigh and decided to change tack. The faster this box emptied out, the faster I'd regain my solitude.

"Do you miss him?"

Though Anita had had the audacity to ask me the question, she wasn't brave enough to look me in the eye. Her attention was focused on the books, which she was flipping through to check their condition.

"You lasted three weeks without asking! That's impressive."

"Not really," she admitted. "I asked other people, but no one can get it out of you."

"I might as well tell you: it's not very discreet to stop talking as soon as I arrive anywhere!"

I got up from my chair, determined to ensure that Anita left. I didn't feel like having this conversation. I was already having trouble not thinking about Maxime, and talking about him wouldn't make me feel any better. I knew Anita wouldn't let up. She didn't approve of my decision, nor did she approve of Maxime surrendering.

"I'll lock the door behind you," I called, hoping she'd get the message.

"Sarah!"

"I'm tired… I'll finish tomorrow."

Anita reluctantly got up and heaved a sigh of disapproval. I felt like being alone and wanted to wallow in bed, with a book. They, at least, never disappointed me. They didn't ask questions or turn my life upside down in the space of a few weeks.

"See you tomorrow, Sarah."

She left the bookshop with one last wary look. I closed up behind her, shut off the lights, and took refuge in my little apartment. Once I was safe and in complete darkness, I allowed myself to squeeze out the tears welling up in my eyes.

Leaving Maxime had been the hardest and easiest decision I'd made in my life. I knew we were destined to live in two different worlds. His Parisian life was blossoming and his career was well worth some sacrifices, including our love story. He loved his profession, and I loved mine. I wouldn't have been able to live without books, and I suspected he would have been unhappy to be so far from Paris. Maxime would have gotten bored, and I didn't want to make him resent me for everything he had given up.

Damien was busy looking after his daughter, who was recovering well, and was staying deliberately non-committal on the brief occasions when we did talk. I imagined he didn't want to rub salt in the wound. Anita and Baptiste were watching over me, hiding the front pages of celebrity magazines from me as much as possible. Élise had gone back to her student life in the capital. I almost envied her. At least she had the chance to see his face.

Without him, the apartment seemed desperately empty. My routine had settled back to the same old: the bookshop, dinners at the restaurant, customers, car boot sales. The rhythm started again, but I was shaky. I hadn't lost my enthusiasm or my desire, but now I was looking for the meaning in what I was doing. I'd told Maxime that I loved living here. And that was true. I'd loved living here with him. I'd enjoyed our dinners and conversations. I'd been honored when he entrusted me with his secret.

And now that I was alone, I was trying to get back to normal. I had been trying for three weeks now, in vain. My usual techniques weren't working; sticking your head in the sand had its limits. Especially when you lived in the place you wanted to avoid. A place filled with memories, and the presence of someone who was hopelessly absent.

Taking refuge in books had worked at first. I found that the first twenty pages of the fifteen books I'd started had let me suppress images of Maxime. Then, invariably, everything came surging back.

His kisses.

Our embraces.

His disconcerting way of looking at me.

His laugh, so rare and so lovely to hear.

If I'd had the courage to face my darkest thoughts, I would have told Anita that yes, I missed Maxime. I missed him like you miss air when you're underwater.

At the bookshop, I put on a neutral face, I made change, I smiled. In the apartment, I suffocated. Every corner of this place revealed a part of Maxime I would have preferred to forget.

Tonight, probably because Anita had brought up the subject, the pain was more intense and weighed on me like a stone. This was new for me. I'd felt loss before; I'd already had to come to terms with several abandonments. I knew how to do it. Time and work allowed me to bury that sickening feeling in a corner of my brain. But losing Maxime was a thousand times worse.

Maybe because I was the one who had chosen for us both, maybe because being in love with someone isn't as idyllic as they would like you to believe, maybe because I knew he was going on with his life while I was dragging around my pain and emptiness, with the unpleasant premonition that they'd end up destroying me.

After two hours of fruitless struggle to find sleep, I went back down to the bookshop. I finished sorting and putting away the books and rearranged an entire set of shelves. I did all I could not to stop in front of the framed Perdican speech that Maxime had given me. Around one o'clock in the morning, I finally fell asleep and woke up a few hours later … curled up on the sofa in the reading nook.

"Okay, that's enough," I grumbled.

I got up and stretched my entire body. Now I'd be tired *and* achy. Great. I hated what Maxime had made me into: a poor, tired girl who couldn't accept a decision she'd made herself. I'd become a cliché, a girl in full heartbreak mode, unable to cope with her normal life.

I finished the night in my bed. Deciding that I'd suffered enough was one thing; making the suffering end was something else. So that night wasn't any better than the others and I woke feeling as shattered as ever. To make matters worse, today was my birthday, and I'd have to endure the threat of celebrations and the worried looks of my friends.

I opened the bookshop at ten o'clock, deciding that caffeine would be my best ally for the day. I put the tables out on the pavement, keeping an eye on the weather, which was rather uncertain lately.

"Let me help you," offered Frédéric, joining me briskly.

"Oh, thank you."

Within a few minutes, the pavement was furnished with tables and chairs. He even helped me set up one of the new shelves Maxime had ordered against the window, stopping in front of the row of books wrapped in brown paper.

"Mystery picks, huh?"

"Giving a book a chance is important."

He stared at me for a bit, while I became lost in more memories of Maxime. Though the idea behind the mystery pick books had confused him at first, he'd taken special care to ensure that this shelf was always perfectly tidy and attractive.

"Do you have a minute?" asked Frédéric.

"Sure."

He scuttled back to his shop and returned with a glorious bouquet of peonies. He handed it to me proudly, before adding, "Happy Birthday."

"Thank you. You shouldn't have."

"Specially ordered for you. They have your name, they're called Sarah Bernhardt. I thought—"

"They're lovely," I interrupted him. "I … I'm going to put them in some water."

Even more urgent than the water was getting away from Frédéric. My birthday was a perfect excuse for flowers and an even better excuse to try to get back in my life. I didn't want to let him believe there was a chance. When he finally left the bookshop, I sighed with relief.

The rest of the morning passed without incident. I had lunch at Baptiste's and once again had to argue about the lack of festivities for my birthday.

"Has he called?" he'd asked as he brought me my coffee.

"No. He's busy," I'd lied, to excuse Maxime.

"Even when I'm busy, I talk to my wife every day."

"Since you live and work together, that seems easy enough to accomplish."

"Ah, you see, you want him to come back! I knew it!"

He'd left my table without another word, wearing a victorious smile. I preferred not to contradict him. The prospect of having to fight my friends all day exhausted me. They'd eventually get tired of the birthday but then there would be something else.

In the afternoon, I took delivery of some new boxes of books, retrieved from a house that had recently been sold. The former owners were doing their best to clear the place out quickly, without haggling over prices. I was emptying the contents of the third box when a delivery man showed up with a package.

"Sign here!" he prompted me, showing his phone screen.

I did so and collected the square package from his hands. The delivery guy grunted and left without even giving me time to thank him. I hefted the package and shook it. No sound. I opened it carefully and found, stuck in between several layers of bubble wrap, a package wrapped in brown paper.

I pulled it out delicately, finding the same type of label I used for the mystery pick books. "Happy Birthday" was all that it said. I unwrapped the book and discovered a nineteenth-century edition of *The Lady with the Camellias*, by Alexandre Dumas. It was Maxime.

In the box, I searched for a card from him, but in vain. The book would have to do. I flipped through it and breathed in the delicious scent of aged paper. I was touched that Maxime had remembered my birthday; that he gave me this book – and not flowers – overwhelmed me to the point of tears. The pain of our separation was as fresh as if it had just happened.

I spent a while admiring my present, settling comfortably onto the sofa in the reading nook. Obviously, my good resolution from the night before evaporated without me even trying to stick to it. So when, an hour later, I saw the delivery man reappear, I leaped to my feet to greet him. This time, he didn't need to remind me that I had to sign for the package.

He'd barely left when I tore open the outer wrapping, then the brown paper.

Peony in Love, by Lisa See.

I burst into a loud, hearty laugh. Frédéric's peonies faded in comparison with this gift. Once again, I flipped through it, looking for a note. But there was nothing. Swallowing my disappointment, I set it on the counter, already checking my watch and hoping for another delivery.

And there was one: *The Black Tulip*. Then another: *The Name of the Rose*. And yet another. The delivery guy didn't have to say a word anymore. I jumped on him almost before his truck had parked. *Purple Hibiscus*.

"How many more are there?" I asked.

"You tell me," he replied, annoyed.

At 6 p.m., he finally dropped off an entire box of second-hand books. I rejoiced.

Better than all my Christmases put together, this apparent treasure hunt thrilled me. I hadn't felt this good since … since him. I had to admit it. Knowing that these books came from him only bolstered my excitement and joy.

After opening everything up, I grouped the books together. There were about thirty works, all with flowers in their titles and all second-hand. They had nothing else in common: there were classics, much more recent titles, hardcovers, paperbacks, reprints, and first editions. I lined them up against each other on the counter and admired them.

Damien entered the shop and didn't even bother to greet me.

"I know you're sulking in your corner, but you won't refuse a dinner invitation, will you? I promise not to talk about him!"

"With pleasure!"

I was practically humming with joy. It was ridiculous. Maxime made a brief reappearance in my life, and I once more became cheerful. Damien stared at me as though a third eye had sprouted on my forehead.

I felt my smile fade. Loving Maxime made me happy, but not being able to be with him tore me up.

"Did Élise leave you some books?" asked Damien.

"Élise?"

Damien grabbed one of the books and turned it to show me the spine. There I saw, perfectly visible, a stamp like the ones you see on library books. These had obviously been sold to make way for new stock.

"That library is in the 9th arrondissement. She's studying right nearby, isn't she?"

My heart skipped a beat. I checked the other books and, unsurprisingly, saw the same stamp. It was the sign I'd been looking for all afternoon, another form of tattoo, just as indelible, which would show me the way. Maxime wasn't as much of a mystery as he thought.

"Well, shall we go eat?"

"Is there still a service area on the motorway, just past the toll booth?"

Taken aback, Damien stayed silent. I gathered my cardigan and the keys to the bookshop, then pushed him back outside. By chance, I'd put on a decent pair of shorts and judged myself presentable. I locked the door, surreptitiously observing Damien. He watched me, bewildered.

"So, that service area?"

"Uh, yes. But…"

"We'll eat something there. We're going to Paris."

"What?"

I was already in his truck when Damien finally managed to move from the spot. He shook his head and got behind the wheel. I was champing at the bit, jiggling my feet and checking the time on my phone. I had to see Maxime right away – it didn't matter how late it was, I just had to see him.

"With all I've done for you, you should consider naming your first-born after me," Damien said, not at all joking.

When we got to Paris, it was dark and cool. Damien groused about the Parisians' driving while I clutched my seat and prayed I wouldn't die. We got lost twice before finding the Drouot library, where the books came from.

He parked in a spot reserved for buses, and it was only at that moment, when the frenzy and fear died down, that I realized what I was doing. We'd covered more than two hundred and fifty miles in the middle of the night on a whim, all because of a theory based on the stamps on some books.

Though at the bookshop everything had seemed clear and certain, in front of this tall building made of steel and glass, I had my doubts. Maxime had been sincere with me. Being friends didn't interest him. For my part, I was starting to wonder if the prospect of abandoning my life in the village really was more unbearable than going on without him.

"Are you sure?" Damien asked me.

"Not really, no. Any advice?"

"I'm going to tell you exactly what I said to my wife once: do what you want, as long as you have no regrets."

I stared at the entrance, almost hoping it was locked. Facing Maxime was going to take all my strength. I knew he wouldn't give me a chance to run away, that making me come here was already a sign. If I went to him now, there would be no turning back.

"That's good advice," I murmured.

"My wife divorced me right after that."

His smile was fleeting but I detected a hint of bitterness. Though Damien seemed to have dealt with his divorce very well, he hadn't managed to have a relationship since. His daughter had become the center of his life.

I squeezed his hand, consoling him silently.

"Thanks for tonight. And for everything else, too," I added, with a smile.

It was thanks to him that the bookshop was still open, thanks to him that Maxime had burst into my life, thanks to him that I'd understood the message hidden in his books.

"No problem. I just didn't see it turning out like this!"

"Like this?"

"Well, you here and us … back there."

My heart shriveled up painfully. In one sentence, Damien had just summed up my dilemma. It wasn't about Maxime anymore. It was about me, exclusively, the choices I had to make, what I wanted to do with my life. I'd told Maxime that I didn't want him to be disappointed or deprived of his career. I'd lied to myself. By pushing Maxime away, by sending him back home, I'd chosen to stay safe, to change nothing about my life. I'd been afraid, afraid to throw myself into real life, without the possibility of closing the pages of my book if a scene frightened me.

"I don't know if… Well, there's the bookshop and … well, all of you."

"We'll survive, I assure you. As for the bookshop … I

think you should look toward the future, Sarah, and stop acting like that bookshop is your whole life."

"It is!"

"It's a part of your life. The one that connects you to your past. It's your hiding-place. I don't blame you, I hide in my vineyards at the slightest opportunity. But maybe it's time to move on."

I glanced toward the library again. I loved Chateaurenard. I loved knowing everyone's habits, being able to joke with the summer visitors, combing through the various car boot sales to unearth new treasures.

But I loved Maxime.

I loved him with his imperfections and doubts.

I loved him the way people love in books, unselfconsciously, no holding back.

"Do you think he's inside?" I asked, studying the upper floors.

The moment my eyes returned to the entrance, I noticed a masculine silhouette appear in the light of the streetlamp. My heart raced immediately, unable to restrain itself. After three weeks without seeing each other, I didn't know where to begin. Damien brought me back to reality:

"I'm going to get a hotel room. I'll call you tomorrow, okay?"

I nodded, my throat much too tight to make the smallest sound. I opened the door, which creaked in protest, and found myself face to face with Maxime. His jacket and blue dress shirt accentuated the square shape of his shoulders. His open collar revealed a tiny piece of his tattoo.

With his brow furrowed and jaw clenched, he still exuded the same magnetism. But in his eyes, something had changed. His eyes were no longer as dark and his body was relaxed.

"Let me guess, he gave you flowers?" he asked.

"Yes."

I hazarded a smile. Apparently, Maxime and his usual sarcasm were ready to shove me back into my corner. That almost reassured me about the rest of our conversation.

"I told you he would. Nice guys are predictable."

"And you told me you'd give me books. Thank you, it was … unexpected and perfect."

"I was hoping you would come."

He crossed the short distance between us and stroked my cheek with his thumb. I shivered and pretended my legs hadn't just abruptly transformed into quivering jelly. With one gesture, Maxime had erased the painful memories of these past three weeks.

"You took your time," he added in a whisper.

I didn't know if he was talking about tonight or the previous weeks. Arms at my sides, I was hesitant to touch him. But I wanted to assure myself it was actually real, that the sensual heat diffusing through my body wasn't a product of my imagination. I could smell him and finally grabbed his shirt to keep from falling.

"I didn't notice the stamp at first."

"Come on, I have to show you something."

He stepped away from me but caught my hand in his. My heart jumped again at that long-awaited contact.

"You know the code?" I asked, as he opened the library door.

"Élise works here."

"You pulled some strings?"

"A bit."

He shot me a conspiratorial grin as we climbed the stairs. Maxime was acting like he knew the place like the back of his hand. He pushed open a heavy wooden swing door and we found ourselves plunged into darkness.

"Not afraid of the dark, I hope?"

"No."

My voice quavered, but he didn't react. I had no idea what we were doing here in the middle of the night. I was lost and tried to concentrate on what I was feeling: Maxime's hand in mine, the parquet under my feet, the familiar odor of paper and dust.

"What are we doing here?" I finally asked.

"We're celebrating your birthday. Wait here."

He kissed the back of my hand before dropping it. The next instant, a multitude of tiny lamps lit up a large room, furnished with shelves and books. The library was spacious and extended toward the back of the building. I swiveled around, seeing reading areas for children and a work room.

"Are we allowed to do this?" I fretted, walking over to Maxime.

"We can do anything, Sarah. If you want to."

He slipped behind me and helped me take off my cardigan. He took off his jacket and tossed both garments onto a chair. His hands ran over my hips and he pressed his chest against my back. The stampeding of my heart began again, but it wasn't the same emotion anymore; it wasn't excitement, nor desire. This time, I was nervous, anticipating another unexpected maneuver from Maxime.

"I thought about what happened," he confessed, behind me. "And what you said to me."

His voice vibrated against the skin of my neck and another warm, delicious shiver went through me. He walked me down the large central aisle of the library. Our footsteps echoed and you could hear our shallow breathing.

"You're right, I love my career," he continued.

"Maxime…"

"But what I feel for you is … different."

We reached the middle of the aisle. On the left, a large window with plants in it looked outside. Some string lights had been hung there, giving it a fairytale look. When I turned to the right, I froze.

"Is this how they do it in your books?"

For several seconds, I remained speechless, trying to remember how to breathe.

"You … you're the one who…?"

"I set the table, but the dinner was delivered," he reassured me with a laugh.

"We're going to eat here?"

"Well, I'm very hungry. What do you say?"

My stomach was tied in too many knots to answer. Maxime had prepared a table out of a dream, with candles, flowers, and white porcelain. *Like in a book.* Or like in *Pretty Woman* … except my opera was a library.

"Sarah?"

"Actually, I … I'm a little lost. I thought you were annoyed at me!"

"I was, that's true," he admitted with a smile. "I hated our last dinner, I hated that you stood up to me. But that's also what I love about you. That you stand up to me and don't let me get away with my usual nonsense."

"Lucky for you I like bad guys, too."

"Lucky for me, indeed. But I also know that you love books. So, I told myself I'd give you some."

"So, did you wrap them yourself?"

He suddenly seemed embarrassed. I went over to him, touched by his gesture. I didn't dare imagine the time and energy expended to successfully get me here. He'd overcome his anger but he was still Maxime, with all his emotions on the surface.

This was where we were meant to be. Another first kiss, another chance. I'd finally understood and I was sure of myself. No regrets, no desire to go back to my solitude. I wanted him, thorns and all.

"It took me for ever," sighed Maxime, running a hand through his hair. "But, since you're here, let's say it was worth it."

"It was very good," I reassured him.

"I didn't wrap all the rest."

"All the rest?"

"Those."

He indicated the space around us. I stared at him, astounded. I must have misunderstood.

"Those?" I repeated. "You mean…"

"The ones in the library."

My heart skipped a beat. Or maybe two. I reeled back, as if absorbing the shock of an uppercut to the jaw. My back hit a shelf and I was delighted to find a semblance of support.

"You mean that … this place is…"

"I bought it. City Hall wanted to get rid of it, and I wanted you back."

He looked into my eyes. I felt dizzy. Or seasick. My whole body was trembling and the floor seemed to almost buckle under my feet. I wiped a hand across my forehead, trying to collect my thoughts.

"So, you said to yourself … you were going … to give me this place?"

"I realized that I wouldn't be enough to make you abandon the bookshop. So yes, there are books, and there's me. I come in several volumes and a million chapters."

I felt myself blush like never before. I had no more breath, no more air, and barely the strength to stand. What kind of man could give a woman a library, while acting like it was all normal?

"You were wrong," I murmured at last.

His eyes clouded, and I went over to him to remove his doubts. He regarded me cautiously, his surge of confidence from the beginning of the evening now flown away.

"You're reason enough. All by yourself."

"Really?"

His eyes lit up like a child's under the Christmas tree. I smiled at him and suppressed emotional tears. Him giving me books was touching; him giving me a library was unreal.

"I want you to have this," he said, hugging me. "I'm sure you could work miracles here, take in second-hand books, launch a community library, or even…"

I shut him up by pressing my mouth against his. His hands clamped around my waist and lifted me against him, then set me on our dinner table. The porcelain fell to the floor, and I almost burned myself on a candle. Maxime took advantage of my surprise to slip his mouth over mine, and I let out an unselfconscious moan. That kiss was the air I'd been lacking for days.

I'd never made love in a library but there was always a first time. I unbuttoned his shirt and helped him get it off. My heart started up again, riding the night's roller coaster of emotions with disconcerting ease.

"This time is really the first," whispered Maxime. "The one that makes you blush," he added, rubbing his thumb over my cheeks.

"A new chapter."

I laid my hand on his tattoo, the thorny vine securely enclosing his heart, and deposited a furtive kiss there. After suffering for three weeks, after lying to myself for so long, and especially after discovering that Maxime had bought this place for me, there was no going back.

"It really is for you," he said, as I followed the ink on his skin. "I want you to stay, Sarah. I hate living without you. Shit, I forgot the music!"

He escaped from my embrace and turned on a little speaker hidden in one of the shelves. Immediately, "A Groovy Kind of Love", an old song from the 1960s, filled the library.

"I already told you that you're enough!" I laughed as he came back toward me.

"I wanted to rise to the occasion. Is it…?"

I rediscovered the taste of his lips, silently answering his question. I was floating; I was soaring so fast I thought I might explode. His hands slid underneath my thighs and grabbed the backs of my knees. He pulled me against him and abandoned my lips to press his forehead to mine.

"I'm high on you," he confessed with a smile.

"I'm high on you," I replied.

He melted onto my lips and laid me down on the table. For the first time in my life, I decided to follow the path I knew by heart, the one I knew I would never, ever get tired of.

The one made of ink, briars, and adrenaline.

Epilogue

"You really think I should do it?"

I shoved the script over to Mathilde. We'd been sitting in this café for a solid hour, talking about our respective plans. Between her move and my shoots, it had been several weeks since I'd spoken to my agent.

"It would be a shame to pass it up," she said with a smile. "The production will be outstanding, with a cast to match. Frankly, Maxime, it's a great opportunity."

"If you say so."

"You don't seem convinced!"

She waved the waiter over to get a refill on our orders. A tea for her, an espresso for me. I rubbed my hands together, trying to chase away a fit of nervousness. To talk with Mathilde, I'd had no other choice than to join her at this café near the train station. Constantly followed around by photographers, I avoided public appearances as much as I could. Despite Sarah being here for nearly a year, they still followed me. But my anger rarely flickered now, and if it did I just reminded myself that there were worse things happening in the world.

"I assure you, Maxime. It's an excellent choice. Why are you so worried?"

"I'm not worried."

Mathilde laid her hand on mine; my fingers were clenched and my body tense. She gave me a maternal smile and my anxiety went down a notch. My agent knew me well. Sometimes, she even managed to take me down a peg or two. I decided to change the subject.

"What time is your train?"

"In twenty minutes. Enough time to remind you of your schedule."

"Great," I said playfully.

She shot me an amused look and opened her diary. She cursed when business cards and a mass of Post-Its fluttered out, and groaned even more when a photo of her son slipped onto the table. I didn't know how she managed to stay so focused when even her diary showed her natural tendency towards chaos. I promised myself I'd give her a new one for Christmas.

Conscientiously, she paged through the next two months. I had to provide a few interviews for a movie, present an award at a festival, and do a shoot for a fashion magazine.

"What about tonight?"

"My answer hasn't changed."

"I really would have liked you to meet this English director. He doesn't come to Paris very often…"

"Non-negotiable. Sarah's putting on her play tonight."

Once in Paris, Sarah had lasted two months before embarking on a new theatrical project. After re-opening the library as a community library and second-hand bookshop, she'd hit it off with a local teacher, and within a few weeks the idea of putting on a play with teenagers had blossomed. I wouldn't have missed this evening for the world.

"Fine. As you wish."

"So you're not going to force me?" I chuckled.

"Will you change your mind if I insist?"

"I don't think so."

"So why would I exhaust myself? Managing you is already very tiring. When I can, I save my energy."

She glanced at her watch and slipped her diary into her bag. I paid our bill and walked Mathilde to her train.

"Are you sure everything's okay? You seem a little distracted."

"Everything's fine," I assured her, half-heartedly.

"Is it Sarah? Listen, I know she doesn't like this notoriety around you, but we can find solutions and help you…"

"Sarah is fine. She's on a roll. Honestly, she's fine," I repeated to Mathilde, confronting her suspicious look.

"Your train is going to leave, you should get to your seat."

She shook her head and then burst out laughing. She readjusted the strap of her bag on her shoulder and crossed her arms over her chest.

"Two evasive maneuvers in less than thirty minutes. Do you take me for a rookie?"

I held my hands up in front of me in a defensive gesture. Mathilde was much too clever not to notice that I was more nervous than usual.

"I hate actors! Are you really not going to tell me?"

"No."

"You're not going to end your career, I hope?" she fretted.

"No," I laughed.

"Good."

She tried to feel reassured, but I could clearly see the cloud of worry in her eyes. Simon's death had made her even more over-protective than usual. She worried even more about me, constantly interrogating me about my private life, as if she were afraid history would repeat itself. There was no chance that would happen with me: Sarah protected me from myself.

"Everything is fine, Mathilde. Get on this train before it leaves."

Reluctantly, she did so. I waited for her to sit down and give me a discreet wave before I left the platform.

Mathilde didn't need to know what was on my mind. She'd find out sooner or later.

I walked through the train station and wandered into the bookshop. I stopped in front of a shelf of paperbacks and scanned the titles. I smiled briefly: I'd finally found a solution to what had been bothering me, and by extension, that had alerted Mathilde.

Actually, I wasn't worried at all.

On the contrary, I was at peace. But like any actor about to go on stage for a big role, I had stage fright. The good kind, that put you in a trance and sharpened your mind.

Buying the book let me relax a little. It was surely a sign from the heavens, one of those little straws in the wind that had guided me toward Sarah.

After a quick detour to the apartment, I settled in at the back of the tiny theater Sarah had rented. She'd obstinately refused my help, even though I could have found her a place three times as large. But Sarah cared about her independence and had even forbidden me to help her at the bookshop.

"Come on, Sarah, that's ridiculous, everybody knows we're together," I'd pointed out to her. "I don't see the problem in helping to pull a few strings."

"Integrity: does that mean anything to you?" she'd asked, a little grumpy.

"Sort of."

I'd then pushed away the hair hiding her face and

done all I could to keep my gaze locked on hers. I'd pressed my body against her and slowly made her retreat until her back met the door to our bedroom.

"I don't want to stay here without doing anything, asking you to help me. It goes against everything I am. And if we ever… Well, if you decided that…"

My lips had found the skin of her neck, while my hands had edged their way underneath her sweater. With a sigh, Sarah had yielded.

Almost.

"Maxime, stop that!"

"Stop thinking I'm going to leave you one day."

"Why?"

"Because it won't happen."

I'd promised myself as much as her. Sarah was a wall between me and my old demons. She'd saved me from myself, my anger, my rage, my shame. With every note she left me – from the shopping list to notes of encouragement – I felt myself come alive again. Moreover, I kept them with pride, all displayed like trophies on the walls of our bedroom.

I clutched the book I'd bought at the train station tight against me. I'd had time to cover it in brown paper and create its label. My nerves were still there, enhanced by a touch of adrenaline. I knew she'd like it.

The play went off without a hitch, and I even found the work of one young recruit very convincing. To the crowd's applause, Élise presented the actors for their curtain call. Shyly, Sarah appeared on stage. I whistled as loudly as I could, and the applause redoubled in intensity. In my girlfriend's expression, I saw pride mixed with joy. She was beaming with happiness, and the actors thanked her warmly.

The hall emptied out little by little, and despite some looks, nobody dared speak to me. I must have still been a bit scary. So much the better – it was Sarah's night, and I didn't want to steal the spotlight from her.

"Did you like it?" she asked as she joined me.

I helped her put her coat on as I nodded.

"It was fantastic. That girl, the one who played Juliet, she's wonderful."

"I know. She's not keen to sign up for acting classes though. Her parents don't really have the means."

"Have her enroll, I'll pay if I have to. And I'll talk about it with Mathilde."

We left the hall hand in hand. The evening was warm enough to walk the whole way. I pulled Sarah against me and kissed her on the forehead.

"Bravo! I'm proud of my brilliant girlfriend."

"It's just an amateur thing. I'm going to resume my normal life among the books."

"Speaking of books, I have this for you."

I suppressed a new wave of nervousness.

Nevertheless, Sarah immediately perceived that something wasn't right.

"Is everything okay?"

"Totally. You should open it."

She turned the book around every which way, tracing the shape with her fingers. She burst out laughing when she saw the label. My breathing almost stopped when she froze in the middle of the street.

"Mystery pick?"

"For a change, yes."

My voice quavered pitifully. But Sarah didn't hear it. She was much too focused on the book's label and the two keywords I'd written.

"'Fantasy epic'?"

She frowned and ripped the brown paper, like a child tearing the wrappings on a present far too long awaited. She made sure to step into the light of a streetlamp, and I had plenty of time to see her cheeks turn pink. She glanced at me incredulously.

"Fantasy epic," she repeated tonelessly.

"You should open it."

She did so and discovered, in a jewelry box nestled in the hollowed-out pages, the ring I'd chosen for her two months earlier. I went over to her, just as she read my request on the first page of the book. Once again, she glanced at me. I saw a few tears barely hiding her stunned look. I took the book out of her hands and removed the ring to slip it onto her finger, repeating:

"Fantasy epic… Well, the fantasy part is right, and I hope it's an epic."

"You butchered *The Lord of the Rings,*" she whispered.

"We'll watch the movie!"

"Sacrilege! The book is always better."

That simple exchange dissipated my doubts. Sarah's stubbornness, her convictions, her blushing. So many reasons to link my life to hers. So many reasons confirming that I couldn't live without her anymore.

"Marry me," I whispered against her lips.

Her whisper against my mouth was barely audible, but it made me feel like I was walking on air again. A whisper better than any shout. A whisper that was going to make me happy until the end of time.

YOUR NUMBER ONE STOP
ONE MORE CHAPTER
FOR PAGETURNING BOOKS

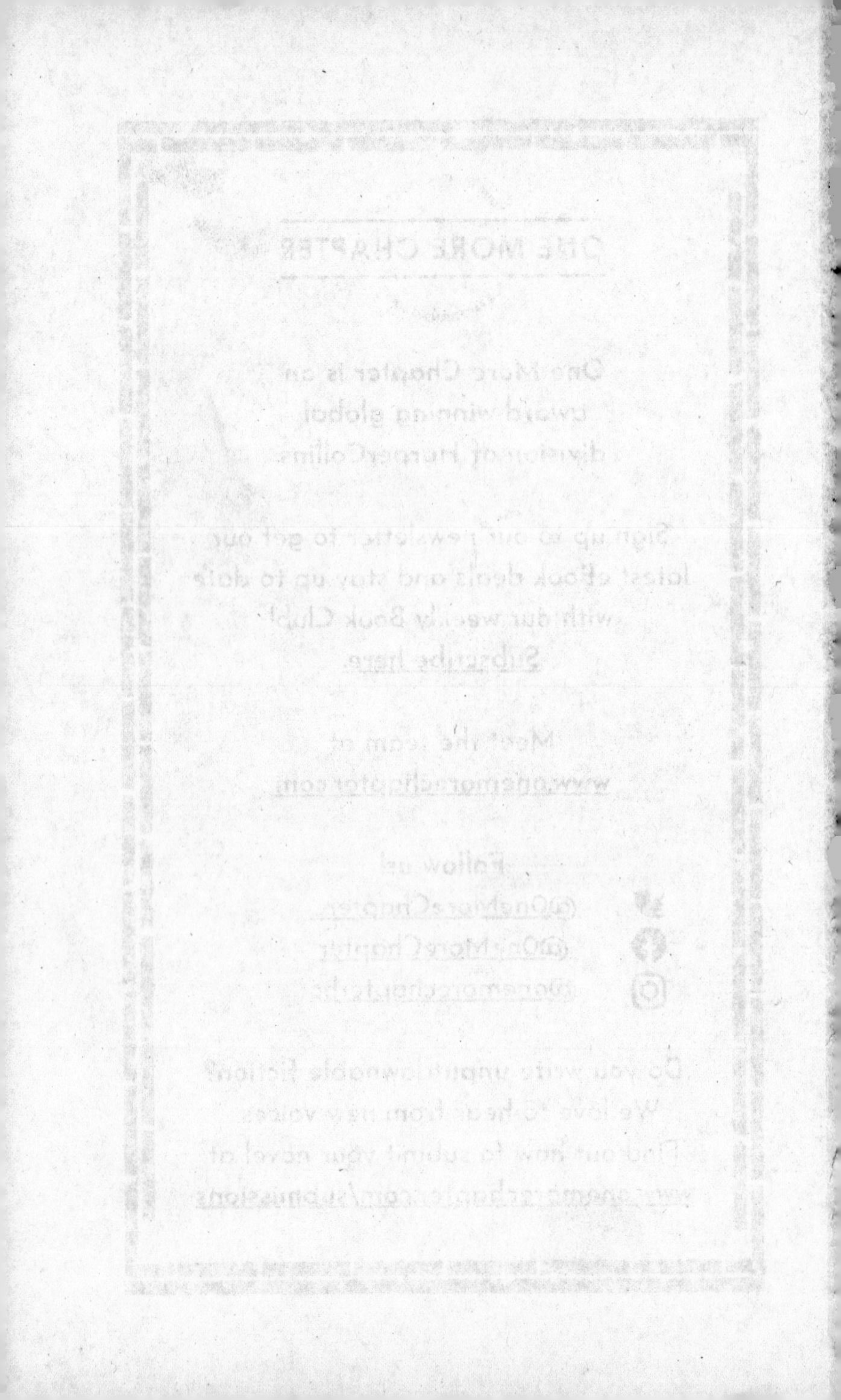